WATCH ME BLEED

A DI FRANK MILLER NOVEL

JOHN CARSON

DI FRANK MILLER SERIES

Crash Point
Silent Marker
Rain Town
Watch Me Bleed
Broken Wheels
Sudden Death
Under the Knife
Trial and Error
Warning Sign
Cut Throat
Blood from a Stone
Time of Death

Frank Miller Crime Series – Books 1-3 – Box set

DCI HARRY MCNEIL SERIES
Return to Evil
Sticks and Stones
Back to Life
Dead Before You Die
Hour of Need

Where Stars Will Shine – a charity anthology compiled by Emma
Mitchell, featuring a
Harry McNeil short story –
The Art of War and Peace

MAX DOYLE SERIES

Final Steps
Code Red
The October Project

SCOTT MARSHALL SERIES

Old Habits

WATCH ME BLEED

Created with Vellum

For my friend and fellow writer, John Walker

PROLOGUE

Two years ago

He didn't feel the pain. That would come later.

Right now, all he felt was the fear.

His face had been rammed sideways into the back wall of the confessional. The little dark room was supposed to be his alone, his little sanctuary where he could do God's work.

This man had invaded it, bringing violence with him.

'Did you hear what I said?'

Father Will Beam was praying, feeling comfort in knowing that a higher power than this killer was looking after him; praying so hard that he had blocked out the other man's words.

'Yes... yes, I heard what you said.'

The knife was still pressed against his left cheek, perilously close to his left eye. His right cheek was flattened against the wall.

'Repeat it.'

It might have been a screwdriver, but he was sure it was a knife. His letter opener. 'I... you...'

The man took an impatient breath. 'I'm only going to tell you one more time. If you tell the police you saw me, and who I am, then I'm going to come back and kill you. Do I make myself clear?'

'Yes.' The priest was shaking, trying to focus on his prayers while concentrating on this man's words.

'Repeat it.'

'If I call the police, you'll kill me.'

'Good. Get on your knees and face the wall.'

The priest felt the man's breath on his face he was so close. The knife was pressed even harder into his face, giving him a preview of what was about to happen should his orders not be followed. 'I'm going to step back, Father. Don't do anything stupid, or you'll end up like her in there.'

The priest didn't see the punch coming, but a gloved fist connected with the side of his jaw, and he felt everything go out of kilter. As he slid to the floor in the dark, he pictured the dead woman lying on the floor in his office. He couldn't remember her name, and then he blacked out.

When he finally came round, he didn't know how much time had passed since he had been punched, but he felt cold and stiff. He got to his feet, and made his way through to the office at the back of the church.

She was gone. He remembered her name now; Cathy Graham, one of his Sunday school teachers. She was dead, but whoever killed her had taken her somewhere else.

Then Beam saw something that made him shiver even more.

The killer had left a Polaroid photo of Cathy on the mantelpiece. Taken after her death.

He picked up the phone, waiting for the man to come crashing through the door, telling him he'd failed the test, that now the knife was indeed going to be shoved into his heart, but nobody came back in.

Will Beam walked on unsteady legs back to the office door, and stepped out to a place where he could watch the front door while he called the police.

As the operator connected him, he looked up at the black eye looking back at him. The one witness who could prove that somebody else had been here.

The security camera.

The one and only, but it might be enough.

'Hello? Police? I'd like to report a murder...'

ONE

'I heard you've finally given up smoking. It's about time,' Detective Inspector Maggie Parks said, turning her nose up. 'It's a filthy habit.'

Detective Chief Inspector Paddy Gibb was holding a packet of cigarettes, but hadn't taken one out. 'I'll remember this insubordination when it's time for your annual appraisal. That'll look good on the application when you're looking for a cashier's position in Tesco.'

Maggie, the head of forensics, came out of the house with her photographer. 'Nothing wrong with Tesco. My sister works there.'

'That's good. She can put in a word for you.'

Gibb tugged up the collar of his coat. There was nothing redeemable about October. The sky was grey, and it was just cold and miserable.

A car pulled into the side of the road, and Detective Inspector Frank Miller got out with another detective.

'Here's the part-timers,' Detective Sergeant Andy Watt said, coming out of the house, squeezing past a uniform and a suited-up forensics officer, a female detective following him.

'Sorry I'm late, boss,' Miller said.

Gibb held up a hand. 'If it involves recovering from getting pished or exhaustion due to activities of a sexual nature, spare me the details.'

'I couldn't get the car to start.'

'I would have blamed it on wee Emma taking a tantrum before going to school, but whatever. Angie, this is Frank *I-couldn't-get-my-arse-out-of-bed* Miller. And DS Jimmy Gilmour. This is DS Angie Rivers. This is her first day with us. Don't break her.'

The two detectives shook hands with the new member of their crew.

'Nice to meet you, sir,' Angie said.

'Likewise.'

'Lost the battle, eh, sir?' Gilmour said, nodding to the pack of cigarettes in the boss's hand.

'I don't need every smartarse making a comment. For your information, I'm just holding them.'

'Oh. Good for you, sir.'

'Too late, Gilmour,' Watt said. 'You don't have to prove you're an arse licker. He already knows. Maybe you'll get a job collecting shopping trolleys beside Maggie Parks in Tesco.'

'What?' Gilmour said.

'Never mind,' Gibb said, before Watt could reply. 'How's Monty doing?'

'Not good at all, sir, I'm afraid. He's still on life support.'

'Give Connie my best, son.'

'I will do. Thanks, sir.'

'Right, children, get into the house and have a look for yourself.' Gibb pointed with his free hand. 'And get overshoes on.'

Gibb held Angie back while the other three detectives entered the house. 'Monty is Judge Montague Chase. He's Gilmour's ex-wife, Connie's, uncle. He had a massive stroke last week. Jimmy needs our support just now, and we're not just a team, we're a family. Sounds clichéd but it's true.'

'I'll bear that in mind, sir.'

'Okay. Let's go in.'

It was a large, detached Victorian in Succoth Avenue, in the upmarket area of Ravelston, just west of Edinburgh's city centre. A big house with big rooms, and the ghosts of children who'd played in them a hundred years ago.

'The victim's Ashley Gates. Thirty-one years old, divorced according to the neighbours, and lives on her own,' Gibb said, as he followed the others through to the back of the house. He shoved the cigarettes back into his pocket. *Later, you little bastards. You're all mine. I'll smoke the fucking arse off you.*

'Who found her?' Miller asked.

'A neighbour out walking her dog. She saw the front door open.' He stopped in the hallway. 'Through to the living room.'

DS Hazel Carter was standing talking to one of the pathologists, Kate Murphy. They were standing close to the pool of blood that had soaked into the beige carpet in the middle of the room. 'Morning, Frank.'

'Hi, Kate.'

'Morning, sir,' Hazel said. She was five months pregnant, and starting to show a little.

'How are you feeling this morning?' Miller said, noticing how pale she looked.

'She's swell. Get it? Swell,' Watt said, imitating a baby bump.

Hazel shook her head and patted her belly, a wry smile on her face. 'I'm pregnant, so I've got an excuse. What's yours, Andy?'

'She got you there,' Miller said.

'I keep throwing them, and you keep knocking them out of the park,' Watt answered, winking at her.

Gibb looked at the other detectives. 'Forensics have searched the whole house, and the garage and the shed. No sign of Miss Gates at all. Now, this not being rocket science, it's safe to assume she was killed here and taken somewhere else.'

'How do we know her identity if her body isn't here?' Gilmour asked.

'Take a look up on the mantelpiece,' Miller said, staring at the object.

He looked over, and saw the Polaroid. 'Oh crap.'

'Oh crap indeed,' Gibb said. 'I had forensics look at it, but I told Parks to leave it there. I wanted you all to see it *in situ*. Including the back-shift.' He looked at Gilmour and Miller.

Miller walked forward and had a look. The instant photo was propped against a small photo frame. It showed the figure of a woman, lying on her back in the middle of the floor with her throat cut, the knife laying across her neck.

'If she wasn't dead when he took it, she wasn't far off it,' Kate Murphy said. 'But, as you can see from the blood pattern, she bled out while she was lying down. There's spatter on the wall at the side of the mantelpiece. It looks as if he hit an artery, and she went down on the carpet.'

'Any idea how long the blood's been here?' Angie asked.

'Although the blood's dry, it hasn't been dry for that long. So I would say she was murdered in the last twelve hours.'

Miller looked at Watt. 'Andy, you need to go and talk to Will Beam. See if he can tell us anything. Take Gilmour.'

Watt and Gilmour left the house just as Kim Smith was walking in.

'Good morning, Kate. Paddy.' She smiled at Angie, waiting for an introduction.

'Kim, this is DS Angie Rivers. Angie, this is Dr Kim Smith, an investigator with the PF's office and liaison manager.'

'Hi, Angie. Call me Kim. I'm also Miller's other half.'

Angie smiled. 'Pleased to meet you. And don't you mean his *better* half?'

'I like you already.' Kim turned to Gibb. 'You said this case could be linked to another one.' She looked at the photo staring back at them. 'Ah. Will Beam.'

'Who's Will Beam?' Kate asked.

'This was before you came to Edinburgh, Kate. Before Kim was here, too, but she's been briefed,' Gibb said.

Miller looked at her. 'He's a priest. A woman was murdered in the office in his church. He lived in the manse behind the church, and he was out for the evening. He came back early from visiting a parishioner and noticed the front doors of the church were open. One of his Sunday school teachers had been preparing her lesson for the following Sunday, and should have been gone. Beam walked in on the killer.'

'Was he harmed?' Kate asked.

'No, he was hiding in the confessional. He thought he hadn't been spotted, but he had been, and he was cornered. He was told that if he called the police, he would be next. He had a knife held to him. He said the killer hit him, and he blacked out.'

'Was he ever a suspect?' Angie asked.

'No. We got no forensics from him either.'

'I'm assuming the killer was never caught.'

'Or heard from again.' He looked at the Polaroid sitting on the mantelpiece. 'Until now.'

'How long ago was this?'

'Almost two years ago. It was my father, Jack's, last case, just before he retired. He thought he was going out on a high, but we all felt at a low point when we got nowhere.'

'And he was never able to identify the killer.'

Kim walked up to the photo, and stared at it for a second. 'I think I know this woman.' She turned back to the group looking at her, as if she were the ringmaster now. 'She's a lawyer. Ashley Gates.'

'That's her alright,' Gibb said. 'This is her place.'

'Jesus, she was a really nice woman. I didn't know her socially, but we chatted when she was in our office. My mum and her were good friends.'

'Kim's mum is also the procurator fiscal, Norma Banks,' Gibb said.

'Any idea where she is?' Kim asked.

'None,' Kate said. 'Forensics did a sweep, and there's nothing. He killed her here, and took her with him.'

'I can have that photo bagged as soon as you're finished.' Maggie Parks said, as she walked in.

'Maggie's leaving us,' Gibb said. 'She's going to be working for Tesco in the near future.'

'You wish,' she replied.

'Hey, nothing wrong with Tesco, remember? Your sister works there.'

'I'll get her to put in a word for you.'

'That's my line.'

Miller looked at Maggie. 'Let me take a photo of it on my phone.' He walked over to the fireplace, and took a couple of photos, one of just her face. 'Have we found a next of kin yet?'

Gibb took out his notebook. 'Mum and dad. They live in Morningside. I got the details from the neighbour. She had them as an emergency contact.' He read the details out to Miller, who copied them into his own notebook.

Maggie Parks stepped forward, carefully picked up the photo, and put it into an evidence bag. Inside the frame it was sitting against was a photo of another young woman.

Somebody had taken it out, and drawn something on it before putting it back.

Round the woman's neck was the crude drawing of a noose.

TWO

They took Kim's car up to Morningside, into another upscale neighbourhood. Angie sat in the front with Kim, while Miller looked out for the address.

'There it is. Number twenty-four.'

The house in Braid Avenue was a large, detached stone property that looked massive from the outside, fronted by a high stone wall. Kim pulled into the driveway, and parked up.

A woman appeared at the door as they all climbed out into the biting wind. 'If you're selling religion, they're not interested,' she said.

'Mrs Gates?' Miller asked, having a feeling that it wasn't.

'No, I'm her housekeeper. How can I help?'

Miller took out his warrant card, held it up for her to see as he approached, and introduced the two women.

'We need to speak with Mrs Gates, if she's in.'

'They're both in, her and her husband. If you'd like to come in.'

They stepped into the large entrance vestibule, and waited for the woman to shut the front door. 'My name's Janet. We get a lot of people selling religion around here, despite the signs saying they'll be shot if they come to the door.' She smiled at Miller. 'I'm kidding. About them being shot.'

They followed her into the entrance hall, the increased temperature welcome. It was large with a staircase on the right. A long hallway was in front of them, with doors on either side.

'If you'd like to go in here on the left, I'll fetch Mrs Gates.'

'Thank you,' Kim said, and they trooped into the room.

'Feel free to have a seat,' Janet said, from the doorway. 'Would you like coffee?'

'No thanks.' Miller felt the news they were about to deliver didn't warrant it looking like a tea party.

Janet left, and a few minutes later, another woman appeared. The mother, Miller guessed. The three of them hadn't sat down, and Mrs Gates looked uncomfortable. Miller held out his warrant card as he had done to the housekeeper, and made the introductions again.

'Please, sit,' Ethel Gates said, and this time they did. She sat opposite them in a wing-backed leather chair. 'What's this all about, Detective Miller?'

'Is Ashley Gates your daughter?' he asked.

'Now you're scaring me. What's this all about?'

'Can you answer my question, please?'

'Yes, she is. What's wrong?'

'I'm sorry, but we have some bad news; it appears that Ashley was murdered.'

'What? Oh my God! Stanley!' she screamed, and jumped up out of her chair. Kim was the first up, followed by Angie. Miller was last.

They heard feet thudding down the stairs just before a man burst into the room.

Oh Christ, Miller thought, when he saw who it was. No wonder he had such a big house.

'Mr Gates?' Miller said.

'You know damn fine well that I am. I know you. Miller isn't it?'

'It is. These are my colleagues, Dr—'

'This isn't a social gathering, Miller. Why's my wife screaming?'

'Stanley, Ashley's dead!' Mrs Gates shouted.

'What?' He took another step into the room as if the carpet was hiding a minefield. 'What are you talking about?'

'He just told me Ashley's been murdered.'

'*He* did?' Gates said, pointing to Miller, as if the detective was the one who had perpetrated the crime.

'Mr Gates, will you please have a seat?' Kim said.

'You as well. Your mother's Norma Banks, isn't she?'

'She is, yes.'

'I'll be right on the phone to her, bloody—'

'Enough!' Angie said, in a loud voice. 'You both need to sit down. We need to ask a few questions. We're sorry for your loss, but there's a murderer out there, and the sooner we talk to you both, the sooner we can get on with our job.'

Clearly, Gates wasn't used to being spoken to like that, especially by a female, and it was enough to derail him for a moment.

'Detective Rivers, could you go and get Janet's details please,' Miller said, and watched her leave the room.

'Please sit down, sir.' Kim indicated the couch.

Gates sat, his now-weeping wife next to him, while the others remained standing.

'What happened?' he asked, the wind now out of his sails.

'We believe she was murdered in her living room sometime in the last twelve hours or so,' Miller said, as he sat on the chair closest to them.

'Oh my God, not my little Ashley,' Mrs Gates said. 'Where is she now? I have to go and see her.'

'Let them tell us,' Gates said, grabbing his wife's arm.

'Take your hand off me! Haven't you done enough?'

Gates looked at Miller briefly, before putting an arm around his wife and holding her close.

Miller looked right back at him. 'Look, this isn't going to be easy, but—'

'I'm a barrister, Miller. My life isn't easy. Give it to us straight, man.'

'The killer took Ashley with him. We don't know where she is.'

'What?' Ethel Gates said, her motherly instincts kicking in. Her baby was gone, and now she wanted blood. 'What do you mean, he took her?'

A Queen's Council barrister and a mother, both staring at him, but he had faced worse. 'He killed her, and took a Polaroid photo of her, leaving that behind for us. Then he took her with him. We haven't found her yet.'

Ethel turned to her husband. 'What does he mean, Stanley?'

'Try and stay calm, love,' he said, showing the first sign of empathy towards his wife.

'I'm sorry, I know this is tough, but we need to ask you some questions,' Kim said.

Gates nodded. 'Go ahead.'

'Do you know of anybody who would want to harm Ashley?'

'Apart from the scum she put away? Nobody springs to mind, and she didn't mention that she was having difficulties with anybody.'

Then Ethel looked at her husband, as if mentally asking his permission to say something, and some form of invisible code passed between them. 'There was Dan Herdan.'

'Is that her boyfriend?' Kim asked. 'We believe she was divorced.'

'It's her *bit of rough*, as she liked to say,' Gates said, his face turning red with anger. 'If I find out that bastard touched her...'

'You'll give us a call,' Miller said.

'Will I?' Gates said, clearly indicating he wouldn't.

'Tell us about this Herdan man,' Kim said, taking notes.

'He's a blue collar worker. A taxi driver of all things. She couldn't have gone for the brain surgeon, oh no. That would have been too fucking—'

'Language, Stanley,' Ethel said, showing who really wore the trousers in their house.

'Sorry. No, that would have been too easy. She did that to get back at me, because I lectured her about meeting somebody nice after her divorce.'

'We want grandchildren, and Ashley said that wasn't going to happen anytime soon. She said she didn't want kids, that her career came first. Then she started dating that horrible man. And then a few weeks ago, she told me... she... was pregnant.' Ethel couldn't hold it together any longer, and started crying hysterically again. Gates still sat with his arm around his wife's shoulder.

'I'm really sorry we have to ask these questions, Mr Gates,' Kim said, 'but it may help us find your daughter's killer.'

'I know how this game works, young lady. Ask away. We'll do anything we can to help.'

'Do you know how we can get in touch with this Dan Herdan?' Miller asked him.

'No. We don't know anything about him. Except he drove for a living. Bloody taxi driver indeed.'

'No address?'

'I just said so, didn't I?'

'Where's her ex-husband? And do you have any details for him?'

'His name's Arthur King. He's also a QC, and a showboating bastard. *King Arthur* he called himself. I hated him, and he knew it.' This time his wife didn't correct his language.

'Do you know where we can find him?'

'I'll write his address down. I can't remember the exact details, but I have it in an address book. I'll give it to you before you go.'

'Do you know if either man was violent towards your daughter?' Kim asked.

Gates gave a brief laugh. 'If they had been, they would have regretted it. Ashley went to kickboxing, and she had a temper. She told King in no uncertain terms that if he ever laid a finger on her, she'd kick his teeth out. She was quite feisty, my daughter.' Gates gave a brief smile, obviously proud of that fact.

I wonder which parent she got that from, Miller thought. 'What about Herdan?'

'I told you, we never met him. We argued over it one day, and I told her she was throwing her life away. She could marry a judge, for God's sake. They're not all ninety years old. In fact, there was one who was quite keen to take her out, but she didn't like him. He's married to somebody else now.'

'How long has she been divorced?'

'About four years.'

'Was it a rough divorce?' Kim asked.

'No. Again, Ashley made it clear to him what would happen if he messed her about.'

'Can I ask you the reason for their divorce?'

'Has this any relevance?'

'It may show a motive for your daughter's murder.'

'King was fooling around on her. He met another woman, and slept around behind my daughter's back. She came home early one day and caught him at it.'

'So it was acrimonious?' Kim said.

'There was the usual shouting and swearing, mainly from Ashley,' her father said. 'King couldn't care less. He's from money. He gave her the house in the settlement, and a ton of money. He kept his Porsche 911. German crap. I wanted her to drive British, but she had one of those tiny Fiat things.'

'They're not interested what kind of car she drove, Stanley,' Ethel Gates said, her sobbing subsided and her voice low.

'Yes, quite. So they went their separate ways, and that was that. Ashley went out with a couple of men – and no, I don't have their names – but one was a banker, and one was a businessman. They were no fun, she said, and then she met this taxi driver after he drove her home one night in his cab.'

'And she was still dating him now?' Miller said.

'As far as I know,' Gates said. His mind seemed to drift, as if he was imagining Herdan suffering a traumatic injury at his hands.

Miller took his phone out. Opened up the photos app and showed them the picture he'd taken of the photo in the frame in

Ashley's house. 'Could you look at this woman's face, and tell me if you recognise her?'

They both shook their heads.

'Who is she?' Gates asked, taking his arm from around his wife's shoulder.

'I don't know. It's a photo in a frame in your daughter's house.' He didn't elaborate about the drawing of the noose round the woman's neck.

'Probably a friend.'

'I thought we knew all of Ashley's friends?' Ethel Gates said.

'We obviously didn't know enough about her,' her husband said.

Miller waited to see if there would be any more information forthcoming, but there wasn't. 'I'd appreciate it if you could get me the address of Arthur King now, please.'

Gates got up, and came back with a piece of paper a few minutes later which he handed to Miller. 'That's his office address. And his home address. He lives in one of those new flats down at Newhaven. Good God. Newhaven.'

'Those are very nice flats,' Kim said, not impressed with Gates' snobbery.

'Exactly; *flat*. Moving from a big house in Ravelston to a flat by the sea. Sounds like bloody Blackpool.'

'Well, we'll be in touch when more information becomes available,' Miller said. Gates was still standing, watching him.

'I'll be on to your superior, Miller. I don't like the way that girl spoke to me.'

'Stanley, she's very nice, and you *were* upset. I think we've more to worry about than a detective raising her voice to you.'

'Whatever.'

'If you can think of anything else, please contact the MIT offices at High Street station.'

'We will,' Ethel Gates said, standing up and stepping close to her husband.

'I'm sorry about this, but I do need to ask—' Miller started to say before Gates cut him off.

'We had dinner with a couple of our friends, we went to their place for drinks afterwards, stayed until about eleven, got a taxi home – Fast Cabs – and then we went to bed. I'm not in court today, so I'm going into my office late.'

'Thank you.'

When they went into the hallway, Janet, the housekeeper, was hovering, waiting to see them out.

'Detective Rivers is waiting outside,' she said. Gates closed the door to the room behind him.

'If you need to contact us about anything you remember, please don't hesitate,' Miller said, in a low voice, handing her one of his business cards.

In the car, Angie sat in the back seat like a spoilt teenager.

'We do things differently down here,' he said.

'It was just like a verbal slap, to get them to focus.'

'He's a QC with friends in high places. He's not somebody you want to tread on to get up the ladder.' He took his mobile phone out, and made a call. Waited for the person on the other end to answer. 'Before you know where you are, there won't *be* a ladder.'

He hung up, and waited for the person on the other end to get back to him. After she called, he thanked her, and made another call. A few minutes later, he had the answer he had been looking for.

THREE

'There it is,' Gilmour said, pointing to the church on the other side of the roundabout. It was at the intersection where East London Street met the bottom of Broughton Street. A part of Edinburgh where estate agents could blur the lines of whether a property was in the New Town or not.

'I've been here before, Jimmy. My ex-wife used to drive me mental whenever we would go for a drive. Back-seat driver didn't even begin to describe how she was.'

The church loomed up on their left as Watt turned off the roundabout and took a left into the car park at the side of the church. It went downhill and round to the left and they stopped in front of the manse doors, the priest's house attached to the side of the church.

'What a godforsaken place,' Watt said, squinting against the cold.

'I think God would disagree with you there, detective,' Will Beam said, standing at the door of his manse. 'Come away in. I've got the kettle on.'

Watt looked at Gilmour as the priest moved back indoors, leaving the front door open.

'Thank Christ for that,' he said, under his breath, as they both walked into the manse.

Watt shut the door, and they stepped into the warmth of the vestibule. Beam came back through from the kitchen.

'It's been a long time, Detective Watt. Good to meet you again, Detective Gilmour. How are things with you both?' He smiled at them as if they were two of his own parishioners.

'We're both well.'

'But you're not here for a tour of the church, so I'm guessing you're here on official business. Come away through to the lounge, and I'll fix the coffee.'

He led them through to a living room with a large screen TV. 'Sixty-five inches. Samsung Ultra HD 4K. Donated by one of my parishioners. A Christmas gift. Here, let me turn the sound down.'

There was a talk show on, and Watt had to admit that the picture was superb. 'And here's me with just a twelve-inch black-and-white.'

'Away with yourself. I'll bet you have the latest gear, DS Watt. I can tell a man like you has exquisite taste. In TVs, and in women.'

'Were not here to talk about...' he started to say to Beam, but the priest had disappeared into the kitchen through a doorway from the living room.

'I had one of those TVs. I left it with Connie. Rachael likes to watch the cartoons on it.'

They sat down on the settee.

'And now you're fuc—'

'Sugar?' Beam asked from the doorway.

'No. Just black for me,' Watt said.

'Same for me thanks,' Gilmour said. They watched the priest disappear back into the kitchen.

'As I was saying, I hope she's worth it, Jimmy.'

'Who?'

'That piece you're shacking up with.'

'Piece? That's my girlfriend.'

'Fucking girlfriend. More like a piranha on two legs. Why doesn't she come round to the pub?'

'Things are a bit strained at the moment.'

'Look, sometimes you think you can settle down with a woman because you're having a good time, but the real test is when you wake up the next morning when you have a hangover. Do you still feel the same way as you did the night before when you were blootered and doing a conga line?'

Gilmour knew Watt was talking sense.

Beam brought in a large plate of Tunnock's Tea Cakes and Jammie Dodgers, and put it down on the coffee table in front of the two detectives. 'I don't know about you lads, but I can't have my elevenses without a biscuit.' He walked back into the kitchen, and Gilmour picked one up.

'You're not seriously going to eat one of those, are you?'

'Of course I am.'

Watt leaned in closer. 'He might have gobbed on them.'

'Don't talk pish. They're still wrapped. Besides, I'd be more worried that he's gobbed in the coffee.'

'That's true,' Watt said, grabbing a teacake. 'If my coffee looks like a homemade cappuccino, I'll throw it about the bastard.'

'Did I hear you say you like cappuccino, DS Watt?' Beam said, smiling as he brought two mugs of coffee in.

'I was just saying how expensive those coffee places are nowadays.'

Beam set the coffees down on the table next to the biscuits. 'That's why I always make my own. I'm not penny wise and pound foolish.'

He walked away to fetch his own cup as Watt bit into the biscuit.

'How fucking cosy is this?' Gilmour said. 'Tea and biscuits when we're investigating a fucking murder. This feels way off for me, mate.'

'Relax. *You catch more flies with honey than vinegar*, is the old saying. We don't want to come in here like a steamroller, and scare the poor sod. We just start a conversation, and then coax more out of him. Psychology, Jimmy.'

'Good point. But he didn't tell Jack Miller anything when he was in charge of the investigation two years ago, so there's not much chance of us getting anything out of him.'

'We can only try.'

'And if we're shitting through the eye of a needle tonight, we can always come back tomorrow and boot his nuts for him.'

'Amen.'

Watt finished the teacake, balled up the foil, and flicked it across to the other side of the room.

'Fuck's sake, Andy,' Gilmour said, shaking his head. 'He's going to wonder where the wrapper went.'

'Fuck 'im. He'll never know I had one.'

Beam walked back in, sat down, and watched as Gilmour ate his own teacake more carefully, not as if it was the last one on earth, as Watt had.

Fuck me, Watt mouthed at Gilmour when the priest was distracted by the appearance of a famous soap actress on TV.

'Oh, let's listen in. I love her,' Beam said, before the policemen could object. He put the sound on again. Watt grabbed another teacake, and sat back with his coffee.

After ten minutes of listening to the actress spout drivel, Beam looked back at the two detectives. Watt had almost forgotten why they were there.

'So, who died?' Beam asked, trying not to look worried, and failing.

Watt looked at the priest. 'What makes you ask that, Father?'

'It's clear why you're here; somebody died, and you want to know if I can help you.'

'Somebody did die, yes, and we do have some questions.'

'Where did he leave the Polaroid, if I may ask?'

'We can't give much information right now, Father. The death occurred last night, give or take. However, we *would* like to know if you were contacted. Either today, or any time since he spoke to you two years ago.'

'Killed on a Sunday night.' Beam looked between the two detectives. 'It was the murder of a young girl, and you found a photo of her.'

'If you could just answer the question, please, sir,' Gilmour said.

'No, he didn't contact me. Not after the last time, nor this time. That's not to say he won't, but so far, he hasn't.'

'If he does, please get in contact with us again.'

'I will. If he lets me live.'

'Has anything else sprung to mind in the time since he attacked you? Sometimes, people remember things, long after the incident,' Watt said.

'Nothing, I'm afraid. Just what I told you at the time.'

'If he threatens you, just call us. I'd like a word with him, if he has the guts.' The detectives stood. 'Thanks for the coffee,' Watt said. 'I think my colleague had two teacakes.'

'Well, who's counting?'

Beam watched them from the door for a moment as they walked back to their car. The priest closed it as Watt got behind the wheel.

'He'll fucking think I flicked that wrapper across to his curtains now,' Gilmour said.

'I think they were foosty anyway.'

'So you had two just to make sure?'

'I'm not the one watching my weight, Jimmy boy. My girlfriend likes a bit of meat on the bones.'

'She'll think you're a keeper, then.'

'I wish I'd gone for a pish before we left,' Watt said, as they drove out of the car park.

Father Will Beam sat back and drank his coffee. He hoped the policemen hadn't been able to tell how nervous he was. He'd wanted to shout out, *He was here! Last night, he was here!* But he couldn't discuss what somebody had said to him in the confessional.

He hadn't looked at the man's face, but his words had terrified him.

The threat had terrified him.

More so, because he thought he knew the man.

Will Beam just hoped that he wasn't standing outside now, watching two policemen leave. He'd think that he, Beam, had called them. Then he was a dead man.

FOUR

Stanley Gates didn't know where Dan Herdan lived, but being a taxi driver, his name was easy to retrieve from the Police Scotland Taxi Examination Centre. As well as putting the black cabs through the road test, they held the taxi driver's knowledge test there, and all taxi drivers had to be registered with them.

Including Dan Herdan.

So Miller pulled up in front of a house in Carrick Knowe, on the west side of the city. There was a taxi parked in the driveway. And an older, but clean-looking, Mercedes C-Class. Angie stepped forward and banged on the door.

A bleary-eyed man, his hair tousled as if he'd just got out of bed, was tying a dressing gown as he opened the front door a few minutes later.

'Dan Herdan?' Miller asked, holding up his ID.

'What's it to you?' Herdan hated the police, more so since he'd been caught on a speed camera going through a red light in his cab. He'd tried to explain in a letter that it had been wet, and had he stopped, he would have been through the *Stop* line and blocking the road, but would they listen?

'Yes or no?' Miller said.

'Yesssss. Now what do you want, I'm trying to get some sleep?'

'We'd like to come in and speak to you.'

'Is it urgent? I mean, can you come back later?'

'No we can't,' Angie answered, starting to get impatient with Herdan.

'Well, you'd better come in then I suppose.' Herdan stood back, and let the detectives in. He showed them into the living room, and Miller looked at the magazines and old newspapers scattered about on the settee. 'It's my housekeeper's day off,' Herdan said, as he saw Miller looking at the mess.

'I'd like to know where you were between nine o'clock last night and nine this morning,' Miller said.

Herdan shrugged. 'Working. Driving around. I own a black cab. Why?'

'Ashley Gates was found murdered in her house this morning.'

'Ashley's dead? Murdered? I never touched her. It wasn't me! I never touched her!'

'We'd like you to come down to the station to answer some questions, Mr Herdan,' Kim said.

'I haven't done anything. Why are you arresting me?'

'We're not arresting you. Yet. Get dressed.'

Herdan was sitting next to his lawyer, drinking a cup of coffee, as Miller and Paddy Gibb walked into the interview room. The two detectives sat opposite as a uniformed officer closed the door and stood guard.

Miller looked at the man, and his eyes kept going to the tuft of hair that stuck up at the back of his head as if somebody had stuck a feather there and he didn't know about it.

Herdan had calmed down a bit now, even seeming to be a little cocky.

'Tell me where you were last night,' Miller said to him.

'I already told you, working.'

'So tell me again.'

Herdan looked at his solicitor, who nodded. 'I finished my shift around three o'clock because it was dead quiet.'

'And then you went round to her house because you were angry with her,' Gibb said.

'I told you, I was cruising around. I got a job at two fifty going to Trinity then I finished after that. I went straight home.'

Miller looked at Gibb, who nodded to him. They were checking out Herdan's story with Edinburgh Cabs.

Herdan shook his head. 'It was one of those on-off relationships. We split up a few weeks ago, but I knew she would come running back.'

'How old are you, Mr Herdan?' Gibb asked.

Herdan looked at Gibb with the same look he had just given Miller. 'Forty-two, what about it?'

'Ashley was thirty-one. What did she see in an old man like you? Do you seriously think if she found somebody younger than you, she would want to go out with you again? What was wrong with your relationship with her? Couldn't you satisfy her?'

Herdan laughed. 'Nice one, Inspector Gibb. Do you expect me to lose my temper and have a go at you? Is that it? Well, I'm sorry to disappoint you, but I'm not a violent man. I get hot-headed at times, but doesn't everybody? I wouldn't lose my temper enough to kill somebody, especially somebody I had feelings for.'

'It's *Chief* Inspector.'

Somebody knocked on the door, and a young WPC walked in. 'Sorry to disturb you, sir.' She handed Gibb a sheet of paper before retreating. He read it, and passed it over to Miller.

Edinburgh Cabs had confirmed that Herdan was logged on in the central zone at two o'clock, but hadn't picked anybody up until two fifty.

'When was the last time you saw Ashley?' Miller said.

'Last night.'

'You said you'd split-up from her,' Gibb said.

'That's right. We *had* split-up, but I called her in the afternoon and asked her if she fancied a drink when it was my break.'

'What time is your break?'

'Anytime I want. I told her to give me a call, and I would log off and have a drink with her. We could have a chat, and see where we went after that.'

'So what time did you meet her?' Gibb asked.

'It was around ten. She was having a drink with her friends at the Phil.'

Gibb looked at him. 'Where's that?'

'The Philosopher? On George IV Bridge. Dearie me, you're a copper and you don't know the pubs?' Herdan smiled, and sat back in his chair.

'It's not as if I go drinking with wee lassies like you do. They have a special wing for prisoners like you in Saughton.'

'I never touched her. I only went to that pub 'cause Ashley was having a drink there. Even though she's in her thirties now, she still likes to act like a student, if you know what I mean.'

'No, I don't know what you mean,' Miller said. 'Why don't you tell me?'

Herdan leaned forward again, and clasped his hands together on the table. 'She liked it a lot. Sex. She wasn't fussy who she went with. I missed the things she used to do to me. I wanted more.' He took his hands off the table, and looked at the two detectives. 'She couldn't get enough, and I don't doubt for one second that she was being entertained by other men when we were apart.'

'And that didn't bother you?'

'Ashley was a free spirit. I just wanted to be a part of her life.'

'Tell us about last night in the pub,' Gibb said.

'She didn't want to meet me at first. Told me it was all over, and that I should just accept it. But I sweet-talked her into it. And by that, I mean I told her we could work things out.'

'And how was she when she met you?'

'Things went fine. Despite that little bitch trying to interfere.' He looked at the two detectives. 'Patricia Wilkinson. Her best friend. The two of them are like twins.'

'And she was there in the pub?' Miller said.

'She *works* in the pub. She wasn't pleased to see me, I could tell, but she was there to serve me. Ashley seemed pleased to see me though. All smiles and hugs. Mind you, she'd had a few by the time I got there.'

'So what happened next?'

'We talked. Things were going fine. She told me we could go out on Friday, just for a few drinks, have a meal and talk things over. See where we went from there.'

'And you didn't fight or argue?' Gibb said.

'No. In fact, things were quite good. Yes, I know we've argued before, and had some arguments in public, but Ashley is very... passionate. Was.' He closed his eyes, and hung his head down. When he looked at them both again, his eyes were shining with unshed tears.

'How long were you talking for?'

'About half an hour. *Patty-the-mouth* saw us go. She can tell you. I left Ashley at the door, and she told me she was going back in. I got a call, and the last time I saw her was just after ten thirty.'

Gibb was writing notes.

'Was anybody else taking an interest in her in the bar?' Miller said.

'Ha. What man wouldn't want to take an interest in her? She was gorgeous, smart, had a fantastic figure. Any red-blooded male would want to take her out.'

Gibb knew there was nothing else they could do about Herdan, and they had nothing to charge him with. He looked at Miller, and nodded: *wrap it up.*

'Right, Mr Herdan. You're free to go, but we may need to talk to you again, so don't leave the area.'

Herdan and his lawyer both stood, and they trooped out behind the uniformed officer, leaving Miller and Gibb alone.

'What's your gut telling you, Frank?'

'That it's fifty-fifty, Paddy. Maybe he was nice to her in the bar, drove away, and then went to her house to kill her. We don't know exactly what he said to her outside. Maybe she told him to fuck off, and he took exception.'

'I'd like somebody to go to his cab office, and see if they can keep tabs on him as he's driving about.'

'It's worth a shot.'

Gibb looked at Miller, pausing for a moment. 'I took a call from Stanley Gates earlier. If Angie Rivers keeps that kind of behaviour up, she'll be on the next train back to Aberdeen.'

'She was just a bit over-enthusiastic.'

'She can tell that to Percy Purcell when we send her packing.'

'I had a talk with her. She won't be doing it again.'

'See that she doesn't, Frank. I'll keep her here with me while you and Kim go to Ashley's office. Get Ashley's ex-husband checked out as well. He was in court this morning, but he's due back in his office this afternoon. I had somebody check.'

'I'll get onto it. I'm waiting for Andy and Jimmy to get back.'

'Make sure we pull out all the stops on this. And keep a tighter rein on Rivers when you're out with her next time.'

'To be fair, it did shut him up,' Miller said, as they left the room.

FIVE

It was after lunch by the time Watt and Gilmour got back to the investigation suite, where Miller and Kim were, along with the others. Angie Rivers sat at her desk typing up a report.

'The prodigal sons return,' Gibb said.

'Traffic was a nightmare,' Watt replied. 'And we haven't had lunch. Is it okay if me and Jimmy go to the canteen?'

Gilmour was hanging his overcoat up.

'What is this, a building site? Five minutes work with an eight-hour tea break? No you bloody well can't go to the canteen. You were only down the fucking road.'

'Before you two write your reports, give me the breakdown,' Miller said.

Watt perched himself on the edge of his desk. 'Beam said he wasn't contacted and I tend to believe him. He's scared though. Something's worrying him.'

'Maybe just the memory of that night two years ago. We'll keep in touch with him though, in case something springs to mind.'

'Right, you two may as well go and talk to a bartender by the name of Patricia Wilkinson,' Gibb said. 'If she's not there, get an address and go talk to her. I want to know what went on between Ashley Gates and Dan Herdan, the boyfriend, in the pub last night.'

'What pub, sir?' Gilmour asked.

'The Philosopher.'

'Oh, I know that place,' Watt said. 'It's mainly a student bar on George IV Bridge.'

'Oh, yeah, I've been in there a few times with Lauren,' Gilmour said.

'That doesn't surprise me,' Watt said, 'considering she's a student nurse.'

'She's mature, Andy.'

'So how old is Ashley's boyfriend?' Watt asked.

'Forty-two,' Miller answered.

'Ashley was thirty-one,' Gibb said, 'and Patricia was her friend, so that's why they were there.'

'If Herdan is telling the truth, then we have a new window for Ashley's time of death; he said he left her at the pub's entrance at ten thirty, which checks out with his cab company, who said they sent him a job at ten thirty-six. Now, it could be that she went back in, and if so, we need to know when she left, and if anybody was with her. Find out what the time was. If not, then the window is between ten thirty last night and nine this morning. Get to it, you two. Don't be all bloody day. And take Hazel with you. She needs some fresh air.'

'Aw, does the wee lassie want to go out and play?' Watt said.

'Piss off.'

'Dearie me, I didn't know *trucker's mouth* was a pregnancy side effect.'

'Just for that, you can buy me an orange juice in this pub.'

Gibb shook his head as the three detectives left the room, heading downstairs.

'Can you and Kim go to Ashley's office now, Frank?'

'Sure.' He'd just entered his office to grab his overcoat when there was a knock on the door. He turned round.

It was Angie.

'Come in, Angie.'

She came in and closed the door behind her. 'Sir, I just want to apologise about this morning. I jumped in with both feet. Trying to make too much of a first impression, I think.'

'Don't worry about it. Gates already called and complained to Gibb. I told him I'd had a word with you, which is no lie. He thinks you got a slap on the wrist, but I don't jump all over my team here.'

'I appreciate that, sir.' She put her hand on the door handle. 'I work hard, and I respect my bosses. Give me a chance and I'll work prove it to you.'

'I know you will. If Percy says you're a good copper, then that's good enough for me.'

She smiled, and left the room. Then Kim came in.

'Flirting with the staff, Miller?'

'I'm just keeping you on your toes.'

'Don't be a pig, Miller.'

'I'm kidding, I'm kidding.' He shrugged his coat on. 'Come on, let's you and I go to Ashley's office. Gibb wants you there, so you can report back to your mother.'

Nobody messed Norma Banks about, and even though the PF was Kim's mother, she made sure things were done by the book.

Kim drove while Miller contemplated.

'Penny for them,' Kim said.

'I was actually thinking about our first anniversary of meeting each other.' He looked at her and smiled. 'I know we didn't start dating until the summer, but we can have as many anniversaries as we like.'

'You're going to dump me, aren't you?' she said, feigning sadness.

'I wouldn't dare.'

'Ha ha. Correct answer, Miller. Now tell me what you're thinking.' She drove down the Mound, heading for the New Town where Ashley Gates' office was located. She went straight over George Street with the statue of King George IV standing in the middle of the street, commemorating his visit to Scotland in August 1822, the first king to do so since Charles II in 1651.

The lights changed and she turned left. 'There's still time to back out. I know I have Emma, and though you treat her like a daughter, I don't want you to feel trapped.'

'You're worrying too much. If I didn't want to be with you, then I wouldn't be with you. But I do.'

Moray Place consisted of townhouses in a circle, built in another time when architects knew how to design something that would last for centuries.

The one belonging to Merton, Sibbald, and King was one such building. Kim pulled the car in and put the police sign in the windscreen.

'I think we should get one of these,' she said, as they walked towards the front door of the office. The sky was a steel grey, and the air was cold and damp.

'Right, let's go and see what Ashley Gates' boss has to say for himself.

SIX

'*Welcome to Scotland – Bars open round the clock!* That's how visitors should be greeted at Edinburgh airport,' Andy Watt said, as he and Gilmour pulled up to the doors of the Philosopher. Hazel had her head resting against the window in the back, gently dozing.

'She looks knackered,' Gilmour said.

'Just let her sleep there. She's up all night with Bruce. He has nightmares every night, poor bastard.'

'I'd be having nightmares if I'd been through what he went through.'

Watt looked at the Gothic structure, and the gaudy neon lighting of the sign hanging above the door. Inside, the main bar was large, with a balcony up above running round in a semi-circle.

The bar was quiet, just a few lunchtime drinkers with low music being piped in. The techno stuff would be kept for later on.

'I watched an American documentary on the AA. Some perverts go there to take advantage of women. The *thirteenth step* they call it. There's some mucky bastards out there,' Watt said.

'There are tables up on the mezzanine. They serve good food in here. And there's another bar downstairs,' Gilmour said.

'Oh, I forgot, you like mixing it up with the wee schoolies.'

'I'm in my late-twenties, Andy, and Lauren is twenty-four.'

'*Death by shagging*. That's what Kate Murphy will write on your death certificate. Mind you, that's not a bad way to go.'

They walked up to the bar, Watt introduced them, and they showed their warrant cards. 'We're looking for Patricia Wilkinson,' he said, to the female bartender.

'You've found her.'

'I need to talk to you about your friend, Ashley Gates.'

'Jesus Christ, what has that arse done to her now? He hasn't hurt her, has he?'

'Who are we talking about, Miss Wilkinson?' Gilmour said.

'Big brave Dan Herdan. He was her boyfriend.'

'Is there somewhere we can talk in private?' Watt said.

'We can talk through the back. I'm the manager, so we can talk in my office.' She looked over at a man who was clearing a table. 'Les? Can you take over? I need to go through the back.'

'Sure.'

Patricia led the detectives to one end of the bar, through a door into a back corridor, and then into her office.

She went behind the desk and sat down, inviting the two policemen to sit in the other two chairs.

'You're a good friend of Ashley's?' Watt said.

'I am, yes. Why? What's wrong?'

'I'm sorry to tell you that Ashley's dead.'

'What?' Patricia sat with her mouth open for a few seconds, her face ashen. 'Oh my God! What happened? Did that bastard hurt her after all?'

'I'm sorry to say that she was murdered. We don't have any suspects at the moment, but we'd like you to confirm she was here last night with you.'

Patricia nodded, opened up a desk drawer, took out a pack of cigarettes and lit one, blowing five minutes of her life into the air. 'I knew something would happen to her if she went out with that wanker again. He gives her nothing but grief.' She reached into another drawer, and brought out a half-bottle of whisky. Waved it at the detectives in an invitation to join her. They both shook their heads, though Watt hesitated for a fraction longer than Gilmour.

Patricia poured herself a healthy measure, took a good chug, and slapped the glass down on the table. 'Have you arrested Herdan?'

'We're pursuing several lines of enquiry,' Watt answered. 'What makes you think he would hurt her?'

'I went out with him for a little while. He's great fun, spends his cash, but when he has too much to drink, he turns into one of those blokes who like to go fighting. He's not a happy drunk. He tried it once too often with me, so I called it quits with him.'

'Now, about last night; was she here?'

'Yes. I work most Sundays, and if Ashley's not doing anything, she'll come along.' She looked at Watt. 'I refuse to speak about her in the past tense. I can't believe she's gone. I *won't* believe it. She's my best friend, for fuck's sake.'

'It's understandable, Miss Wilkinson.'

'Call me Pat.'

'Pat. We need to go over what time Ashley was here last night.'

Patricia sucked on the cigarette as if she was trying to take the filter off. 'Let me see; she came in around eight thirty. We chatted. She had a few drinks then she said Herdan was coming in to talk to her. He wanted to get back with her.'

'How were they when they were in here?'

'He was pleasant, and they were having a laugh. But you know how it is; you're always a different person until you start going out with somebody. Then the real persona starts to show through. He was just being nice because he wanted her back.'

'What time did he come in?' Gilmour asked.

'I think it was sometime shortly before ten.'

'What time did he leave?'

'It wasn't that long after. He didn't seem too happy. Ashley went out with him, but then she came back in a few minutes later. She said Herdan had been sent a job after he logged back on to his system.'

'So Herdan left, and Ashley came back in. What time did she leave?'

'Around eleven thirty. Same as always when she's working the next day.'

'What time do you close?' Gilmour asked.

'Midnight on a Sunday. One o'clock the rest of the week.'

'Did you actually see Ashley leave?'

Patricia sucked harder on her cigarette, and flicked the ash into an ashtray that had magically appeared from the drawer as well. Watt was waiting for the finale when a rabbit would be pulled out.

'Yes, I did.' She drank more of the whisky. 'I saw her go out the door. She stopped and waved. The last time I ever saw her.' Her lip started to tremble, but she masked it with another draw of her cigarette.

'How did she get here?'

'By fast black. She used taxis to get around all the time. She said it was better than trying to find a parking space, and she didn't have to worry about having a drink.'

'So it's safe to say she might have jumped in a cab last night.'

'Definitely. There's no buses that go past her house on a Sunday, and she wasn't driving.'

'So Herdan could have picked her up.'

'It's possible.'

'We'll need to speak with other members of staff who were here last night, if you could give us their details.'

'I will.' A computer screen sat on one side of her desk. She stubbed out her cigarette, typed, and ran the mouse about until the printer sitting on a cabinet off to one side spat out a sheet. She grabbed it, and laid it down in front of her.

'Who was on with you last night?'

'Les and a few of the others. I'll highlight their names.' She took a yellow highlighter, and drew it across the sheet a few times.

Watt sat forward. 'I need to ask you this; was Ashley a bit promiscuous?'

'What makes you ask that?' Patricia said, furrowing her brow as she slugged back the rest of the whisky.

'Her father described Herdan as Ashley's *bit of rough.*'

'No, of course she wasn't. She was young and single so yes, she did go out with men, but she didn't let them shag her in the toilets if that's what you mean.'

'It's not. I had to ask.'

'She was young and divorced, and liked the company of men.'

'Thank you,' Watt said, as they stood. He took the sheet from her, and folded it away into a pocket. 'I'll have some of my colleagues follow up on this.'

At the door to her office, Patricia stopped, and looked at Watt. 'You'll get Herdan for this, won't you?'

'If it was him.' They left the warmth of the pub, and got into their car.

Hazel had slumped over on the back seat, as if she'd died in her sleep, and didn't move when they got back in the car.

'Hazel!' Watt shouted.

'Huh?' she said, with a start. She ran the back of her hand over her mouth. 'God, Andy, I don't know what happened.'

'You fell asleep. You're fine. Just lay back down again. I'll tell you when we're back at the station. First, though, we're going to get a quick bite to eat. Workmen on a building site, indeed.'

'Two teacakes not enough to satisfy you then, Andy?' Gilmour said.

––––––––––––––––––

Patricia sat back in her chair, and watched as the office door opened and a figure walked in.

'You didn't tell them about us?' he asked.

'No, of course not.' She stood up. 'You'd better go. I don't want you coming in here again. It's too risky.'

The man nodded. 'I'll call you.' He turned to go when Patricia caught his arm. 'I love you.' She kissed him hard.

'I love you too.'

He slipped out quietly.

SEVEN

Inside, the reception area was in what might have been a family room back in the days when kids played with wooden toys instead of video games. Now, the room was filled with several desks with young women staffing them.

'I'm DI Frank Miller. This is Investigator Kim Smith with the PF's office. We'd like to speak with somebody regarding Ashley Gates.'

The woman nearest the door wiped her nose with a paper hanky. 'It's such awful news. Mr Gates called and told Mr King the news. We're all devastated.'

Miller looked at the other two women behind the desks, both younger, only one of whom seemed to be devastated.

'Perhaps we could speak to Mr King?'

'I'll call through.'

Less than a minute later, she said they could go through. The girl who wasn't too upset was asked to escort them, perhaps because she was the junior member and her duties included running out for ciggies to the corner store and escorting police officers through to the boss. She walked towards Miller, looking at him as if he was accusing her of the murder.

'This way. Sir.'

Her accent was pure Edinburgh, but not that of someone who had been educated at George Heriots. It was the same as that used by an airport security officer just as she snaps the rubber gloves on.

He and Kim followed the girl out into the hallway outside the reception.

'Did you know Ms Gates?' Kim asked.

'Aye.'

'You don't seem very upset at the news,' Miller said.

'Is it against the law to not cry when you hear that somebody's dead?'

Usually Miller heard this kind of tone when the interviewee was sitting opposite him in an interrogation room. 'No, but usually people don't have such a cavalier attitude when they hear of a colleague being murdered.'

The girl stopped. Turned to look at them both. 'A what?'

'Usually people are upset,' Kim said.

'Aye, well, those other dafties in there might be spilling their crocodile tears into their cup of tea, but I know what Ashley Gates was really like.'

Miller turned round to make sure they were out of earshot of the front office. 'Care to elaborate? Off the record.'

The girl visibly relaxed, and leaned in a bit closer, keeping her voice low. 'She was a slapper. Took it from any man willing to give it to her.'

'Is this hearsay?' Kim said.

The girl smiled, a vicious smile, full of vitriol. 'I saw it for myself up at the Palais. I was there with my pals a few weeks ago on a Friday night, just for a laugh. It's *Grab a Granny* night on a Friday, and all those sad old tossers are in there, hoping for a bit on the side before going home to the wife.'

'And Ashley was in there?' Miller knew of the club. The Palais de

Danse was originally a dance hall in the 1920s farther along Fountainbridge. It closed as a dancehall, and was turned into a bingo hall, but then it fell into disrepair. The name was resurrected for the nightclub round the corner in West Tollcross, opposite the fire station.

'Yes, she was. Making a real arse of herself. Bagging off with guys old enough to be her dad. Young guys who were in there to take the piss out of older people. You name it, she had her tongue down its throat.'

'Do you know if she had a boyfriend just now?' Kim asked.

'Yeah. First battalion The Royal Scots. But I overheard her on her phone in the little coffee room we have. She was talking to a man. All but shoving her tongue through the phone.'

'Was this Dan Herdan?' Miller asked.

'I know where you're going with this, Inspector, but no, this wasn't Herdan. Not at first anyway. She hung up and made another call and *this* one was to Herdan. Knocking him back for the first one.'

'Didn't she make any attempt to hide her conversation?'

The girl curled her lip. 'We don't even exist to her. I mean, didn't. We were just shadows flitting about the building. I could walk into that room, and she could be getting it on the conference table and she wouldn't bat an eyelash. We're here just to run about after the suits. So, no, she didn't hide any of her conversation. Only covered the mouthpiece on her phone to tell me she wanted her coffee black. I hadn't even gone in there to make her a coffee, cheeky cow.'

'So what about the first man she spoke to? Did you get a name?'

'No, but he's a doctor. And he drives a Jag. Black.'

'You got that from the call, or you saw it?'

'He picked her up that same night. I didn't see him because it was dark by the time we finished, and it was raining and the lights were on in the office. But I saw it pull up.'

'And you could tell it was a Jaguar?'

'I might come from Pilton, but I know a Jaguar when I see one. It was an F-TYPE. The sports car.'

'Registration?' Miller asked, without much hope.

'I'm good, but I'm not that good.'

'How did you know it was the doctor picking her up?' Kim asked.

'I heard her calling him that. She asked him to come round and pick her up after work. I mean, I'm assuming that was the guy.'

They heard a door opening upstairs. The skylights on the roof at the top of the stairwell lit up the whole stairway through the wrought iron stair railings. The openness also let sound come down.

'If you think of anything else...' Miller said, handing her one of his business cards.

'Sharon.'

'Sharon. Give me a call. You've been very helpful. You should think about a career in the police if you get fed up here. You have an eye for detail.'

For the first time, the girl smiled. 'You never know, Frank. We'd better go through though.'

She led them through to an office tucked away in the back, off a tight corridor. She knocked and waited.

'Come!' they heard a voice shout.

Sharon opened the door, and poked her head in. 'The police are here.'

'Oh Christ,' they heard King mumble, as if he'd been caught with his pants down. 'I said to wait five minutes. I'm finishing something up here.'

Sharon turned back to Miller, and shook her head. 'Wanker,' she whispered, and walked away.

Miller walked in with Kim. 'Mr King?'

'The very one.' He made no effort to stand or offer his hand.

'I'm DI Miller. This is Investigator Smith with the PF's office.'

'Ah, yes, Kim. Norma Banks' daughter. I've heard her talking about you. Come in and grab a pew.'

They sat on the seats facing King at his desk. 'We believe you heard the news about Ashley.'

'God awful thing. I can't believe she's gone.'

'So tell me, Mr King,' Kim said, but King held up a hand.

'Call me Arthur.'

'You worked here with Ashley?'

'I do. Did. Although we were divorced, we were still friends. We were really rather civil to each other.'

'Her father said you got divorced because you were fooling around on Ashley.'

'Did he now? Well, that wasn't what we were putting out there. *Grown apart* is what we agreed on, if she got the house. However, she didn't screw me to the wall, as she could have, because by the time we were getting a divorce, I discovered she too had been messing about behind *my* back. So it was a relatively amicable split.'

'So you didn't hate your ex-wife?' Miller asked.

'What? No, of course not. Just ask anybody in here. In fact, we grew even closer. Ash was my best friend. I got on so much better with her after we got divorced.'

'That's not what her father thinks.'

'He needs to try and not think too much. He works in a different office, so he didn't see how Ash and I interacted.'

'What about her co-workers here? Did any of them have a grievance with her?' *Like Sharon, who thinks your ex is a hoor?*

'Oh God, no. She loved every one of them, and I've never heard anybody say a bad word against her.'

'Had she received any threats from anybody? People she helped put away?'

'Nothing. She would have told me if she'd had a letter or something, but she didn't seem upset or unhappy about anything.'

'I need to ask you this, sir, just as part of our enquiry—'

'I was in London. Staying with my sister and her husband over the weekend. She's just had another baby, and I went down to see my new niece. I flew up on the shuttle this morning. I'll write down the details, and you can check them out, including my flight details.'

After a few minutes of looking into his phone and scribbling notes down, he handed Miller a piece of paper.

'We won't take up anymore of your time, Mr King. I'm so sorry

45

for your loss.' This time, Kim shook King's hand, but the QC gave no indication he wanted to shake with Miller.

Outside, Miller stood on the pavement while Kim fished out the car keys. 'What do you make of him?'

'I wouldn't like to go up against him in court.'

'I would like to go up against him in an interrogation room,' Miller said, as Kim unlocked the car. He hoped there was some flaw in King's alibi, but knew deep down there wouldn't be.

Whoever killed Ashley Gates, it wasn't her ex-husband.

EIGHT

The place stank of oil and dirt and... death?

Obviously death. This place was Hell's anteroom. The furnace dried the air out so your lungs had to fight for every scrap of fresh air.

The furnace itself was through in the back, hidden behind rubber doors. The receiving bay door allowed vehicles to reverse in only so far. The old, soiled hospital linen would then be carted through, and the furnace man would put the fabric into the fire, along with all the medical waste bags.

Doctor Mitchell Robb wasn't interested in the furnace this afternoon though. It was a room *off* the furnace area that he was interested in.

'This is creepy,' the nurse said, as she squeezed his hand tighter.

They were in a small corridor that linked the other side of the furnace room with the main hospital, the arterial entrance for the cages that came down with the waste.

'It adds to the excitement, don't you think?' Robb said. He had a large canvas bag slung over his shoulder, filled with sheets.

'It kind of does, actually.' She giggled, as he led her along to the end. 'Are you sure he's not here?'

'Every day like clockwork.' Robb looked at his watch, feeling the usual stirrings below, his own excitement level through the roof. 'He has a manky little office, and I called it before we came down. When he's on lunch, the answering machine kicks in.'

Suddenly, she stopped, jerking Robb's arm back. 'How do you know he's not just busy? What if he's really there?'

'I'll make up some story.' He smiled at her, but she wasn't convinced.

Fuck me, the condom's practically bursting out of the packet all on its own. 'Listen, if he's there, I'll pretend I'm showing you how everything works, as if I'm giving you a tour of the hospital.'

She hesitated one second more before giggling again. 'Come on then.'

The door was simple, and marked with an old sign that had oil stains on it. *Private.* Robb turned the handle, and walked into the room.

'And this is the eating area,' he started to say, but saw it was empty.

The nurse smiled. Spotted the corridor beyond the other side of the door. 'Tell me what this place was again.'

'Before they built the new wing, this was the accident and emergency bay. We worked long hours, and there was this room where you could grab a few hours' sleep. It was needed when we were doing seventy-two hours straight. It was used by the furnace guy when the A&E was moved to the new location round the corner. Nobody comes down here now.'

He locked the door behind them. There were still several chairs and the coffee table in front of them. They'd been left behind in the move, but had seen better days. They're probably luxury for the furnace man, Robb thought, as he made his way over to the other door.

A small TV sat up on a shelf, with a cable TV box underneath. It was silent now, like a big eye looking down on them. A small fridge stood against another wall, with a microwave on top.

A little table was against the back wall with two chairs at it.

'Why would he go out if he has a microwave in here?' she said.

Robb smiled, and mentally gritted his teeth. 'Maybe he likes a liquid lunch. Maybe he prefers to go to a café.'

'What if he's away out for a couple of cold pies that he can heat up here?'

Robb pulled her towards him, and kissed her. Then he pulled away. 'Well, we can stand around here waiting for him to come back, or we can... go through to the Royal suite.'

'You sure the door's locked?'

'Here, let me reassure you.' He walked over, grabbed one of the chairs, and tucked it under the door handle. 'Happy?' he asked, as he turned towards her, but she was already unbuttoning her uniform.

They walked down the short corridor to the third door, and Robb opened it. The single bed was still there. He opened the bag, and took the sheets out, spreading them on the bed. A pillow next.

'I know this is hardly the Ritz, but can you feel the buzz?' He almost winced, realising it sounded like *Can you feel the bugs?*

There was a window on one wall, high up, but big enough for egress during a fire. Robb saw her looking at it as if she was contemplating her escape from a psychopathic captor.

Her uniform was open, and she stepped out of it. 'Oh, I can feel the buzz alright, honey.'

Robb had hinted that there was the possibility of flying down to London to stay in the real Ritz, but being the pig that he was, he had brought her down here for a bit of *try before you buy*.

She shrieked a little as she climbed naked between the cold sheets. Robb dropped his scrubs in record time, almost peeling the condom wrapper off with his teeth, and seconds later, he was under the sheets with her.

A record seven minutes later, he was on his back, sweating.

'How was that, lover boy?' she said.

'Pretty...' *fucking average,* 'amazing.'

'I can't wait 'til we get to the Ritz. We can shag all day. In between shopping trips that is.'

But Robb wasn't listening. He was already thinking about the new Jaguar F-PACE that he had planned to test drive at the weekend. The F-TYPE was nice of course, but he liked the idea of the SUV. German cars were nice too, but he was thinking of sticking with the Brit—

'...before I'm listed as missing.'

'What? Oh, yes, yes, we'd better get going,' he said. The nurse was already out of bed and dressed before Robb had a chance to light up a cigarette, if he had smoked.

'Call me tonight. Maybe we'll have a drink.'

'Sure I will,' he said, before she leaned over and kissed him. Then she left, almost running, either because she was full of adrenaline, or she was already planning her new wardrobe for London.

He got up and dressed, the Ritz in London the furthest thing from his mind. Then he threw the sheets into the bag. He strode along the corridor, through a set of rubber doors, to the receiving area, where trucks brought soiled linen and waste bags to be burned. There was another set of rubber doors that separated the furnace area where the cages were lined up, ready for the furnace. They were already filled with the bags, which would all be grabbed and thrown into the fire. One more wouldn't be noticed.

He was just about to go through one of the rubber doors – the top half of which were transparent, but old and scratched – when he caught sight of movement near the furnace. The furnace man. He hadn't gone out for his lunch after all.

He stopped for a moment, and Robb thought he had been spotted, but then the other man carried on emptying a cage and throwing the medical waste bags into the furnace. The furnace man looked over at the doors.

Robb ducked below the transparent part of the door. What was he going to do with the bag of soiled sheets?

He slowly raised himself, half-expecting to see the man's face peering back at him, like in the movies, but the man was over by the furnace.

The giant gas-powered machine, just like in a crematorium, was designed to burn a lot of soiled sheets and scrubs, as well as the medical waste. The grimy man had on a pair of thick gloves, and he grabbed the handle of the steel door. That too had thick glass in it, which Robb could see as the man stood to one side. The furnace would be on, but Robb wasn't sure at what level.

The furnace man looked back towards the door again, and Robb ducked. Then inched his face back up again. Then the man turned back to the door again, and this time, started walking towards it. Robb ducked, and hurried away, only standing up straight and running when he thought he was out of view. He tossed the linen bag on top of a cage with plastic bags in it. The furnace man would think some lazy porter had slung it there.

Back into the corridor, and right along, back the way he had come. Into the stairwell, and up the stairs. There was a lift next to the stairway door, but he didn't want to be seen standing there.

Porters brought the dirty laundry down, not surgeons. There was no logical explanation for him to be down here.

The door to the corridor on the first level didn't come out onto a ward but an ancillary corridor. *Behind the scenes at the hospital* might have been the title if Robb were a documentary producer. However, he was a serial shagger, who was starting to know this area like the back of his hand. He wandered along, made a few turns, and came out through one of the doors the porters used, well away from the wards and surgical suites.

Even if one of them bumped into him, he would ignore them and carry on as if nothing happened.

Robb stopped as one of his phones rang. He took out his real one, and saw the name on the screen. Jess.

He ignored it. She would think it was in his locker, and that he was in surgery saving somebody's life. Not downstairs shagging one of the nurses.

He walked along to the surgical suite, his mind on what excuse he would use to get out of a shopping trip to London.

NINE

Gibb was standing at the whiteboard, with all the team members in attendance.

'Ladies and gentlemen, your attention, please. We still don't have any idea as to where Ashley Gates' body is. We have still to identify the female in the photo on Miss Gates' mantelpiece.'

He pointed to the blow-up of the photo attached to the board. 'Nobody seems to know her. Is she the killer's next victim? Or is that drawing of a noose round her neck meant to throw us off the scent? I want every avenue explored to try to find her.'

Miller stepped forward. 'We spoke to Ashley's boss, who just happens to be her ex-husband, Arthur King, and he gave us the usual, *I don't know anybody who would want to hurt her.* She was a good worker, and she was a good defence lawyer. A QC like her old man, albeit a junior one. We want to look through her case files to see if she had any threats from family members of victims. Maybe Ashley represented somebody in court who got off, and the family blamed her for the verdict.

'Our main suspect is Dan Herdan, a taxi driver, and Ashley's ex-boyfriend. They used to fight a lot, and they split up. Herdan saw

Ashley last night, and spoke to her in the pub. He wanted her to go back out with him, and he says they agreed to meet on Friday to discuss matters. He left the pub, and got back into his taxi. However, we spoke to another member of staff at the lawyer's office, and she says Ashley was fond of men. Very promiscuous. Maybe she had jilted somebody who wanted to take things further. We had Herdan in for questioning, but we had nothing to hold him on, so he was freed.'

Angie Rivers spoke up. 'This afternoon, we went along to the Edinburgh Cabs' office, and spoke to the manager there. He looked up the electronic log records for Herdan's cab last night. He was sent a job just after ten thirty, just like he said. He had quite a few street pick-ups, and was given a load of radio jobs.'

'So he has an alibi until he finished his shift at three o'clock?' Miller said.

'For most of the time. The manager said the dispatcher sent him a job at twelve forty-five am, then he re-zoned in the west zone at three minutes past one. The job he'd been sent was dropping off at Balgreen Road. The funny thing is, he was sent a job at seven minutes past one for a pick-up off St John's Road, but he didn't claim it, and he was dumped.' She looked at the other officers. 'That's the technical term they use for when a driver is sent a job on the computer and he doesn't press the button to accept it.'

'Did he say why he didn't claim it?'

'Sometimes they just aren't fast enough. Say a driver steps out for a pee, and he misses the job, if nobody else has claimed it, he can talk to the dispatcher and explain, and he'll get it. Herdan didn't talk to the dispatcher, and at one oh nine am, he logged off.'

'Is that unusual?' Gibb said.

'Apparently, a driver can log on and off as often as he likes. If he wanted to go for a meal break or something, they don't have to explain. It was unusual at that time of the morning though. If you've had a quiet night, and want to go home, then you log off for the night, which is a different code, and the dispatcher knows you're finished.

Herdan was logged off as if he was away for something to eat. But he'd already been logged off when he met Ashley in the pub.'

'What about GPS?' Watt asked.

'This company is relatively small, and like other cab companies, they're owner operated. It's run by a committee, and the drivers don't think it's worth the expense at this time. Other bigger companies with hundreds of cabs have them, but not Edinburgh Cabs. All they have is the computer, which tells them where the drivers are, but that can be tricked.'

Gibb rested his backside on a table. 'A computer that can be tricked? Tell me more.'

'Well, because the company relies on the driver to hit a button as they pass through each zone, they can cheat. For example, if a driver is in the central zone, heading for say, Haymarket, and he sees a job in Corstorphine, he can hit the button to say he's now in the Haymarket zone, and then hit the button to say he's in the west zone. In effect, he's claiming a job in the west when he's really not there. Tricking the computer.'

Miller looked at her. 'So, I'm assuming it can't tell that he's at Haymarket one minute, and then in Corstorphine the next?'

'That's right. That's because the west zone boundary isn't that far from Haymarket. It doesn't measure time, so it doesn't know he can't physically get there in such a short time, it just knows that there's a cab in that zone and the driver has claimed the job. So now it's up to the driver to get there as fast as he can.'

'And nobody knows he's cheating?' Hazel asked.

'Sometimes they do. Each taxi is assigned a call sign, like the numbers you see on the back of a taxi window. Herdan is Zulu thirty-nine, so he has the little orange digits zed three nine on his back and front windows. The computer shows who accepted the job, so if he's taken the job for Corstorphine and somebody sees him blazing through Haymarket, they know he's cheated to get the job.

'If a committee member is driving, then he's for the high jump, with a likely suspension from the radio for a week. If it's not a committee member, then that driver can choose to ignore it if it doesn't affect him, or report the driver, but most don't report their colleagues because they're all at it.'

'So when *did* Herdan log back on?' Kim asked.

'At two forty-two am. He was sent a job at two fifty-one, and he logged off for the night at three twelve.'

'What zone was he in when he logged back on?' Gibb asked.

'Still in the west.'

'What zone is Ravelston in?' Miller asked.

Angie looked at her notes, which contained a map of Edinburgh the manager had given her with all the boundary lines for the zones highlighted on it. 'The west.'

'So let me get this straight,' Miller said, going to the board, 'Herdan logs off at one oh nine, and nobody questions it, then he logs back on at two forty-two, still in the west zone, which takes in Ashley Gates' address. No questions asked, like, *Where have you been for the last hour and a half?* Nothing. And he gets one more job, and then calls it a day.'

'That's it,' Angie said.

'Couldn't he just have been picking up street fares?' Kim asked.

'If he was, his computer would have told the dispatcher that as soon as he switched the meter on, and then he should have logged in what zone he was going to, in case there was a job out that way. But he was logged out of the system, and it's connected to his meter, so his meter wouldn't work if he was trying to drive without the dispatcher knowing where he was going.'

'So, in theory, he could have driven over to Ashley's house, done her in, taken her away with him to God knows where, and then logged on again as if nothing happened.'

'Pretty much.'

'Wouldn't the taxi have been in a mess?' Gilmour said.

'Have you never puked in a taxi before, Jimmy?' Watt said. They all laughed. 'Not that I'm talking from experience, mind, but the floors are rubber and the seats are vinyl, so they can be washed out quickly if a punter does throw his ring. Then it's a quick turnaround and they're back on the road.'

'Don't forget the sheets were off the bed, and not in the washing machine, and a rug was missing from the dining room, so we're theorising that he wrapped her in the sheets and then the rug. So it's not as if she'd be spewing blood all over the back of his cab.'

'Right,' Gibb said, 'it's getting late, but I'd like a couple of volunteers to go over to the cab office and watch where Herdan goes. We know he could cheat on the computer, but we can always try to build a picture. See if he logs off, and what zone he's in when he does. That sort of thing. It doesn't have to be all night, just for a few hours.'

'I'll do it,' Watt said. 'I've nothing on tonight.'

'Good man, Andy. Anybody else?'

'I will,' Angie said.

'Good job. Just for a couple of hours, maybe around nine tonight. Call it in if there are any shenanigans. Otherwise, we'll see you in here tomorrow.'

TEN

Jack Miller crossed High Street onto the North Bridge, heading for home, when somebody put a hand on his shoulder. Maybe it was the detective in him, maybe because he was six foot five, or maybe it was just because he was quick-tempered, but whatever it was, he turned round, his fist primed to punch his would-be mugger.

The man laughed. 'Jack! It's me. Tony!'

Jack reined it in as he recognised the younger man. He took off a glove, and shook the offered hand. 'Jesus, I didn't recognise you for a minute there. How you doing?'

Tony Matheson laughed again, and pumped Jack's hand. 'I'm doing great, Jack. How are things with you?'

'Never better,' he replied, putting his glove back on. 'I'm retired now, and loving it.'

'I heard! Good man.'

'I was just heading home for a beer. You fancy joining me?'

'Sure. I just had a couple with an old buddy of mine, but there's room for more.'

'That's the spirit. Come on, it's in here.'

They went into the Royal Mile Mansions and up to the fifth floor.

'It's been such a long time, Tony. How've you been living?' Jack said, as they entered the apartment.

'Quietly. Well, not quite so quietly, but you know what I mean.'

'I've only seen you a few times since... well, you know.' Jack took off his jacket, Matheson did the same, and they hung them on the wall hooks.

'Since my dad died, Jack?' Matheson smiled. 'It was a long time ago. My mother's at peace now too, so I'm an orphan.' He laughed. 'It's called *life*. You can live it moping about feeling sorry for yourself, or you can make the most of each day.'

'You were, what, fifteen when your dad died?'

'Almost fifteen. He was a good cop, just like you. He would have been here with us having a few beers.'

'I liked him a lot. He was always willing to go the extra mile.'

'And that's what got him killed.'

They went through to the kitchen where Charlie, the cat, was waiting to be fed. Jack put dried food out for him.

'This is a nice place you have here.'

'Thanks, but it isn't mine. I just live here. With my son and his girlfriend and her little girl.'

'How is Frank?' Matheson said, beaming a smile.

'He's doing very well. He's a DI, and he just turned thirty last month. He'll go far.' He reached into the fridge, and brought out two tins of lager. They cracked them open. 'Cheers.'

They sat at the kitchen table. It was getting dark outside, so Jack put a light on.

'Is Frank still working?'

Jack put his can on the table. 'Yes. His girlfriend, Kim, works with the PF's office, so she works out of the station as well. They're working a murder case so their hours are long.'

'So what about you, Jack? Anybody special in your life?'

'You heard about Beth, my wife?'

'I did. That was sad.'

'It hit me hard, and I dated a few women, but nothing serious until I met Samantha.'

Tony took a swig of lager. 'Tell me more.'

'It's Samantha Willis, the crime writer. She lives along the landing.'

'Samantha Willis? You're joking!'

'No, I'm not. We've been dating since the summer.'

'Good grief. I've read all of her books. I'm a big fan. You have to introduce me sometime, Jack. Maybe she can sign her latest for me.'

'I will.'

'My dad was an avid reader too. He would have been chuffed at all the eBooks now and Kindle readers. He would have had one.'

Jack smiled, feeling comfortable. 'I remember that. He always had a paperback lying about somewhere. He and George West were both big readers. Sometimes it looked like a library in there.'

'It's nice to reminisce. I miss my old man.'

'It was unreal what happened to him.'

Matheson took a swig of his lager, and then smiled. 'But you know what? That's how he would have wanted it. He wasn't a desk jockey. He died trying to apprehend an armed suspect. He didn't see himself sitting at home and dying of a heart attack in his armchair after mowing the lawn. That wasn't my dad.'

'He was one of the best officers I ever worked with, hands down.'

'He thought the world of you, Jack. Although you were his DI and he was only a sergeant, he thought you were brilliant.'

'There's no such thing as *only a sergeant*. Most of the sergeants I know work harder than the damn brass upstairs.'

'I'll drink to that.' He clinked glasses with Jack. 'I heard about David Elliott. Poor sod. He was around when Dad worked at the station.'

'He just took a bad turn, and ended up paying for it with his life.'

'It's a fine line we walk at times, that's for sure. The line between good and bad. Sometimes we just cross it for a moment and pull ourselves back in time, but others, they jump across with both feet.'

'And Elliott jumped across, and then there was no way back.' Jack stood up. 'A short to chase that down?'

'Thanks.'

He went to the cupboard where he kept his bottle of Scotch, and poured two doubles of single malt. 'So, what do you do yourself these days?' he asked, when he sat back down.

'Cheers.' He took a sip of the malt, and closed his eyes for a second. 'I work as a technician at the Western General down at Crew Toll.'

'Good for you.'

'Advanced Biomedical Technician, is my official title, but all it means is I look through a microscope all day.' He smiled again. 'It pays the bills.'

'So where are you staying these days?'

'I'm still in the old house in Balgreen. I ended up with the place after my mum died. I don't see any point in moving when the house is paid for.'

'That makes sense. The area will slowly come back, and if you hang on to it long enough, you'll make money if you ever want to sell.'

'I will one day, when I retire. I quite fancy the idea of going to live out my retirement in Spain.'

'You ever fancied joining the force?'

Matheson made a face. 'I don't know if I could do it full time, but I'm a Special Constable. I thought my dad would have been proud.'

'I didn't know you were a special. He would have been proud of anything you did.'

'Thanks, Jack. Yeah, I was on duty the night... you know... when Cathy was murdered.'

'Jesus, and now we think he's killed again. Did you read about that poor lassie?'

'I did. It makes me sick to my stomach.'

'They'll catch him. '

'Cheers to that.' He raised his can up again. 'Losing Cathy was hard, but I started dating again. I didn't want anybody thinking I've forgotten about Cathy, but I just felt the time was right. We've been going out a little while now. I'll see how it develops.'

'Good for you. Life moves on. Like it did for me. Nobody would expect you to be a monk,' Jack said. 'Have you seen Frank lately?'

'I've bumped into him a few times, but I haven't seen him for ages.'

'Maybe we could have a few beers sometime.'

'That would be great. I'm based out of High Street, but I'm sent to other stations as needed. Maybe I'll see him around.' Matheson finished his drink. 'Can I use your bathroom?'

'Of course you can, pal. Last door on the left.'

Matheson got up and left the living room, leaving Jack alone with the cat. Jack switched the TV on, and looked at the clock that sat on the fireplace. The gas fire gave off enough heat to keep the cold at bay, but not enough to make him fall asleep.

He took his phone out, and sent a text to Samantha, saying he'd call her later to see if she fancied getting together if she wasn't working. He didn't want to talk to her while Matheson was here.

She sent a reply;

I'm just finishing a chapter. Bite to eat later?

Sounds good.

I'm feeling knackered. A bite to eat at my place?

Great. Let me know when you're done, and I can pick something up.

Thanks, sweetie.

He laughed inwardly at her use of the word *knackered*. She really was earning her *Honorary Scot* badge.

He flicked through some channels, wondering how Frank was getting on with the investigation. He'd called and told him all about the missing lawyer, and how her blood was all over her living room carpet. And the Polaroid.

The thought of Will Beam being threatened made his blood boil.

They'd thought it was a one-off after the passing of time, but here they were, another murder, another photo left at the scene.

Jack looked at the clock again. Tony was taking his time, but he figured it had been more than long enough even if he was doing number twos. He was approaching the time that was a fine line between stinking the place out and lying on the floor having a heart attack.

He got up, and strolled along to the end of the corridor.

The bathroom door was wide open. The small room was empty.

But the front door was ajar.

Tony Matheson was gone.

ELEVEN

Frank Miller could have stayed in by himself with the cat, but that wouldn't have been any fun. Kim was away with Emma to her mother's house, no doubt to talk wedding stuff. *When do you think you'll get engaged?* would no doubt be out of her mother's mouth before the tea had even left the spout of the teapot.

So now he was in Logie Baird's with Jack. Monday night wasn't Friday night busy, but there were a fair number of people in. Not even the cold could stop the Edinburgh folk from socialising.

'I did see Tony a while back. He's doing well for himself,' he said.

'He's even a special.'

'I know. He told me.' Frank paid the barman for the two pints, and they stood at the bar so they could see one of the TVs.

'So tell me, now you have a woman who was murdered, and a Polaroid. Do you think it's a copycat?'

Frank drank some of his pint. 'I don't know. There's always that chance, what with there being a couple of years between murders.'

He looked around the bar. One or two familiar faces were in, regulars who kept the place in profit. The October cold didn't keep them from making the trek to their preferred watering hole. Jack saw

Kate Murphy sitting at a table with Malc Freeman, an undertaker who had recently been given the overflow contract for the mortuary. They seemed to have found chemistry in death.

Kate smiled and got up from the table after Freeman headed out. 'Can I get you both a drink?' she said, when she came over.

'Jack's just waiting for Samantha to text him so they can have dinner. I'll get you one though.'

'You don't have to twist *my* arm too far. G and T, thanks. I just need to pop to the ladies.'

'I can see why people call him *Malkie the alkie* behind his back,' Jack said, as Miller came back with Kate's drink. 'He can put a few away. Hollow legs.'

'He's like us, Jack, just relieving his daily stress.'

'There's just something shifty about him.'

'He's an undertaker. People think all undertakers are shifty. It's their association with death that makes people wary. You wouldn't want to have a pint with somebody one day, thinking that he might be pumping you full of embalming fluid the next. He's not too bad.'

'I don't like him.'

'So you said, after the first time you saw him and Kate chatting in here.'

'He's always flirting with her.'

'That's all it is, harmless flirting.'

'I don't trust him.'

'Neil McGovern has her back. If Freeman starts anything, Neil will have a word.'

'Neil's a good guy to have on your side. And now he's going to be your father-in-law.'

'Don't worry, Dad, I'll still love you too.'

'Piss off.'

Miller laughed as Kate came back. He handed her the drink.

'Cheers, Frank.'

'I'm off now, son. I'll see you later.' Jack left the pub, just as Jimmy Gilmour came in.

'Hi, Jimmy. Pint?'

'Cheers, sir.'

'It's Monday night and we're in the pub, so you can call me Frank.'

'Okay, Frank.'

'I haven't seen you in here on a week night before.'

'I come in now and again, now that I live down in Dumbiedykes. I've been flitting about since my divorce, but now I've settled down there. For a while anyway. So I come in here sometimes.'

'It's better than sitting at home moping.'

'You're right there. Excuse me a minute, I need to use the facilities.'

'Have you ever been married, Kate?'

She looked sad for a moment, looking down at the floor before looking back at Miller. 'No. I always looked after my mother. Until she died.' She couldn't use the word *murdered*. 'I had a steady boyfriend for a while, but sometimes I'd get a phone call from my mother saying she'd fallen, and by the time I got home, she'd be alright, sitting in her chair, right as rain. She was jealous of my boyfriend. It got too much for him in the end.'

'I can see why that would have ruined things for you, but if the guy had thought anything of you, he would have stuck around.'

'That would have been nice, but he found somebody else. A flight attendant.' She finished off the contents of her glass. This was the story she always told. It sounded better than the truth. 'Now I'm thirty-seven, and on the shelf.'

'There's always Malkie the alkie,' he said, and laughed.

Kate elbowed him. 'You're such a pig, Miller!'

'I thought you liked him?'

'I do, but not in that way.'

Gilmour returned. 'Slangevar.' They raised their glasses, and Miller could feel the heat of the whisky going down his throat.

Gilmour's mobile phone rang. He excused himself, and walked

over to a quiet spot. He looked at the display before answering. It was Lauren. 'What's wrong?' he asked.

'It's your ex-wife,' she said. 'She's just been on the house phone.' To Lauren, Connie was usually referred to as *That bitch you were married to.*

'What did she want?'

'She just called asking to talk to you. Maybe she broke a fingernail or something.'

There was an awkward pause, as if Lauren was preparing herself for a fight.

'I'll give her a call,' Gilmour said.

'You do that, and tell her I said we should do lunch sometime,' Lauren said sarcastically. He didn't know how to end the call without including the words *off* and *fuck,* so he just hung up. Then he dialled his ex-wife's number.

'Hello?'

'Connie, it's me.'

There was the sound of his ex-wife crying. Then it stopped suddenly.

'What's wrong, Connie?'

Silence for a moment.

'He got worse, Jimmy.'

The words shot into him like a bolt. 'What did they say?'

They spoke for a few minutes, Gilmour trying to make sense of Connie's words between sobs. She told him she had to go, and he hung up, joining the others.

'Is everything okay?' Kate asked.

'My ex-wife's uncle had a stroke a few nights ago. He's in the Western, and he's just taken a turn for the worse.'

'Does Connie want you there?' Miller asked.

'No. They're working on him right now.'

'Keep me in the loop.' Miller finished off his drink. 'I'll see you later.'

Miller left Kate and Gilmour at the bar, and walked out into a dark night filled with the promise of rain.

Kate peered into her drink for a moment. 'I feel bad lying to Frank like that, Jimmy.'

He gently took one of her hands. 'We're not lying. We just haven't told anybody.'

'It just feels as if we're going behind his back.'

'Listen. Lauren decided she didn't want to be with me anymore. We live in separate bedrooms. When we do talk, it's in loud voices and using the f-word. We're finished. So when you and I fell for each other, we didn't ruin anybody's life.'

She looked at him and smiled. 'You're still going to tell Frank after Lauren leaves?'

'Of course I am. And you know what makes me happy? That you know I still need to keep in touch with Connie. That you don't give me a hard time about it.'

'You have a daughter with her. It's to be expected.'

'It will be a lot easier when things are out in the open. Frank will understand.'

Kate smiled again, and took a sip of her drink. She had fallen for Gilmour in a big way. She thought she could love him. Just like she'd loved the other detective in her former life.

TWELVE

Mitchell Robb was dog-tired when he pulled up to his garage at the apartments. He felt cosseted in his Jaguar though. It was one of the finer things in life, being able to own a brand new Jag. Some of his friends at the golf club had gone over to the dark side and bought German, but those cars were crude. Fine examples of engineering, yes, but so was the Forth Rail Bridge.

The headlights illuminated the garage door, which slowly glided up and out of the way. His garage was third from the left, in a long row. They were joined onto the ones on the other side that faced the apartments. His being the penthouse apartment, he was given two.

His girlfriend wanted the other one, but he insisted she park in the overflow spaces beside the other riff raff who lived in his building.

She thought he was a snob, because he looked down on the neighbours, even though they probably all earned six-figure salaries. To Robb, if you weren't a surgeon as he was, you were driftwood. No, the other garage was for the new Jaguar F-Pace he was planning to buy, although the taxi was sitting in there just now. Maybe his new nickname would be *Johnny Two Jags,* just like the former British Deputy Prime Minister John Prescott.

The engine purred as it took the sleek F-Type inside, the LED headlights almost blinding him as they bounced off the white wall at the back.

He ached after doing the afternoon surgery right after being with the nurse, but it saved him money going to the gym.

The boys at the club would love this story. Bunch of tosspots. They were hardly what you would call real friends, but they laughed at his jokes, listened spellbound to his stories, and bought him drinks.

With the car securely locked up, he looked at the other garage, and wondered if he should take the black out for a spin. The taxi sat inside, waiting for him to drive around, but he really couldn't be bothered. Besides, he was on call.

With the wind biting at him, he cursed the Scottish weather. Preferring his usual brogues, the weather had forced him to wear clumsy shoes with a thick sole. Something the lower classes would no doubt love. Along with their knock-off Timberlands and Caterpillars. At least his were real.

The building had been refurbished, and was in excellent condition when he bought it. The perfect bachelor pad. That memory almost made him cry. Now it was *our own little palace, the place where we can bring up our family.*

At one time, whenever anybody had asked Robb if he had any family, he would always answer, *Yes, a mum and dad.* Even though his folks had started pushing up the daisies a long time ago. It always got a laugh, but now his girlfriend had told him the apartment was going to be filled with the sound of ankle biters running about, shitting and puking, and learning to crayon all over the fucking walls when they got big enough. Maybe they'd even cut the curtains with scissors or wipe snotters on their bed. God knows what they would do.

He stepped into the hallway after unlocking the front door of the building. Stamped his feet on the large, communal doormat. *That's what you are, my old son, a doormat.*

He called for the lift, and waited for it.

No, what had once been his own private domain had been invaded by Genghis Khan's sister. No more coming home for a swift beer and putting his feet up in front of the box, or going to the club with the boys, or even driving his taxi about, trying to pick up women. He stepped into a battlefield every night now.

The lift arrived, and he stepped in. Sixth floor. It would make the fall more deadly if he decided to leap out of his window.

Back when he'd met Jess, he had been driving a Jaguar XK two-door. She had been impressed by the sleek, black bodywork (always black, never red – red was a traffic cop magnet) and had giggled like a schoolgirl. However, she badgered him for ages about moving in, and after he relented, something had obviously flicked a switch in her brain.

'You'll have to get rid of it,' she'd said about the car, barely five minutes after moving her shit in.

His brain nearly had a short circuit when she started talking about his baby like that. 'Get rid of it?' he'd spluttered.

'What do you want to keep it for when we'll be needing a Volvo?'

A fucking what? he had asked her.

'Oh, you know, one of those estate cars that keep children safe.'

Children? What did he want one of those things for? You bought everything for them just so they could wait sixteen years to tell you to piss off, it's my life, and I'll fucking well do what I like.

One of the blokes at his club had one like that, and it wasn't as if you could take it back. They didn't come with a warranty, or a money-back guarantee. No, once they came sliding down the birth canal like they were in a water park, your life as you knew it, was over.

Children frightened Robb. The man who could do surgery on other people's brains was scared of little human beings.

Then his girlfriend had dropped the bombshell. *I'm pregnant.*

He could see now that Jessica Ann Thorn had played him for a fool. She had looked stunning the first time he'd seen her walk onto the ward he was doing his rounds on. Hourglass figure, beautiful brunette hair cut short, but not too short. Her smile was to die for. He knew then that he had to have her.

So he'd pursued her with a vengeance – while pursuing other women too, of course, let's not get silly here – and she had agreed to go out with him.

Robb was touching forty, and Jess wasn't even thirty. When the vultures down at the golf club had learned about her, he had given them his spiel, exaggerating just a little. Which he saw no harm in doing. After all, fishermen didn't brag about catching minnows.

And, for once in his life, Mitchell Robb had felt not only happy to be going out with a woman, but *excited*. He'd told the boys at the club he got a *buzz*. Of course, they had openly mocked him and said it wouldn't last, that the great Doctor Robb would jack her in just like the others.

Maybe it was because they were all married, and he didn't want to slide into retirement sad and alone with only a pair of slippers and the *Sunday Post* for company, that made him agree to Jess moving in. Just to prove a point, that despite living the high life, he wasn't a sad bastard.

Now he could quite happily smack all those tossers in the golf club. Not that he would tell them that the honeymoon was over. No, he lied to them every single time, telling them his Jess was a gourmet chef in the kitchen, and a world-class whore in the bedroom. He knew they thought he was a sexist prick, but keeping up appearances was all-important to him. These were the guys who looked down on you if you didn't drive home after getting pished.

Jess had been playing him all this time. He had told her in no uncertain terms that he was a surgeon, a skilled craftsman who saved people's lives on a daily basis, whose very hands had the power to decide between life and death. He didn't want to come home and find that very small people had taken over command of his TV, and were communicating in a language that consisted of shouting at the top of their voices or crying, or sometimes both.

'Don't be silly,' Jess had told him. 'Children are wonderful things.

Don't you like children?' He was about to reply, *Yes, but I couldn't eat a whole one* when he thought better of it. She was leading him down a path he didn't want to go down, one where waking up in the middle of the night was due to a child crying, and not because an excessive amount of alcohol dictated a trip to the bathroom.

He hadn't backed down. Instead, he'd told her he didn't want kids, that she should get rid of it.

It had seemed perfectly reasonable to him, but she had gone berserk. 'What's the point of being with me if you don't want children?' she had screamed at him one night.

'Well, excuse me, I thought you moved in so we could have the fabulous sex we enjoy every night without having to sneak away for the weekend.'

Then she had changed. Gone was the fun-loving personality, replaced by the inner psychopath that had been lurking there all along.

'You've ruined my life!' she had screamed at him, the claws homing in on his face.

He sighed. That had been weeks ago, and the little sex they had been having had trickled down to a drought. The well was dry.

The lift doors dinged, then opened, and Robb walked along to his apartment, ready to do battle once again.

The place was almost in darkness, just a small LED light on in the open-plan kitchen.

'You took your time coming home,' Jess said, by way of a welcome. She was standing by one of the windows, drinking wine, and looking out at whatever. She had jacked her job in before he'd even had a chance to protest. 'To prepare myself for motherhood,' she'd said, just before her words had wiped the smile from his face.

'So, how's the job hunting going?' he asked her.

'You're very funny.'

'Why is it so dark in here?'

'I can see out the window better.'

'What? Are the stars looking pretty tonight?'

'No, but the police cars are.' She sipped more wine.

'What police cars?'

Jess turned towards him, and smiled at him for the first time in months. 'Your girlfriend's dead. Your other one.'

It was like an ice pick slamming into his gut, making him want to puke blood, just before the point was pulled out, and thrust back in again.

'What are you talking about?' Robb hoped he didn't have his *liar* face on. Jess always said she could tell when he was lying, because a certain look came over his face, and it was a dead giveaway. He looked down at the front of his trousers, hoping he hadn't pissed himself. Now *that* would have been a dead giveaway.

'Your other girlfriend.' She drank more wine, and turned back to the window. 'The slut who lives in one of the houses farther up the road.'

Robb stepped forward and looked out of the window. 'How much have you had to drink?'

He looked out at the police cars that were outside Ashley Gates' house. There was a crime scene van, and people coming and going.

He had come in from the other direction, and hadn't seen any of the police activity. Was it Ashley's house? Yes, it was. Her little red Fiat was in the driveway, *the little roller skate* as he called it. He'd told her that neither of them had a car with a back seat that was practical for making love in.

'She was murdered, apparently. Last night.' She laughed and drank more wine, her eyes slightly glazed over.

Gone was the beautiful brunette who had charmed and captivated him. Before him stood a viper with foul-smelling breath, unwashed hair, and no make-up. The princess was well and truly gone.

'Where were you last night?' she said, a smirk on her face, her mouth going round the wine glass as if she was going to swallow it.

'I was here with you, as you bloody well know.'

'I see the first thing out of your mouth wasn't a denial that she was your girlfriend.'

'You're drunk.'

'So, where were you? Before you came home to me?'

'I was out driving my taxi.'

She let out a hollow laugh. 'Listen to yourself. A surgeon who has a secret life as a taxi driver. How many other surgeons do you know moonlight as a taxi driver?'

'My dad had the plate, and I just kept it on, that's all. You know all that. Sometimes it's great just to get out and about and drive, even if it is a taxi.'

'*Keeping it real.* Isn't that what you once called it?'

'There are worse ways to make a living.'

'Anyway. What was she like in bed? Your little whore. You never did tell me.'

'I'm not going to be drawn into a fight. You and your little jealousies. You were quite happy living that life until not so long ago.' Robb turned up his lip in a sneer, hoping it disguised his *liar* face. Jess had been right, but if she could prove it, her lawyer would have a field day with his bank account, paying child support.. Then his Jag would have somebody else's arse sitting behind the wheel, and he'd be lucky if he could keep the taxi. He'd have to use it to get to work, which would look magic.

So you get a taxi to work every day, Mitchell?

Yes, and as it so happens, I drive the fucking thing here.

Super-duper. Catch you later, old friend. Much later.

Not to mention those toss bags at the golf club having a good chuckle behind his back. They were already mocking him by calling him *Daddy*.

'I might not have been a surgeon, darling boyfriend of mine, but I do have a little grey matter between my ears.'

A little bit of floss between your teeth wouldn't go amiss. 'You get paranoid at times. Why don't you just sit and watch TV, and put the wine bottle away for tonight?'

'I went over there, you know.'

'Where?'

'To the house. Today. I watched with the other nosy neighbours.' She turned to face him again. 'Why did you have to go behind my back? Wasn't our little group fun enough? You had to go the extra mile. Once a month wasn't good enough for you. And it was you who got me into all that stuff.'

'Come on, let's sit down.'

'I spoke to the police, you know.'

Robb felt his face going pale. 'You didn't make up a story, I hope. Didn't tell them a pack of lies because of your insecurities.'

'The policeman who was standing guard at the end of her street. Very nice man. He wouldn't tell me anything, but I heard a reporter saying that the young woman was murdered. It's been on the news.'

Fuck. He'd been listening to his iPod in the car again, getting down with some dance music. He had different playlists for different moods; dance for when he wanted to drive fast, ballads for when he felt like taking it easy. And Pink Floyd for when he felt like *keeping it real*.

'Listen, Jess, come and sit down. Let me make you a coffee.'

She ignored him. 'I told the policeman I wanted to talk to a detective because my husband knows the dead woman, and he didn't come in 'til late last night.' She turned to face him, but she wasn't smiling now. 'Or I should say, the wee hours of this morning.'

She walked away from the window and sat at the dining table, next to her bottle of wine. She topped her glass up.

Robb looked down at the police cars. At Ashley's little red car, and felt something catch in his throat. From up here in the penthouse apartment, they had a bird's-eye view of their neighbours. Of the comings and goings of the people who probably earned more than he did. But he didn't care about that. Nobody knew who he was, and he didn't talk to them. It was the sort of neighbourhood you had to live in for fifty years before they said *Good morning* to you.

He pulled the curtains shut.

Jess was sitting watching the TV, although it had been muted.

'Should you be drinking, considering.'

'Considering what?'

'That you're pregnant.'

'Who cares? Not you. You probably care more that your little slut friend is dead.'

'At least when I went over to her place, she didn't lecture me. We just went to bed and had a good fuck.' Now his tongue was in the driving seat, and it was hard to keep quiet.

Jess threw the wine glass at him, but he ducked, and it missed, landing on the carpet without a sound, spilling the contents on its way.

'You know something? I called my sister today. Right after I went over to talk to the police. I told her I'm leaving you. I'm going to have this baby, without you. All I ever wanted was a child anyway.'

'You have a cheek calling Ashley a whore!' Robb said. 'You're the one who's a whore. All she wanted was a good time, but you wanted to snag yourself a husband. You're the only fucking whore I know. Getting yourself pregnant like a little schoolgirl. Fucking bitch.'

'Fuck you. My stuff's already packed. I was just waiting for you so I could tell you to fuck off to your face.'

'You know what? Just get your stuff and get out. I'll find myself another little whore as soon as you're gone.'

Jess stood up. 'Good luck. But by the time I'm finished with you, no nurse will want to drop her knickers for you again!'

'I'm away out. Be gone when I get back.'

THIRTEEN

Frank Miller was standing at the crossing waiting for the lights to turn in his favour, when he felt a hand grab his arm above the elbow. It only took a fraction of a second for him to register it and prepare for his training to kick in.

'If I was a Russian spy, you'd be dead by now,' a man's voice said to him.

He was already pulling away and turning when he saw Detective Superintendent Percy Purcell smiling at him.

'Percy, what are you doing here?'

'I was on my way to Logie Baird's when I saw you come out.' The crossing turned to green for them to walk. 'Come on, let's go into the Mitre and have a swift one. I want to talk to you.'

The pub was almost opposite Miller's regular, and he went there with Kim now and again. Inside, it was quiet, with a TV playing in one corner. Miller got two pints of lager and they sat at a table.

'It's good to see you again, Percy. A bit unexpected though.'

'This is my new home. I'm your new head of MIT.'

'What?' Miller said. 'They told us we would have a new boss by next month. I didn't know it was you who'd got the job.'

'It was all hush hush. I just got word yesterday that the job was mine.'

'That's brilliant news. What made you want to come back down here?'

'To be honest, I just want to get away from Aberdeen. Too many bad memories there for me.'

'What about Dennis Friendly?' Miller said. 'He didn't give you any grief when you were last down here because you were investigating somebody. But he's above you in rank. Aren't you worried he'll try to make your life a misery?'

Purcell laughed. 'I start tomorrow. The first day of Friendly's short transfer to Tulliallan. He'll be there for a month, and then quietly bow out. Turns out that, as he worked closely with David Elliott, some people think he knew more about Elliott than he's letting on. Between you and me, he was given the chance to take early retirement, or one of my colleagues from the north would be coming down here to give him a roasting. And then his career was finished.'

'Who'll be taking his place?'

'I don't know. They haven't told me. All they said was I'll be heading up Edinburgh MIT, doing the work of two men for the time being. Whoever gets Friendly's job will be in overall charge of all aspects of CID.'

'Is Suzy here?'

'She'll be here later.'

'Will she be working with us?'

Purcell shook his head. 'No, she's going to be working in HQ at Fettes. We had to disclose our relationship, so we can't be in CID together anymore.'

'That's a stupid rule,' Miller said. 'Kim and I work together, and it works just fine.'

'You work for different departments. Kim's not with the police.'

'True. At least you'll both be here,' Miller said. 'Is she coming down soon?'

'Not right away. They asked me to come down here early so I can liaise with the team back home, and Suzy is my eyes and ears up there.'

Then Miller knew. 'He struck up there too, didn't he?'

'Yes, he did. Last Thursday. We've tried to keep a wrap on it, and released a press statement saying a woman had been found murdered in her own home.'

'It must have worked as I didn't see anything on the news about a murder similar to ours.'

'That's the thing, Frank; murder is more commonplace now, and there are such terrorist atrocities going on in the world that a wee thing like a murder in Aberdeen hardly blips on the radar.'

'Who was it?'

'Michaela Savage. Mickey to her friends. Her folks couldn't get a hold of her, so we sent round a patrol car to do a welfare check. They found blood spattered on the walls, a rug missing, and a Polaroid sitting on the fireplace, showing her with her throat slit.'

'And no body to be found.'

'No body. As soon as they heard about your murder this morning, they sent me down. Not to take over, but to liaise with you boys.'

'I wonder why he chose Aberdeen?'

'I wish I knew. Hopefully we'll find out.'

FOURTEEN

Kim was just putting Emma to bed when Miller and Purcell walked in.

'Percy!' Kim said, smiling when she saw the detective. 'What are you doing here?'

'That's all I get? Not, *It's wonderful to see you again?*' He smiled at her as she rushed at him.

'Don't be silly. Of course it's wonderful to see you again.' She gave him a hug.

'You'd better release me. Your boyfriend's just come in the room. Pretend I'm a plumber or something.'

She laughed, and slapped his arm. 'Where's Suzy?'

'If somebody can put a kettle on and let me get my jacket off, all will be explained.'

Miller made the coffees. When they were settled, Purcell relaxed, but in the same way Mama Bear might relax while her cubs are playing.

'Paddy Gibb's retiring next month as you know, and now that David Elliott is dead, they gave me the job of running MIT. Dennis Friendly has been shoved sideways for the time being, and he'll be replaced soon by somebody who will be in charge of CID. A chief super. I'm still superintendent.'

'So, essentially, you're doing the job of two men,' Kim said.

'Basically. Police Scotland needs to stay trim, and by combining my roles, it means I get to shuffle a lot of paperwork and still be centre stage. They're looking for somebody now, so it won't be long.'

'So; Suzy. Where is she?'

'Still up in Aberdeen.'

'Is she coming down here?'

'She is, but she won't be CID. She's going into operations as a uniformed inspector. There was a post going down at Fettes, and she thought there would be a better chance of her coming down here if she took that. Plus it's a promotion for her.'

'Percy had to tell them about their relationship,' Miller said, relaxing in the armchair.

'It's the way it goes. I'm serious about her. She moved in with me at my dad's house. We're getting our own place down here.'

They heard the front door opening and closing before Jack came into the living room with Samantha. Purcell stood up, and for the second time that evening, a woman threw her arms around him.

'I need to buy more of this aftershave,' he said, after Samantha pulled herself away.

'It's so good to see you, Percy.'

'You too, Sam.'

'Good to see you again, son,' Jack said.

'I'm here a month earlier than expected. I wasn't supposed to start until November.'

They all sat down.

'Is Suzy here?'

Purcell explained again. 'This is hush hush, but I'm here because of the murder this morning.'

'There's been one in Aberdeen too, hasn't there?' Samantha said.

'There has. How did you know?'

'I'm a crime writer, Percy. It's easy to figure out why you came here; if you're a month early, and your girlfriend is still up there, they needed your input on the murder this morning.'

'Go to the top of the class. That's exactly right. Our victim was killed in the early hours of Thursday morning. Before three fifteen. There's a clock on the mantelpiece that's in the background of the photo he took of our victim.'

'This is terrible. But good news that you're coming down here for good. Where are you staying?'

'They got me a room in the hotel down in the Grassmarket. I wanted to be near the station.'

'You could stay at my place.'

'Mm, tempting as that sounds, Sam..." Percy said, with a wry smile, "Besides, Police Scotland is picking up the tab. And I don't want Jack asking me outside.'

'If you're sure.'

'I am, honestly. I'll be there until I find a place to live. I'm getting help with that, too.'

'How's your dad doing?' Jack asked.

'Lou's fine. With Suzy being there, he has her for company just now.'

'Is he going to make the move down here too?'

'No. He already moved up there when I moved to Aberdeen, and I did tell him he could come back, but he's settled now, and he has a girlfriend.'

'Good for him.'

'They chatted some more before Purcell got to his feet. 'Listen folks, I'm knackered, and I still have to Facetime with Lou to make sure my dog, Bear, hasn't eaten the couch.'

'Bright and early tomorrow to meet the troops,' Miller said.

'Absolutely. I'll get an update from Suzy first, to see if they're making any headway up there.'

'But you think he's down here, and they're definitely linked.'

'I do.' He said his goodbyes.

'One more thing, Percy,' Jack said.

'What's that?'

'Trying to move in with my girlfriend? Outside, now.'

Purcell laughed. 'I'm too tired to fight. We can talk about it over a beer tomorrow.'

'Count on it, son.' He smiled, and shook hands with the big detective.

Frank showed Purcell out then came back into the room. 'I wonder what the Aberdeen connection is?' he said.

'You need to go through Cathy's background again. If they're linked, it'll be there somewhere,' Jack said.

'I'll do that tomorrow.'

FIFTEEN

DS Jimmy Gilmour groaned as he heard the alarm clock going off. He reached his hand out in the dark to try to silence it, and then it went off by itself. Then came on again. The phone. It was as if a jolt of electricity had hit him as he grabbed the handset. His blurred eyes made out the green digits of the alarm clock. Twenty minutes past two. The early hours of Tuesday morning. Christ.

'Gilmour,' he said as quietly as he could, thinking it was control looking for him.

'Jimmy, it's me.' It was Connie, his ex-wife. She was crying, and barely making sense.

'What's wrong, Con?' Her name was Constance, shortened to Connie. Only Gilmour called her Con.

'It's Uncle Monty, Jimmy. He's dying.'

'Where are you?'

'I'm at the Western.' She told him what ward she was calling from. 'Try to hurry, Jimmy.'

'I'll be there as soon as.' He hung up, and tried to get out of bed as quietly as possible, gritting his teeth as the bed springs creaked. When he looked over at Lauren's side, he saw it was empty. Fuck. He felt his heart racing faster now. Had Lauren been mugged and was now lying down a close? Was she in the hospital? He tried to calm himself down. No, she was pissed off at him that was all. She had probably stayed over with a friend.

By the time he'd used the bathroom and got dressed, it was two thirty. He tried calling Lauren's mobile phone. It kept on ringing until it went to voicemail, so he left her a message telling her where he'd gone.

Edinburgh on an autumn night was like having a wild animal for a pet, familiarity on one hand, uncertainty on another. Few souls were walking about as the cold gripped the city.

Night buses trawled the streets, as did taxis, and a few drunks, driving themselves home because getting pulled over *won't happen to me*. After the divorce, Jimmy had left the house in Chancelot Mill, and moved into a flat in Dumbiedykes. Now, it was only Connie and his little girl, Rachael, who lived in the house. He missed it.

He drove up High Street, and down the North Bridge. Princes Street itself was like a runway, waiting for the next plane that wasn't going to arrive. The car was an old Vauxhall Astra. Another thing he'd left behind when he'd left was his car.

Now he was outside the Anne Ferguson building, in the grounds of the Western General Hospital, a blue edifice tacked onto the original hospital, looking very much like a Lego building. He parked right outside the front doors on the double yellows.

He wanted a coffee from the downstairs café, but it was closed so he headed through to the back corridor. Outside the two lifts, a directory hung from one wall. He quickly scanned it, and found what he was looking for. Ward 55. Acute Stroke Unit.

He took the lift up to the next floor, and walked along the corridor into the ward, the building seemingly deserted. It was warm in here, a reprieve from the cold. He looked through the windows in the corridor, at the small garden courtyard that was surrounded by the windows from the wards. The light from the corridor windows was bringing the garden to life, giving it form in the dark, where it normally would lay dormant until sun up.

Bay number 2 was on the left. When Gilmour looked in through the open door, he wouldn't have recognised the man lying in the bed if he hadn't seen the name written on a small whiteboard on the door.

Connie sat in a chair on the far side of the bed, holding her uncle's hand. A spot lamp on a swivel arm was the only source of light, pointed at a corkboard on the wall behind the bed.

Montague Chase looked as if he could have been sleeping.

'Hello, Con,' Gilmour said.

'Oh, Jimmy,' she said, getting up. She threw her arms around him, and he held onto her, feeling her warmth through her sweater. He could feel her body wracking with the tears that were flowing. After a couple of minutes, they parted.

Connie stood back, and wiped away the tears.

Gilmour looked at the old man. It was obvious he was gone.

'He passed away ten minutes ago.'

'God, Connie, I'm so sorry.'

She cried into his shoulder for a few minutes. Then she straightened up and sniffed. 'The consultant wants to talk to us. I was waiting for you to come so you could listen to him. They've been telling me stuff, but I can't really take it in.'

'That's understandable. It's times like these that your brain turns to mush.' He glanced quickly at the old man again, not believing it was Monty lying there. 'Let's go and see if we can find somebody, Con.'

He used the hand sanitizer pump that was hooked onto the end of the bed. Looked around the room as he rubbed the foul smelling liquid into his hands. A closed door to the shower room. A small TV up high on a shelf in the corner. It was switched off right now, the remote lying by its side. Monty wouldn't have been able to watch TV anyway.

He looked at the old man's face. The top lip seemed sunken, then he remembered he had a top dental plate, which must have been taken out.

'He had a chest infection, that's why he was on the antibiotic drip,' Connie said, as if the man was still alive. 'He was a bit sick, and some of the vomit went into his lungs.' She started crying again, and Gilmour put his arm around her shoulder.

Poor bastard, he thought, looking at Monty. He'd always got on well with the old man, even after he and Connie had divorced.

Monty would call Gilmour up on occasion, and arrange to take him for a pint. Those had been good days, but they had become farther and farther apart as Gilmour's caseloads got bigger.

He escorted Connie out into the main corridor, and looked around. For a second, it seemed they were the only two people in the hospital. No sounds came from the other bays, no footsteps falling on the vinyl flooring, no beeps from machines wired up to sick people.

Across from Monty's room, posters were stuck on the wall. A chart explaining what cholesterol was, with graphic drawings. Another one describing the effects of a stroke. Gilmour turned Connie away from them and, still holding onto her, walked up to the end of the corridor to the nurses' station. A figure moved into a small ward, seemingly like a ghost. Was it an apparition? Some soul not able to leave the hospital? Gilmour felt a shiver run down his spine. He held onto Connie tighter, pulling her closer. Comforting her, shielding her from the pain she was feeling, shielding himself from the memories of his mother, who had also died in hospital.

Then the figure appeared again. Not a ghost. A consultant. He walked towards them. His hair was jet black, and he stood almost as tall as Gilmour, but thinner.

'Mr Gilmour? I'm Mitchell Robb. I'm so sorry for your loss.' He held his hand out, and Gilmour shook it. He made a mental note to use the hand sanitizer again when he got the chance.

'Pleased to meet you, Doctor.' Gilmour wondered if a consultant was addressed as doctor, or if he'd just made an arse of himself.

'If you'd like to come with me down to the conference room.' He walked past them, and led them back down the corridor. Gilmour noticed pamphlets on strokes. More posters.

Robb led them into a room with a large, rectangular table in it. 'Please, take a seat,' he said. They sat down, and faced a large, widescreen TV that sat on a wall-to-wall cabinet. Robb sat at the head of the table, and leaned back in his chair.

'Mrs Gilmour asked if I would explain what happened to Mr Chase. As you may know, he had a massive stroke. He had two smaller strokes a few years ago, a year apart.' He looked at Connie, who nodded. 'Those were the warning signals.'

Connie stared at him, his words barely forming an impression. Gilmour couldn't see outside the window for the room's reflection in the glass. He turned his attention back to the doctor.

'When Mr Chase was admitted, we gave him a CAT scan to confirm that it was indeed a stroke he'd had. Then we talked with Mrs Gilmour here about giving her uncle a TPA—'

'What's a TPA?' Gilmour asked, holding a hand up. He was starting to sweat now. He opened up his jacket a bit more. It was starting to feel as if he was in an interview room back at his station.

'Tissue plasminogen activator. It's a very powerful clot-busting drug. The new one we have has to be given within three hours. That's the condition of our licence to use the drug. Unfortunately, Mr Chase was just outside the three hour limit by the time he got his CAT scan, so we had to give him some other reperfusion agents to try and break up the clot.'

'It didn't do the job?' Gilmour asked. He looked at Connie. She was staring at the blank TV screen, her eyes streaming.

'Let me show you.' He picked a remote up off the table, and pointed it at the TV screen. It burst into life as the doctor spun in his chair and opened a cabinet under the TV.

The screen was like a giant computer monitor. Gilmour watched as Robb took out a cordless keyboard and started typing on it. Then Monty's scan result came up. Gilmour reached over and squeezed Connie's hand.

'This is Mr Chase's scan. It is a slice-by-slice view. Moving up from the bottom of his skull.' They watched as Monty's brain got bigger and bigger.

'You can see where the swelling of the brain is.'

Where the normal pattern of swirls and trenches were that made up the brain, one side was completely clear of patterns.

A few more slides. Darker areas. 'Those are the spots where massive bleeding occurred. Unfortunately, that's one of the side-effects of a TPA.'

Connie started crying again.

Robb turned to them. 'Mr Chase was on antibiotics and a drip feed. Basically, he was on life support.'

'Wouldn't he have gotten better?' Gilmour asked.

'It would have taken a miracle. If he had survived this, he would be in a vegetative state. He couldn't talk, and his right side was paralysed. He would need care, twenty-four seven. But that's only if a miracle happened.'

'Wasn't he too young to have a stroke?' Gilmour asked.

Robb looked at him. 'People in their twenties can have a stroke, so no, he wasn't too young. *You* could have one.'

Cheery bastard, Gilmour thought, making a mental note to cut back on the doughnuts.

'I can't believe he's dead,' Connie said, dabbing at her eyes. 'He was sixty-eight, and I knew he wouldn't live forever, but it seems inconceivable that he's gone.'

The door of the conference room burst open. A man stood looking at them, his hair unkempt.

'I might have guessed you'd be crawling round here, you bastard!' the man shouted at Gilmour.

SIXTEEN

Patricia Wilkinson left the pub feeling tired, but also as if there was an electric buzz zipping through her. It had been a busy night, nobody had called in sick, and there were no tantrums by the staff. No fights, no drunks having to be thrown out.

And her boyfriend had come round.

She should have been out of here almost an hour ago, but she had let the others go, saying she would lock up. There was only her and one customer after all.

Nobody knew about him. None of her co-workers, her friends. Ashley hadn't known about him either, thank God. She would never have heard the end of it. And her boyfriend's wife either didn't know, or didn't care. She was a raging drunk anyway, and would probably have passed out by eleven he had told her.

'I can't believe you wanted to make love in my office,' she said, giggling as she locked the front door of the pub. George IV Bridge was quiet at this time of the morning, but a few cars went by. The wind was cold, and her face was starting to glow already.

'I want to make love to you everywhere,' he replied, bringing her in close.

'You *are* still going to have that talk with your wife, aren't you?'

He smiled his charming, boyish grin, the one she had fallen in love with right from the start. 'I will, I promise. Things have been bad recently, and she's been drinking even more. It's hard to find a time that she's sober nowadays. By the time I get in from work, she's already sozzled. We had a fight earlier, which is the norm nowadays, so that makes things a lot easier.'

'Do it soon. I can't wait much longer.'

They started walking up the road towards High Street. 'I thought you said you'd wait for eternity?'

'I would. But I want you long before that. I want you right now. You said yourself that you think we're good together.'

'And we are. I can't think of anybody else I'd want to be with right now.' They stopped at the railings where he looked over the side into Merchant Street, which itself ran under the street they were on, leading to the prisoners' entrance to the Sheriff court.

'You promised me you'd tell her last weekend.'

'Things have been difficult.'

'I'm sorry. Of course they have.' She pulled him close, and held him tightly for a moment. Stepping back, she looked up into his eyes. 'It's just that I want you so much. I hate all this running around in secrecy, watching where we go in case somebody sees us.'

He kissed her on the lips, and they started walking again, hand in hand. 'I know, and it's all my fault.'

'It's nobody's fault, silly. I know we have to be careful, or she'll take you to the cleaners. But you have to understand, I've been with men before, but none of them like you. I just want to feel your arms around me. To hear you snore as you lie beside me in bed.'

'Snore? That's a turn-on for you?'

Patricia pulled her hand away from his, and pointed at him, laughing. 'That's not what I'm saying! I meant it's all part of the package. Like I go to bed with rollers in, and green paste on my face. That's something you'll have to get used to.'

'Really? Rollers?'

She laughed again, and grabbed hold of his hand. 'No, of course not. I'm just having a laugh.' She looked at a small café that was locked up for the night. 'Take this place for instance; The Elephant House. I go in there sometimes, and just sit with a coffee and read a book. It's said that JK Rowling wrote the Harry Potter books in there and I've actually read a couple in there. To me, that's magical. So I imagine us being able to go in there and sit with a coffee and talk about books and authors.'

'I'm more of a Samantha Willis man myself. Don't get me wrong, the little wizard has made her a lot of money, but I prefer the old crime novels. And Willis is a local author too.'

They moved on. 'See? That's just the sort of thing I'm talking about. We can discover new writers who we each like and can swap books.'

'I love your enthusiasm, Pattie. I want to wake up next to you more than anything, every single day. To see you smiling at me.'

She let go of his hand, and slipped an arm through his, pulling him closer. 'We can make love any time you want.'

He knew her promise was made out of love, and not because of his athletic prowess, but he loved her for it. 'Maybe not tonight though. I think I put my back out on your desk.'

'It was a thrill. Even though everybody had left, it was different.'

'It certainly was.'

'Are you getting up early tomorrow? Today, I mean.'

He shook his head. 'I can go into the office later. It's not a big deal. Nobody will question me. They'll think I was working at home.'

'Me neither. That means you can come home with me, and we can at least snuggle up on the couch and have a glass of wine. See if we can't tease Mr Rogers there into a second round.'

'Now that you put it that way, I think a nice glass of wine would go down very well.'

'Really? You really will come home with me this late?'

'Of course. My marriage is over, I told you that. She'll be happy with half the house and half the bank account. She doesn't know about the account I have offshore. As long as nobody sees me with you, then she can't make my life a misery.'

'I love you so much.' She kissed him again.

'I love you too.' Then he saw it; the *Taxi* sign lit up orange on the top of the black cab. He hailed it, and the cab swung round and stopped next to them.

'The Shore,' he said, as they stepped into the warmth.

SEVENTEEN

'Christ almighty,' Gilmour said, as Connie's cousin walked into the room. Gabriel Chase was unshaven, his short hair making him look like a thug rather than a respected lawyer. The doctor had jumped up, Gilmour between them.

'What's the meaning of this?' Robb asked.

'Who the fuck are you?' he asked the doctor, pointing at him.

'Shut up, Gabriel,' Gilmour said, taking a step closer. He could smell the drink on Chase's breath.

'What are you doing here? What are you after, Gilmour?' He sneered, and more beer fumes hit the detective.

'Did you call him, Con?' Gilmour said, looking at his ex-wife.

'No, I couldn't get hold of him.'

'Maybe one of the nurses called him, if his name's on the contact list,' Robb said. 'But if you want to stay, then you'll have to behave yourself.'

'You don't talk to me like that. I'm here to see my fucking uncle.'

Gilmour grabbed hold of the front of Chase's jacket, and banged him against the wall. 'You want to stay here, you shut it. Your uncle's dead, so get a grip of yourself. Got that?'

The fight seemed to drop out of Chase, like a balloon that's been suddenly deflated.

'Dead? They just told me to come in.'

'I'm sorry, Mr Chase, your uncle passed away twenty minutes ago,' Robb said.

Gilmour let him go.

'I can't believe this.' Chase ran a hand through his hair.

Robb left the room to ask the nurses to prepare Monty for their last goodbye. Gilmour left the conference room with Connie, and they sat in the corridor on the chairs that were grouped in a corner. He wondered if this was where all the families waited who had been told that a loved one was about to die. Would he himself end up in here one day, with his daughter sitting where he was, ready to say goodbye to him? That thought made him feel hollow inside.

Chase came out, and sat farther down, his head bowed into his hands. He looked a mess.

Gilmour didn't like the man. Connie's father was Monty's brother, and he had died years ago, while she and Gilmour were still happily married. Monty's wife had died, and they didn't have children of their own.

Monty's other brother had one son, Gabriel, and Monty had treated Connie and his nephew as if they were his own children.

Gabriel was a lawyer, but he was often outspoken, and drank more than his liver could handle without there being medical repercussions farther down the road. Monty hadn't trusted his nephew, so he had given Connie power of attorney. Gabriel said he couldn't care less, as long as he got some of his old man's dosh when he kicked the bucket. He would no doubt buy shares in a brewery, via a barstool.

'I'm sorry about that, Jimmy,' Connie said, in a low voice.

'I can hear you,' Chase said, looking up at them. 'You've got a cheek getting him to come here, Connie.'

'Shut your mouth, Gabriel. I'm here for her, so don't let me hear you giving her any of your shite, okay?' Gilmour said.

'Fuck you,' Chase said, in a voice barely above a whisper.

After Monty was made presentable, they went in to see him. He was still lying on his back, but with his hair combed and the covers straightened up.

Gabriel Chase went and held his uncle's left hand. Connie held the right. Gilmour left the room.

After half an hour, Connie came out. 'You need to go home, Jimmy. You've got work in the morning. I'm going home too. I'll come back and see Uncle Monty later.'

'You can come back later today, and I'll have the death certificate made out. Then you can register his death,' Robb said.

'Thank you,' Connie said, and they walked away along the corridor, their shoes on the floor the only sound.

Gilmour glanced back as he opened the door for his ex-wife and saw Chase come out of the room. He was on his mobile phone, talking quietly to somebody. He looked at Gilmour, and then turned away.

Gilmour wondered to whom Chase was talking. The man wasn't married, and Connie hadn't mentioned a girlfriend.

When the door closed behind him, he looked through the glass into the ward.

Chase was gone.

'I'm sorry about my cousin,' Connie said, slipping her arm through Gilmour's.

'It's not your fault he's an arsehole.'

They made their way down in the lift, and out into the freezing cold of the wee hours.

'I came on the bus, Jimmy. I figured it would be easier than trying to find a parking space in the tiny car park. I can get a taxi home.'

'I don't think so. I have Jimmy's taxi right here.' He opened the door of the Astra for her, and closed the door once she was seated. He looked up at the blue building, figuring out in his mind where Monty's ward was. First floor, over on the left. He felt sorry for the old man.

He started the car up, the engine noisy in the deathly quiet of the hospital grounds. The wipers batted away the layer of condensation from the windscreen. He headed up to Crewe Toll, and turned right onto Ferry Road, heading east.

'How's Rachael?' Gilmour asked. He looked at Connie in the darkness of the car. He could feel her eyes on him, and for just a moment, it felt as if they were married again, and had been on a night out.

'She's fine, Jimmy. I took her next door.' Connie's next-door neighbour was Rachael's babysitter when they needed her.

Connie started crying again as they headed for Bonnington. The roads were clear. Gilmour felt the old familiar feeling of coming home when he turned into Connie's street in Connaught Place. Right down to the newer houses they had built on the footprint of the old Chancelot flour mill.

He stopped outside her terraced house. What used to be his house, and he felt a pang of... what? Jealousy? No. Regret. He'd thrown it all away for a piece of garbage. *Frank Miller was right; I have to do what's best for me.*

'Thanks, Jimmy.'

'No problem, Con,' he replied.

'Would you come with me to register his death?'

'Of course I will. I'm sure it won't be a problem. I'll call you when I get up.'

She leaned over in the dark, and kissed him on the cheek. 'I'll see myself in. I'll call you later.'

'Get some rest.'

'I will.' A sudden cold shot into the car as she opened the car door, and not for the first time did Gilmour wonder if he'd done the right thing by divorcing Connie.

EIGHTEEN

When Gilmour got up for a shower later that morning, Lauren was sleeping heavily. He didn't know what time she had come home. He himself had got back at five thirty, so it must have been after that. Now it was eight o'clock, and he felt as if he hadn't been to bed. Which made him even more pissed off with her.

She had seemed tense for a long time, and he tried to think what could have caused the shift in their relationship, but he wasn't doing anything different. Connie always caused Lauren's back to get up and he accepted that, but he couldn't cut Connie out of his life.

He had left her for Lauren, leaving Rachael with her, and he had been happy at first. Felt the buzz from the excitement of moving in with somebody new, but it had worn off quickly. Maybe there was a hint of jealousy in Lauren. They had talked about having a baby together, but she had decided against it.

He got up, showered, dressed, and made coffee.

Lauren came into the room, and ignored him. He felt a rush of anger, but quickly controlled it.

Lauren poured a coffee. She was like a walking zombie

'Are you going into work today?' Gilmour asked.

'Nope. I'm going back to bed after I call in sick.'

'Did you get my voicemail this morning?'

She sipped at the black, steaming liquid. 'What do you think?'

'Where were you last night?'

'Out with some of my friends. Not that I need your permission to go out.' She sneered at him then walked out, back to the living room. It was as if Lauren had died, and now her evil twin had come to stay.

It was bright outside, the sun streaming through the windows and the wind had stopped scattering leaves all over the place. Gilmour poured more coffee from the pot, and put some bread in the toaster. Walked over to the living room door, and saw Lauren sitting on the couch, cradling her coffee cup.

'Lauren, what's up with you recently? Is it something I've done?' he said, standing in the doorway, trying to break the ice.

'It's something you've *not* done. Like, get rid of your ex-wife.'

'What, you want me to put her in a suitcase and dump her out in the Forth? Would that make you happy?'

'Don't be fucking stupid. You know perfectly well what I mean.'

'We've been through this already.'

'Enough said, then. I know where I stand.'

'Her uncle died. She's trying to keep it together.'

'Good for her.'

Oh fuck off. The phone rang. Gilmour answered it. After a few minutes, he went back into the kitchen. 'I have to go.' He finished his coffee.

He strode up Holyrood Road, and felt the icy wind sting at his face, making his eyes water by the time he reached Frank Miller's building on the corner of the North Bridge. He pushed the buzzer.

'It's Gilmour, boss. Do you have a minute?'

'Of course. Come on up.'

'I'll get you a coffee,' Miller said as Gilmour entered the apartment. 'Sit down.'

Gilmour sat at the table. 'Hi, Kim. Hello, young lady.'

'Hi, Jimmy.' Kim looked at Emma. 'Say hello to Detective Gilmour.'

'Hello, Detective Gilmour. Do you have a cat?'

Gilmour felt his breath catch in his throat for a moment. *I have two cats,* he was about to say, but caught himself in time. The cats were Connie's now. 'No, I don't have any cats. I know you do though. Where is he?'

'Brushing his teeth. I've decided he's coming to school with me today.'

'Is he now, missy?' Kim said.

'Yes he is, Mum. We have to bring something into school that we love. I want to take Charlie in, because I love him.'

'Honey, he doesn't want to go out into the cold.'

Miller put a coffee down for Gilmour, who had loosened his jacket. 'Thanks, boss.'

'Oh, Mum, please?' Emma said.

'Why don't you take a soft toy in?' Gilmour said. 'One that you love. That way, your friends will see something that means a lot to you, and soft toys don't mind the cold. It's what my little girl did.'

'Oh, Uncle Jimmy, you're so clever!' Emma said, getting up from the table and coming round to hug him.

Kim smiled at her daughter. 'Go and brush your teeth, or we'll be late.'

The little girl ran away from the kitchen.

'Thanks, Jimmy, you're a lifesaver. How is Rachael, by the way?'

'She's fine, Kim. But I came round here with some bad news.'

'Monty?' Miller asked.

Gilmour nodded, and took a sip of his coffee. 'He died earlier this morning.'

'I'm sorry to hear that, Jimmy. Is there anything we can do?'

'I'd like to go and help Connie to register his death, and go and see the undertaker.'

'That's fine. Take whatever time you need. I'll square it with Paddy.'

'I'm sorry, too, Jimmy. I met Monty a few times, and he was a good friend of my mum and dad.'

'Connie was his only niece, but he has a nephew, Gabriel. He's a lawyer, but he's a real mess.'

'I know him,' Kim said.

'Me too,' Miller said. 'A weasel of a man.'

'Well, Connie has power of attorney, and is one of the executor's of his will, along with Monty's lawyer. She's going to see him first thing so he can release a press statement. *The Caledonian* will want to run an obit piece on him. Then I'll go to the hospital with her so we can pick up the hospital death certificate, register him, and then see the undertaker after that.'

'Listen, Jimmy, take the day off. And if you need more time, just ask.' He looked at Gilmour for a moment, as if unsure whether to ask the next question. 'How are things with you and Lauren this morning?'

Gilmour drank more coffee, enjoying the taste, needing the caffeine. 'I hate to say this, but I think it's over between us.'

'Oh, Jimmy,' Kim said, putting a hand on Gilmour's arm. 'People go through bad patches. It might work itself out.'

He kept quiet about seeing Kate Murphy, and finished his coffee. 'I'd best be off.'

'Keep me in the loop,' Miller said, as they walked down the hallway.

#Percy Purcell stood looking out of his hotel bedroom window into the Grassmarket. A place that brought back memories of a case he'd helped Frank Miller work on just a couple of months ago. When it was warm outside. Now summer had left, and autumn had come in with a vengeance.

The grey sky was the backdrop for the castle across the way.

Traffic was starting to build up for the morning. He let the curtains go; glad he wasn't an office worker.

He sat down on the small couch, opened his iPad, and called Suzie on Facetime.

'Hello, lover boy,' she said, when she answered, smiling at him.

Purcell put on his best Sean Connery accent. 'Well, good morning to you too, Miss Moneyfanny.'

Lou, Purcell's father walked into the frame. 'Here, enough of that talk. One day in Edinburgh and you've a mouth like a truck driver.'

'Thanks for invading our privacy, Lou.'

'I've not got rubber ears.'

Suzy smiled, and turned to Lou. 'Sorry about that. We're just kidding around.'

'That's okay then.' He briefly patted her shoulder. 'Just don't let him corrupt you. If he starts giving you lip, refer him to me.'

'Oh, big man when you're at the other end of the camera,' Purcell said.

'I'll be on the next bus down to the big city and skelp your arse. See what Suzy thinks of you then when you're squealing like a wee lassie.'

'Of course you will. Then you'll have Bear hanging off your ding dong. We'll see who has tears in his eyes after that.'

'I'm away for coffee. This conversation has plumbed new depths. But remember one thing; this is a lady you're living with, so treat her like one.' Suzy smiled at Purcell as Lou left the kitchen.

'You're right, Dad. Sorry, Suze. I'll watch my mouth in future. I reckon I'm not used to being with a nice woman. I am missing you though. I wish I had a photograph of you.'

'That's funny, I didn't figure you for *A Flock of Seagulls* kind of guy.'

'Just don't tell anybody.'

'Take a photo now. I'll put on my best smile.'

He whipped out his iPhone and snapped a picture of her. 'Now, just pout a little bit.'

'I will not, you filthy sod.' She smiled at him.

'Percy!' Lou shouted. 'I might not be in the same room, but I'm not deaf!'

Purcell stuck two fingers up at the screen. 'So, how's my boy this morning?'

She picked up her iPad, and showed Percy his German Shepherd eating. 'He's being a good boy. I took him out this morning. It's freezing so we didn't go to the park.'

'I need to get him a jacket.'

'Percy, he's a German Shepherd. He'd be embarrassed to wear a poodle jacket.'

'It could be a camouflage jacket, not a pink one.'

'Still. He has a thick coat already.'

'I know, I spoil him.'

'And he'll be spoiled in Edinburgh too, just not with a jacket.'

'Okay. You win.' He sipped the coffee he'd made. 'So, how are things going at your end?' Meaning, tracking down Michaela Savage's killer.

'We're not making much progress. We're checking out friends, family, and colleagues, but we've struck a blank with her family. Basically, she only has her parents, who live in Edinburgh. The only connection I can see between our killer and the one down there is Edinburgh itself. She lived there, and decided to move up here.'

'Maybe he knew her and tracked her down. I don't think this is random, Suzy.'

'Me neither. I'll keep on it up here, but I think you're going to have more luck down there.'

'Me too.'

'How are you settling in?'

'The hotel's great, but it's not like a proper home.'

'I've been looking at places for rent, and I made a little list. I'll email them to you. Maybe you could check out the ones you fancy. You know Edinburgh better than I do.'

'I'll check them out at lunchtime. Right now, I'm going down for breakfast, and then I'll head up to the station.'

'Are you missing me?'

'Of course I am.'

'More than Bear?'

'Well, it's about even.'

'Would you rather he warm up your bed at night?'

'Okay, you win; I miss you more.'

'Good call, Purcell.'

'Right, honey, I'll get away now. I don't want to be late.'

'Take care, Percy. The last time you were in Edinburgh, somebody tried to kill you. Twice.'

'I can look after myself.'

They signed off, and Purcell knew inside that Michaela's killer was down here. He'd hunted her down like an animal and killed her, just like he'd killed Ashley Gates.

NINETEEN

Mitchell Robb was in his office, sitting behind his desk with a sheaf of papers in front of him.

A nurse knocked on the door, and ushered Gilmour and Connie in. He would usually have a nurse pass over the hospital death certificate, but since Gilmour was a police officer, he made an exception.

He didn't bother to stand up or offer them a seat when they came in, since this transaction was simple; hand the piece of paper over, spew some nonsense about how sorry he was for their loss and bingo bango, done and dusted.

'So, what happens now?' Connie said.

'Your uncle is down in the hospital mortuary. You'll have to take this certificate to the Registrar's Office on George IV Bridge and register his death with them. They'll give you an official death certificate. Contact a funeral director of your choice, and they'll send somebody to pick him up and take him to their place of business. Then you make arrangements with the undertaker for the funeral.' He held out the certificate, and she took it.

'Not had much sleep either, Doc?' Gilmour said.

'I've not had any. I was on call through the night. I'm just finishing up some of this paperwork, and then I'll be heading home. A day off for me. Sleep then the golf club.'

'You guys play golf even when it's cold?'

'I said the golf *club,* detective. I didn't say anything about playing golf.'

'Ah. Got it.'

'Time for a little unwinding.'

'Right. Thanks for everything you did for Connie's uncle.'

'I wish it could have been more, but such is life. At least he's at peace now.' The words were of little consolation, but he knew the bereaved weren't listening at this point.

'Thank you, doctor,' Connie said, as Gilmour ushered her out.

Robb finished off the last piece of paperwork he intended to do that day. If he left now, he could grab some shut-eye and make it round to the club for a good sesh with the boys. There was a knock on the door, and he thought it was the woman and her ex-husband back to ask another question, but it wasn't; it was one of the lab managers.

'Ah, come in. You have the results, I take it?'

'I do indeed, sir,' she said, smiling as she came into the consultant's office. 'Everything is straightforward; all the tox screens came back negative, and the correct amount of drug was administered.'

'Thank you. Routine, thank goodness.'

'If you need anything else, just call me.'

'I will. Thanks again.' He watched her leave, and sat back in his leather chair, sighing with relief. He had asked her to put the blood screen on fast-track, so he could get the results back quickly. The fact that Connie's ex-husband was a police officer made him nervous. He might decide to come back poking around, accusing him, Mitchell Robb, of wrongdoing. But he had just covered his own arse with the blood screen. Everything had been done by the book.

Robb was keeping his eye on the lab manager. He had seen her about, and he wasn't far away from asking her out. Just a little more time.

He got his jacket on and left the office, telling his receptionist he would be away for the rest of the day. He was off for the next two days, time to relax and get some decent sex in. He'd already made a call and had somebody lined up for a dinner date.

He wiped the leaves off his car while the engine was running, wishing they would build a multi-storey car park so he wouldn't have to do this. And there was the matter of getting the lazy sods in maintenance to sweep the place. This sports car was rear-wheel drive, which wasn't the best for driving on wet leaves. As he got in and felt the heated seats pamper his backside, he made a mental note to call the dealer and enquire about the delivery date for his F-PACE.

He pulled out of the car park, and headed home to Ravelston.

The Jag cosseted him in a way that public transport never could. With the car safely tucked away in the garage, he trudged over to the front doors and wondered if Jess had left yet, just as she'd promised. Well, fuck her, he wasn't going to be lectured to anymore. Their cards were on the table; he'd been screwing around, she'd found out – game over.

He let himself into the apartment.

Stood rooted to the spot for a moment. Then he forced himself to take out his other mobile phone, the one he would throw away after this call.

The person at the other end answered his call.

'I've got a problem,' Robb said.

TWENTY

Percy Purcell stood at the front of the incident room next to Paddy Gibb, looking out at the other detectives gathered in front of him.

'For those of you who have forgotten who I am – or wish you'd forgotten – my name is Detective Superintendent Percy Purcell. When this fine young man retires next month, it will be my ugly mug you'll see sitting in his office. I'm doing double duty, as Superintendent David Elliott's replacement. Detective Chief Super Dennis Friendly is on secondment to Tulliallan, so it's yours truly who is running Police Edinburgh CID, with direct responsibility for MIT. I'm not sure who they'll be bringing in to replace him. Any questions so far?'

Andy Watt put his hand up. Paddy Gibb gritted his teeth.

'Yes, Andy?'

'Will you be reinstating the tradition where the boss buys the coffee and doughnuts every Friday?'

'I think there are enough doughnuts in here. No offence.'

'Offence taken.'

'Right, let me tell you why I'm here a month early; we had a similar murder to Ashley Gates' back in Aberdeen, last Thursday.

We have no suspects, but my team back there are working on it. The only connection we found is that she used to live and work down here. She moved to Aberdeen for work just over a year ago. She isn't married, and her parents live down here.'

'I'm assuming that the MO was the same?' Kim said.

'Correct. At the crime scene, we found a Polaroid photo of her with a knife sticking out of her neck, and there were stab wounds on her torso. The pathologist we work with up there said there was a ninety-nine per cent probability that she was dead. Without a physical body, the rules say he can't give a definite one hundred per cent.'

'What about blood at the scene?' Miller asked.

'There was spatter on the walls and the furnishings. There was an area the size of the rug in front of her fire that was clean and it was outlined by the blood spatter. We're assuming he took her away in this.'

Gibb stepped forward, and pointed to the whiteboard. Three photos had been enlarged and pinned up. 'This is Cathy Graham from two years ago, the woman who was murdered in the church. This is Michaela Savage from the Aberdeen enquiry. And this is Ashley Gates. Let's find out why he waited for two years to grace us with his presence again.'

Miller was standing at the side, and spoke up. 'We're still checking out Ashley Gates' family and friends. Maybe something will become apparent then.'

'Right, so DCI Gibb is still in charge of this case, but I'll be here as liaison. Let's get to it, people.'

As the detectives dispersed, Miller took Purcell aside. 'Hazel Carter will be in later. Bruce is still having problems, and now he's gone and fallen down the stairs, dislocating his knee. Hazel is at the Royal with him. I said I'd run it by you, but she can take the day off if that's okay with you.'

'Of course it is, Frank. He's one of us. Anything we can do to help.'

'She's going to need a lot of help when the baby's born in a few months' time.'

'We'll all pitch in and help her. And tell her if she has a son, I want him named after me.'

'Dick?'

'Go away, Miller.'

TWENTY-ONE

'This just feels so final,' Connie said, as Gilmour slowed down on the bend in the road to wait for a gap in the oncoming traffic.

'I know what you mean.'

If you blinked, you would miss the little lane off Ravelston Dykes Road. It was a private road, with access only to Monty Chase's house and the golf club. At the end, it narrowed into a track where the club's vehicles drove along. Apart from that, it was very quiet.

Gilmour turned into the large grounds on the right. There was a detached double-garage over to the right, with a small, circular driveway leading round to the front door of the house. It was large, if not quite a mansion and L-shaped. A lawn was on the right, between the garage block and the house.

'I remember the Sunday afternoons in the summer when we'd come here and he'd grill us burgers outside,' Gilmour said, as he stopped the car.

'That was fun.' Connie looked over at her ex-husband. 'I'm going to miss him, Jimmy. We had such good times here.'

They approached the front door and Connie used her keys to

unlock. The heating was still running, and the old, familiar feel gripped her as she closed the door behind them.

'What was it the funeral director said again?' she said.

'He said we should pick out a suit for him to be dressed in. People can come and view him in the room at the funeral parlour, and considering he was a judge, he should be dressed appropriately.'

'Did he say anything about underwear? I can't remember. Oh God, I was paying attention, I promise, but it just went out of my head.' She started to cry as they stood in the hallway, and Gilmour took her in his arms.

'I know you were, love. It's hard at these times.'

When she was finished sobbing, she gently pulled away from him.

'I believe he did say to bring underwear,' Gilmour said.

'Okay. I'll go and look out his clothes. Can you put the kettle on?'

'Of course I will.'

The wide hallway made the house feel empty, and Gilmour knew Connie and Gabriel would soon have to get a lawyer onto selling the house. He figured they would both be beneficiaries in the old man's will.

He watched Connie climb the stairs to the bedrooms then walked through to the back of the house, filled the kettle in the kitchen, switched it on, and went for a wander while it boiled.

The living room was large, and looked out onto the back lawn. The property was surrounded by tall, thick trees. Nobody from the golf course could see into the room, neither could the neighbours. He remembered the better days, and mentally ran the movie in his head of his little girl running around the garden.

He opened the curtains wider, letting more light in.

The door to the den was over to the left.

Inside was a desk with an iMac on it. One of the newer ones, the smaller 21.5 inch 4K version. Bookcases lined two walls, and part of the room held two leather chairs facing each other, with a small table in the middle. There was a chess game laid out, all the pieces standing to attention. Gilmour knew nothing about chess.

There was a drinks cabinet behind one of the chairs. Decanters filled with whisky sat on top. Underneath was where the glasses were kept.

He sat down on the high back, leather office chair. Maybe it was because he was a detective, or maybe he was just being nosy, but he started looking through the desk.

There were drawers on either side of the keyboard tray. Not very deep ones, and they both held stationery of sorts. Below the right one was a cupboard, which held reams of paper for the printer that sat on a little stand at the side of one of the bookcases.

Two more handles were below the drawer on the left. The bottom one revealed hanging files. The middle drawer revealed a selection of boxes and some CD cases with handwritten covers in each. Classical composers.

Why would a man who lives in an upper class neighbourhood need copied CDs? Gilmour shrugged as he shuffled through the cases. He didn't see an external CD player, and there wasn't a CD player in the room. *How do you play your CDs, Monty? The new Macs don't have a CD drive.*

The last case didn't have anything on the cover. Gilmour flipped it open.

Some things fell out, and Gilmour started when he saw what they were. He couldn't have jumped more if they were black widow spiders. But they weren't.

These things made his heart beat even faster.

Then he called Frank Miller.

TWENTY-TWO

Even though Kim wasn't a police officer, she was still a part of MIT. So she went to be with Hazel at the hospital, and promised she would get Hagan home safely.

Miller took a pool car. It was a ten-minute drive through the city centre traffic, down Lothian Road from Lauriston Place, cutting through the traffic, past the Caledonian Hotel, and into Queensferry Street.

From there, a few minutes to the upper-class area of Ravelston, the siren blaring, and the lights flashing on his Vauxhall.

Patrol cars had their blue lights flashing as Miller pulled into the private road. Percy Purcell was standing next to another pool car, speaking into his mobile phone. He turned when he saw Miller driving in, and finished his call.

'How's Hagan?' he said, as Miller got out of his car.

'I'm still waiting on Kim to give me an update.'

'And little Percy?'

'I think you're going to be disappointed there, sir. It might be a girl.'

'You can't have too many Percys running about in this world, Frank. It's going to be a boy. I can feel it in my water.'

'That's just a bad pint you had last night.' Their breath was pluming in the cold air.

'I don't remember it being this cold when I worked down here before,' Purcell said, as they walked towards the front door of Montague Chase's house where a uniform was standing guard.

'So what have we got in here, do you think, Frank?'

'I'm keeping an open mind about this. Until I know for sure, everything is as it was.'

The cold air was being kept at bay by the front door, and they left it behind as they stepped into the entrance foyer.

'Jesus, this is going to hit the fan big time. This throws our investigation down a new road, if it's what we think it is.' Purcell stepped out of the way of a forensics officer as the white-suited woman stepped past them and went out the door.

'How many?' Miller asked.

'Four. The Polaroids were in a CD case. Jimmy was sitting down at the judge's desk in the den and being nosy. He said they would have to go through everything anyway, and he was just killing time while his ex was upstairs.'

'Are they just like the others?'

'Come and see for yourself.'

They walked through the living room to the den where Maggie Parks was working, along with the forensic photographer. Jimmy Gilmour was standing looking out the den window.

'This is a real mess,' Gilmour said to Miller.

The four Polaroid photos were laid out in a row on the desk.

'You can pick them up if you put your gloves on,' Maggie said. Miller and Purcell snapped a pair on each, and Miller gingerly lifted one of them.

The woman's face looked back at him. Her eyes were lifeless. He placed it back on the desk, and lifted each of the others. They were all the same woman, somebody they'd known for over two years. Cathy Graham. They were similar to the one they'd found in Will Beam's office, only these showed different details. Taken from different angles.

'Show me where you found them,' he said, to Gilmour.

Gilmour walked over and pointed to the drawer. 'They were in that CD case in there. Just sitting there. Not hidden away, but just sitting there. As if he would take them out now and again and have a gander at them. I was just interested in what sort of music he listened to.'

'We don't know they're his,' Purcell said, putting the last one back and nodding at Maggie to bag them.

'We'll run them for prints at the lab before giving them back to you boys,' Maggie said, as she put them in evidence bags.

'So what does this mean?' Gilmour said. 'That Connie's Uncle Monty was a killer? That somehow he attacked Will Beam in the church and scared the living daylights out of him?'

'We don't know what it means yet, Jimmy. Where's Connie?'

'Still upstairs with Andy Watt and the new girl.'

'DS Rivers.'

'Yeah, her.' Gilmour started to pace the room. 'You know, my little girl was here with us years ago, playing in that fucker's garden. Was he watching her? Planning to do something to her? I mean, he's a filthy fucking—'

'Enough, sergeant,' Purcell said. 'Go and wait in the kitchen. Make yourself a cup of coffee or something, but try to stay calm until we find out what's happening here.'

Gilmour left the room.

'You know he'll have to be taken off this investigation?' Purcell said.

Miller nodded. 'I know. We can't have somebody on the case who has clouded judgement.'

'I'll make a call later and see what we can have him working on. I want him on different duties right now, Frank.'

'The first thing we're going to have to do is take Connie in for questioning.'

'There's no way of getting around that, my friend. Take her away now while we have Maggie Parks go through every inch of this place. And I want somebody to go through that old bastard's life with a microscope. And I don't want any pish from the Lord Advocate on this or I'll have that old tool banged up in a heartbeat.'

'I'll go and tell Jimmy we're taking his ex in.'

'This might be my first day here, but I won't be taking any crap off the team. If he starts any nonsense, I'll have him removed from MIT permanently.'

'I'll take care of him.'

TWENTY-THREE

The photos had been copied, and were laid on the table in front of Connie Gilmour in interview room one.

'I swear to God, I've never seen those photos before.'

'You were Monty's niece. You mean to say you didn't go snooping?' Purcell said.

It was hot in the room, hotter than was necessary, but this room was designed to make people talk, not feel as if they were on their annual holidays to Tenerife.

'Never.' She was bent forward in her chair, hands clasped between her legs as if she needed to get close to the photos. To look into the eyes of the dead woman.

'Your uncle was a judge. How long ago did he retire?' Miller said, although he knew the answer. The object of the exercise was to get her talking.

'About eighteen months ago.' Connie sat back, and Miller could see her eyes were red from crying.

'How often did you go round to his house?' Purcell asked.

'Recently or before?'

'Before what?'

'My divorce.'

'Both.'

'We used to go round there on a Sunday when Jimmy was off, and then it was almost every Sunday when he joined CID. I used to take Rachael round on my own sometimes, but not as often as before.'

'Why?'

'It wasn't the same. Especially after he retired.'

'In what way?'

She looked at Miller before answering. 'Too many memories of the good times we had before my marriage went sideways. I still had to go and see him though. He's the only family I have, and he didn't have kids of his own.'

'Do you know how often Gabriel went to visit him?' Miller asked, having briefed Purcell about Connie's cousin on the way over to the police station.

'I don't know. He didn't talk much about him, except to moan.'

'How did Gabriel get on with his uncle?' Purcell asked.

'Monty treated him like the son he never had. He was talking on the phone with his brother one day, Gabriel's father, and they were arguing. Monty was furious with his brother. It wasn't much later that Gabriel's father died, and Monty felt bad.' Connie paused a moment and then carried on, 'Gabriel's a good lawyer, but he messes about with too many women, drinks too much. Monty always expressed an opinion on that, and Gabe didn't like it. He loved the old man, but he felt he was a bit too interfering at times.'

'Is he married?' Miller again.

'No. He's never been married. Monty thought Gabe might be gay. Nothing wrong with that mind, but you know what the older generation are like. But Gabe was always running loose with women. He didn't care if they were married or not, as long as they had fun with him.'

'Do you and Gabe have keys for the house?'

'Yes.'

'Would anybody else?'

'His housekeeper, Janet. She cleaned for him. He cooked for himself, but I think he just wanted the company. So he had her in a couple of times a week.'

'We'll need her details if you know them.'

Connie nodded. Then she looked at the two detectives. 'I think she also works as a bartender in the golf club just round from Monty's house in Ravelston. The Royal golf course. She's the one who found him lying on the floor last Wednesday.'

Miller looked briefly at Purcell before speaking again. 'Do you know if that's the same Janet who cleans Stanley Gates' house?'

'I don't know. Monty just mentioned her a few times without going into details.'

Purcell looked into Connie's eyes, his stare direct and unwavering. 'How do you think he got hold of those photos?'

Her lip trembled before she answered. 'I don't know.' She looked at Miller. 'You don't think he killed her, do you?'

'That's what we're trying to find out. There's no logical explanation as to why he would have them in his desk.'

She put her head back, and closed her eyes for a moment. Then looked at the two detectives. 'If he did, then I wish he wasn't dead. I wish you could have put him in front of his peers to be judged, just like he judged other men.'

'Did Monty know Father Will Beam?' He knew the priest was a friend of Monty's but he wanted to hear her reply.

She looked as if she wasn't sure how to answer at first. 'He used to go to church, but I'm not sure which one.'

'What about Gabriel? Did he go to Father Beam's church?' Purcell asked.

'I don't remember Gabe ever going to church. He was always too hungover on a Sunday morning to go anywhere.'

Purcell ended the interview, and had Connie write down what information she knew.

Back in the inquiry room, Purcell sat down at the computer beside Frank. 'What the hell is this all about, Frank? Montague

Chase employs a woman as a cleaner then two years after her murder, photos turns up in his desk. And he was a judge for God's sake.'

'We'll need to delve more into Chase's background.'

'I think we need to go and see Beam for ourselves. The more we speak to him, the more he might remember.'

TWENTY-FOUR

They would drive over to the church in the morning, but for now, Miller invited Purcell over for dinner.

'Look who else is here,' Jack said. He introduced Tony Matheson to Purcell. 'Tony's dad was one of us, way back when. Unfortunately, he passed away when he was on the job.'

'I'm sorry to hear that,' Purcell said, shaking the younger man's hand.

'It was a long time ago, Percy.'

'Still, it must have been hard losing your dad. He was a good copper.'

'I'll drink to that,' Jack said, bringing through another couple of bottles of beer. They clinked bottles.

The doorbell rang, and Jack answered it. Samantha came in, bringing a bottle of wine.

'This is very nice,' she said, handing the bottle to Kim. 'And look at little Emma. You've got your own little table.'

'Yes, Samantha, but Mummy says I can't have any wine.'

Samantha laughed. 'When you're older, sweetie.'

'Samantha, this is Tony Matheson who I told you about,' Jack said.

They shook hands. 'I'm a big fan,' Matheson said. 'I wish I'd remembered to bring my copy of your latest book.'

'You'll be round here again, Tony lad,' Jack said.

'I appreciate being invited round for dinner.'

'Talking of which,' Jack said, heading off into the kitchen. He had done the cooking, with Kim guiding him.

'So, what do you do for a living?' Purcell asked. He was feeling more relaxed now he had taken his jacket off and had a bottle of beer in his hand.

'I work as a lab technician down at the Western General. Nothing as exciting as you guys. But I am a special constable.'

'I wouldn't call it exciting, Tony,' Miller said.

'It's a lot more exciting than my job. Take that girl who was found murdered. Now, I'm not saying it's not a tragedy that somebody was murdered, but don't you get the buzz inside? I remember my dad saying he always got a buzz when he was working on a case. Isn't that right, Jack?' he said, as Jack came back into the living room.

'What's that?'

'I'm saying that my dad, along with everybody else in CID, got a buzz when you were working on a case.'

'We did. Although it was hard when somebody innocent lost their life.'

'That was the hard part, I imagine, but I'm talking about when you cracked a case. When you caught the bad guy.'

'It's like that for all of us, even now,' Purcell said. 'It'll be a real celebration when we get this joker who's killing people.'

'He has to be stopped, that's for sure.'

'Oh, we'll get him. He thinks he's being clever but he's just another halfwit whose aspirations are greater than his abilities.'

Matheson smiled. 'I do believe my dad said that once. He always thought that even a clever killer was never as clever as the men who were chasing him.' He took a swig from his bottle. 'I miss my old man.'

'We all do, Tony,' Jack said.

'Don't you fancy becoming a regular?' Purcell asked.

'I thought about it, but I have an easy job, to be honest. And I don't think I'd be able to be as good as my dad was. I enjoy being a special though. I've made some good friends. That's fine for me.'

'That's good that you're a special.'

Matheson took Jack aside. 'As I said on the phone earlier, I'm really sorry about bailing out of here yesterday.'

'Don't worry about it.'

'I just got upset, and I didn't want you to see me with my eyes all red. When I used your bathroom, it all came flooding back.'

Jack put a hand on his shoulder. 'Forget it, son. And there's nothing to apologise for.'

Matheson smiled, and they clinked bottles.

'Let me help with dinner,' Samantha said to Kim, and they went into the kitchen.

'You're getting more domesticated every time I see you, Jack,' Purcell said.

'I always wanted to cook, but I worked long hours, like you, so my wife cooked. Now I'm retired, I want to do more.'

'He wants to use the microwave more,' Miller said.

'Says the man who had to go to night school to learn how to use a can opener.'

'Touché.'

They sat down at the table in the kitchen, and Jack dished up the pasta dish he'd cooked.

'Tony there would make a good copper,' Jack said.

'I would have tried for detective grade,' Matheson said, knocking back his beer. Jack fetched him another.

'So, what do you make of this murder?' Purcell asked. 'The one with the disappearing body?'

Matheson's eyes seemed to light up, and he smiled at the detective. 'First of all, I disagree that your killer is a halfwit, Superintendent. In fact, I think he's very cold and calculating.'

'What makes you say that?' He took a mouthful of the pasta dish, and was impressed by Jack's cooking.

'Just by the very fact that he was confident enough to take his victim away, but leave a mess at the crime scene. He also risked getting caught by taking the victim with him.'

'We suspect it was in the early hours of the morning, therefore minimising his risk. It was cold, dark, and miserable. Not many people about. I wouldn't say that took a lot of thought. It sounds to me that he's very cocky.'

'I think the FBI would call him *organised*. He struck in the early hours, minimising his own risk. If the whole point was to take the victim away, I'd say he thought it through very carefully. I'd be looking for somebody who's very intelligent, who has a past history of mental illness.'

'Somebody who was beaten by his mother, maybe.'

'Or who had a controlling wife. Or still does have a controlling wife.'

'See? I told you Tony should have joined the force,' Jack said. 'Anybody for another beer? Ladies? A soft drink?'

They all agreed that they could do with another drink, and Jack fetched them with Miller's help.

'You should bring your girlfriend along next time, Tony,' Kim said. 'I'd like to meet her.'

'I'll certainly put that to her, though she's very shy in mixed company.'

'Tell her we don't bite,' Jack said, as they finished their meal. 'Anybody for dessert?'

'Jack, that was magic,' Purcell said, 'but I fear if I eat much more, the button keeping my trousers up will take somebody's eye out.'

'Room for more beer?'

'One for the road. I have work in the morning, and there's a little lady waiting to get to bed.'

'You can have more beer, Uncle Percy,' Emma said, from her little table.

'That's very kind. If the little lady says it's okay, then I will indeed. But can you make it a short, Jack? You know what they say; you only rent the beer for a little while.'

'What does that mean, Uncle Percy?'

'Frank will tell you, sweetheart. And on that note.' He stood up. 'If you'll excuse me.'

Matheson insisted on helping Jack clear the table.

Afterwards, they moved to the living room, leaving Jack and Matheson alone in the kitchen. Matheson brought out a photo album. A slim one that held some 6 x 4s. 'I didn't think you would mind that I brought these round. I found them in a sock drawer after I spoke to you. They bring back great memories.'

'Not at all, son,' Jack said. 'Let's have a look.'

They sat side by side at the table.

Kim looked over Tony's shoulder. 'Your father was a very handsome man, Tony.'

'Thanks.' He beamed a smile at her. 'You know, I never once remember my old man raising his voice to me. When he wasn't spouting off about what he would do to these miscreants, he would always be up for a laugh.'

'I remember his sense of humour when he'd had a few in the pub. What a laugh we had.'

Matheson flipped through the little album. 'As you can see, he liked a few beers at home, too.' Archie Matheson was sitting back in a chair with his shoes off, sticking his feet out in front of the gas fire, holding up a can of lager in salute to the photo taker, a big smile on his face.

The last photo was of an awkward teenager, almost as tall as his father. Archie was standing, smiling, holding a cigarette in one hand.

'That was on a holiday to Blackpool the summer before he died. He always swore he was going to give up smoking, but he never did.'

'I didn't see any photos of your sister in there,' Jack said.

'I have plenty at home. This album was just me and my dad.'

Kim came in and he looked round at her. 'Thanks for indulging me. I didn't mean to bring the tone down.'

Kim smiled, and put a hand on his shoulder. 'Don't be silly. It's nice to share somebody's memories.'

'It was good to see photos of Archie again,' Jack said.

Kim moved away from the table. 'I'm taking Samantha and Kate Murphy over to see how Hazel is, so I'd better get ready' Kim said. 'Good meeting you, Tony.'

'You too.'

After a few minutes, Kim left with Samantha and Emma.

'I don't remember Purcell, Jack' Matheson asked.

'He worked with our Serious Crimes when your dad was there. You must have heard your dad talking about him.'

Matheson helped load the dishwasher. 'I can't say that I remember. Maybe he just didn't stick out. Like Andy Watt, for instance. Now, there's a character.'

'Andy's never changed.'

When the machine was loaded, and Purcell was sitting with his Glenmorangie, Matheson shrugged his jacket on. 'Thanks for dinner.'

'Off so soon?' Purcell said. He stood up.

'I'm afraid so. I'm meeting the other half, and I don't want to be late. She's shopping for new shoes or something, and I said I'd meet her for a drink in town.'

'Good meeting you,' Purcell said, shaking hands with the younger man. He wasn't the kind to try to persuade somebody to change their mind. Unless that person was in an interrogation room with him.

'You too. Maybe I'll see you again .'

'I look forward to it.'

Matheson left, leaving Purcell with Miller and Jack.

'He's turned out just fine,' Jack said. *Considering his whole family died.* Jack didn't want to bring up the subject in front of Purcell.

Jack went through to the kitchen, and Purcell looked at Miller. 'Sorry to say this, but I don't know Tony at all. Now, Archie, *him* I do remember.' He didn't voice his opinion, but he remembered the older detective as a bumbling idiot who couldn't catch a cold.

TWENTY-FIVE

Jimmy Gilmour heard his girlfriend talking to somebody on the phone, and guessed it wasn't one of her female friends.

'Can't you just have the decency to wait until I'm out of the house before calling your boyfriend?' he said to her when she came back into the living room.

'Why? He's not bothered.'

'I should have known you were a slut when you were shagging me while I was still married.'

'I didn't hear you complain then.' She looked at him, expecting a comeback, but there was none.

'Good luck in your new life. You're going to need it. Not every married man will leave his wife for you. You *did* say you were shagging a married man before me, didn't you? Are you into collecting them?'

She smiled at him, but it was more of a smile reserved for a grandpa with dementia. *Poor bastard.* 'I'm tired of fighting, Jimmy. That's why I'll be moving out as soon as I find a place.'

'Good. Don't let the door bang your arse on the way out.'

She shook her head, and walked away. Just a few weeks ago, she would have been pointing her finger at him, the nail filed almost into the point of a shiv. Now, she looked at him as if he was some sad old sod.

He expected her to slam the front door, but once again, to surprise him, she closed it quietly.

He took out his phone and called Connie's number, but it went straight to voicemail. He sent a text to Kate Murphy, and got a reply almost right away. It made him forget all about Lauren.

After a couple of hours of flipping through the channels on his TV, he got another text from Kate.

He put his jacket on, and braved the cold of Holyrood Road. Down on the right was the old *Caledonian* office building, the space filled by a games company. There was a lot of money in video games these days, and he wished he'd been a lot more intelligent so he could sit in front of a computer, bash out some code, and create a million-pound game.

He was angry at the world just now. What the fuck was old Monty up to? And him being a judge, to boot. And because of him, he, Gilmour, had been taken off the case.

Purcell had taken him aside, and told him he was being transferred. He had a choice; work down in Leith CID, or help Lloyd Masters up at the firearms training centre. Being ex-army, he had chosen firearms.

He was mostly angry with Lauren. He had thrown all his eggs in one basket with her, and now look what had happened. He walked up High Street towards Logie Baird's. Then he saw the silver lining walking across the road to meet him.

'Hi, Kate,' he said, smiling at her. The temperature had plummeted, and now his breath was visible in the cold night air.

'Hi, Jimmy. Where are you off to?' She looked around, keeping up the pretence, and Gilmour had to admit to himself that it gave him a thrill.

'My second home these days. Care to join me?'

She smiled at him, looking good with her hat pulled down over her hair, and her cheeks a rosy red. 'I'd like that.'

'Allow me,' he said, opening the door for her.

The heat was welcoming as they took their woollen hats off and undid their jackets. Gilmour got the drinks in, and they found a table far enough away from the TV. The crowd was thin.

'This is a nice surprise,' Kate said, clinking her glass with his.

'It certainly is.' He smiled at her again, feeling comfortable in her company. 'So, what has the good doctor been up to tonight?'

'Kim, Samantha and I went over to see Hazel and Bruce.'

'How's Bruce doing?'

'He was lucky; his knee only partially dislocated. It slid out and slipped back in again.'

'He's had a rough time of it. I hope to God he keeps it together and returns to us when he gets back on his feet. No pun intended.'

'I heard you've been taken off the case with Monty Chase.'

'I'm too personally involved, Purcell said.'

'You are, Jimmy. Percy's right. If they want to catch whoever's doing this, they have to go by the book.'

'I know. It'll be okay working with Masters though. Maybe a break from MIT will do me good.'

'As long as it keeps that smile of yours on your face, I'm all for it.'

He loved her London accent, and felt himself relaxing more as he listened to her. He didn't know where Lauren had gone, and he didn't care.

After they'd been sitting for a while, Kate looked at her watch. 'I'd better get down the road. Believe it or not, I don't drink every night. This was nice though. We should do it again some time.' There was a glint in her eyes.

'I'd like that.'

Kate stood up, and Gilmour helped her on with her jacket before pulling on his own.

'You don't have to go because of me,' she said.

'It's really no fun drinking on your own. I'll walk you down the road.'

'Aw shucks. Chivalry really isn't dead.' She laughed as they made their way out and headed down the road. Kate slipped her arm through Gilmour's. *For balance* she said. Gilmour didn't fight her off.

'How do you like working up here, compared to living down in London?' Gilmour asked, as they walked down St Mary's Street.

Kate was silent for a moment. Nobody except Frank Miller and Kim knew she was in witness protection, and of course, the man who'd helped her, Neil McGovern.

'I like Edinburgh, Jimmy. It's so different from London.'

'I'm glad you came up here. I'm not shy around women, as you may know, but I feel even more comfortable around you. I know I'm only a copper, and not in your league though.'

She looked at him, puzzled for a moment, as they turned into Holyrood Road. 'What do you mean?'

'You could be married to a brain surgeon. Somebody with his own business. Out dining in fancy restaurants, or going to the opera. Yet here you are, having a beer with some flat foot.'

'I'll let you in on a secret; I don't like the opera. And it's the man I enjoy being with, not what he represents.' She smiled at him. 'So shut your cake hole, Gilmour, and just enjoy the moment.'

He laughed. 'Yes, ma'am.'

'What would Lauren do if she saw another woman on your arm right now?'

'Probably throw a fit. She's out somewhere tonight, and she's moving out as soon as she can. Then we can go public. If you still want to.'

'Of course I do.'

He smiled, and looked at her. 'I'm glad I met you. Lauren's bad news. Never been married. Knows every man and his dog. She's had more pricks than a second-hand dartboard. Oh God, sorry. I forgot I was with a real lady for a minute.'

'I've heard worse.' She pulled herself in closer to Gilmour.

When they were halfway down the road, she stopped. 'You don't have to see me all the way down the road.'

'Are you kidding? I'll see you to your building's entrance.'

When they got there, Gilmour watched as she got her key out. 'Goodnight, Kate.'

'Do you want a nightcap? I don't have any beer in, but I have a bottle of Bacardi. And Coke.'

'Great. I'd love that.' Part of Gilmour wished Lauren could see him going into Kate's building with her.

Upstairs, he settled onto the couch while Kate poured the drinks. She sat beside him.

'You said you've never been married,' he said.

'Did I?'

'The other night. Or did I get that wrong?'

'No. You're right. I've never been married. I'm thirty-seven, hardly a spring chicken anymore. I think the time for settling down passed me by.'

'You obviously have no problem attracting men.'

'It's attracting the *right* man that's the problem.'

'My trouble was I married too young. I was twenty, and in the army. Then we had Rachael, and I left to join the force.'

They had a few more drinks before Kate popped a CD in. 'Dance with me, Jimmy.'

It was slow, romantic music. For the first time in a very long time, Kate felt good. She leaned in closer to Gilmour, and kissed him. Her breathing became faster when he didn't pull away.

Knowing there was everything wrong about this, she danced with him some more before taking him through to her bedroom.

TWENTY-SIX

Miller and Purcell took a cab along to the Royal golf club in Ravelston. It was a stone's throw from Ashley Gates' house and it was this establishment's greens that backed onto Monty Chase's garden.

It was also where Janet was working.

'I wonder what the fees at this place are?' Purcell said, as they walked into reception. A girl was in the coat check-in as Miller and Purcell handed theirs over. Normally, Miller wouldn't have bothered, but it was obvious from the heat that the club had no trouble paying their utility bills.

'It probably costs more than I earn in a month,' Miller said. 'You'd be okay though.'

'A superintendent's salary doesn't stretch as far as you'd think. Besides, golf is just a waste of a good walk. Hitting a wee ball into a hole in the ground with a stick. I could think of better ways to spend a Saturday afternoon.'

'Breaking it down into its basic form, Percy. That's like saying Formula One is men sitting in tin boxes on wheels driving round in circles.'

'Now you're getting it.'

They walked into the main bar, which had a restaurant off it. Miller recognised Janet from the day before. She looked at him, recognition sparking in her eyes as he ordered two pints.

'Detective Miller. What are you doing here?' She smiled, but kept her voice low, as if they were a bunch of union conspirators.

'We wanted a word, Janet. This is Detective Superintendent Percy Purcell.'

'Hi.' She looked around at her colleague, a young man who wasn't exactly rushed off his feet. Indicated she was going to talk to the two men in suits.

They sat at a corner table, Miller with a view of the door.

'We want to ask you a few questions, Janet,' he said.

'About Ashley?'

'About why you didn't tell us that you were also Ashley's house-keeper, and Montague Chase's housekeeper.'

She looked puzzled for a moment. 'Didn't Mr and Mrs Gates tell you I worked for Ashley? I suppose not. And why is it a problem that I was Mr Chase's housekeeper?'

'It's not a problem,' Miller said.

'First of all, I haven't been interviewed, and secondly, Mr Chase isn't connected to the Gates except for being in the same field.'

Purcell smiled at her. 'We were just wondering if you could help us with an enquiry. We just want to run some things past you.'

'Okay. I don't mind helping the police, but I've done nothing wrong.' She fidgeted with her hands in her lap.

'Don't worry, we don't work for the Inland Revenue,' Miller said. 'Or Customs, or whatever it's called these days.'

'I hope you're not suggesting—'

'We're not suggesting anything, Janet,' Purcell said. 'All we want is to have a chat. In a relaxed atmosphere. Or we can go to High Street station and talk there, if you prefer.'

She looked at him. 'No, here's fine.'

'We want to know if you know of any regular visitors to Mr Chase's house. Anybody he was friends with.'

'If he had people calling round, he didn't tell me. Don't get me wrong, we would have lunch on the day I was there, which was a Wednesday, and we would have good conversations, but mostly about books and documentaries. It was last Wednesday that I found him.'

'What about Gabriel, his nephew? Did he ever call round when you were there?'

'Not that I can remember. He's a moron anyway. He thinks his shit doesn't stink because he's a lawyer, but he'll never reach the level Monty was at.'

'Did Ashley know Mr Chase?' Miller asked.

'Yes. I believe he worked in her office before he became a judge. I think she was a junior lackey when he was there.'

'But she didn't go to his house, as far as you know?'

'Not that he told me.'

Miller looked over Janet's shoulder as two men came in. He recognised one of them.

'Ashley Gates' ex-husband just walked in,' he said to Purcell. Janet and Percy both turned to look.

'Arthur King,' Janet said, as she turned back to Miller. 'Prick. Him and that guffy he's with. Mitchell Robb. I made the mistake of calling him *Doctor* one day, and he said that he was a consultant and to call him *Mr* Robb. So I call him Mitch all the time now, just to piss him off. They think a woman's knickers will fall down to her ankles if they so much as look at one.'

Purcell looked back at Miller. 'I'm satisfied, if you are, Detective Miller.'

Miller nodded. 'Thanks for talking to us, Janet.'

'There is one thing. It's probably nothing.'

'We're listening.'

'I want you to know, I don't go snooping in their houses, but when somebody's arguing and shouting at the top of their lungs, well, I don't have cloth ears.'

'You're talking to us in confidence,' Purcell reminded her.

'Stanley Gates was arguing with his daughter one day, in here. She drinks a lot, and she was half pissed and they started at it. She accused her father of having an affair. He had been talking to that doctor's girlfriend, Jess.'

'The guy with King?' Purcell said.

'Yes.'

'So, Ashley thought her father was having it off with the doctor's girlfriend. What made her wonder that?'

'They had been sitting drinking, having a laugh.'

'It's hard to imagine Stanley Gates with a sense of humour,' Miller said, remembering the man's attitude when he'd found out his daughter was dead.

'When he's got a few down his throat, he can be quite witty. Anyway, it was one evening, Stanley was in here with a few of his snobby mates, and then Jess came over and started talking to him. Stanley wasn't much of a golfer, but he liked to socialise. His daughter was in too, with her husband. Mitchell wasn't in, but for some reason, Ashley got mad at her father. King just laughed, but she was furious. Stanley told her to shut up. He carried on chatting with Jess.'

'Do you think Stanley Gates was actually having an affair with Robb's girlfriend?'

'Oh no. I think he was having an affair with somebody else. He called her one night when he was sitting at the bar, and Jess was sitting with Robb.'

'And it wasn't his wife he was calling?'

'Ha. Are you kidding? He thought I couldn't hear him, but the things he said he wanted to do to her? I don't think he was talking to his wife, or they have the best marriage in history.'

'Thanks for that, Janet,' Miller said. 'If you remember anything else, please give me a call.'

'I will. I hope you get the bastard who did that to Ashley. But wait, I *do* have a question.'

'Fire away.'

'Why were you asking about Monty? Do you think somebody murdered him?'

'Oh no, nothing like that. We're just making enquiries.' The stock answer.

Miller walked over to the bar with Purcell. King saw him coming, and smiled. 'Detective Miller. Care for a drink?'

'No thanks. This is Superintendent Purcell.'

'This is a good friend of mine, Mr Mitchell Robb.'

'Mr Robb,' Miller said.

'Are you new members?' Robb asked.

'No, they're not,' King said. Then he looked at Purcell. 'I'm on the new member committee, and I didn't see your names.'

'Well, it's lucky we're not interested then,' Purcell said. 'Although I'm sure a developer would be interested. Not in playing golf, though. Nice bit of parkland you've got in the back.'

'Good seeing you again, Mr King,' Miller said, and walked away to catch up with Purcell, who had started heading towards the cloakroom. 'That's Ashley Gates' ex-husband. King, I mean.'

'The smell of bullshit was getting to me,' he said to Miller, as they were checking their coats out. He took his phone out and called control. Asked for a patrol car to pick them up as they were out on police business and didn't have a pool car. 'Remember this, Frank? The Lothian and Borders taxi service they used to call it.'

Miller laughed. 'I do. And you weren't shy in using and abusing it.'

'That's fighting talk where I come from, my fine friend.' He looked at his watch. 'And we're still on the clock until we get dropped off.'

'So, what did you think of King?' Miller asked, as they stood in the cold of the car park, away from prying ears.

'A high-flying wank box who thinks he's God's gift. Him and his bum chum, Robb. Both of them look like the sort who would be all over

Suzy and Kim if they were in there on their own. All aftershave and flavoured condoms. I've met their kind hundreds of times.' He blew out his breath into the dark air. The side of the club housed the Pro's shop, and the place was well lit. 'Why? What did you think of them?'

'I'm with you, their motto's probably *find 'em, fuck 'em, forget 'em*. The sort who take advantage of women.' He looked at Purcell. 'Kim would kick their heads in, first time out.'

'Did you see King's demeanour? His ex-wife isn't even cold in her grave, and he's in there having a bevy with his mate as if it's business as usual.'

'He's cocky alright. Ashley's father says he calls himself *King Arthur*. Like when people say their surname first then their first name.'

'Pompous fuck. Are you sure his alibi holds up?'

'It does.'

'Pity.' He took his hands out of his pockets as the patrol car rolled in. 'My breath doesn't smell of beer, does it?'

Miller took out a packet of Polo mints, and spread the foil wrapper wide. 'Take two.'

Purcell popped two, and let Miller lean down when the driver rolled his window down. 'We got dropped off by another member of our team, and we need a lift back into town,' he said.

'No problem, sir.'

Purcell got in the back with Miller. 'Have you set a date for your wedding?' Miller asked.

'June third. You're already on the invitation list, if that's what you're worried about.'

'I'd gatecrash it if I wasn't.'

'How about you and Kim?'

'I'm still thinking about it. I think she wants to get married because it would be a more stable life for Emma.'

'You can't blame her, mate. She loves you.'

'Are you and Suzy going to have a big affair?'

'She wants the big, white wedding because it's her first time. Me? A quickie down at the registry and a few pints afterwards.'

'So romance isn't dead after all?'

The patrol car left the golf club and drove down to Corstorphine Road.

TWENTY-SEVEN

Patricia Wilkinson left the pub feeling like going home and sinking into a bath, but at nearly two in the morning, it maybe wasn't such a good idea. The night behind the bar had dragged, and she couldn't stop thinking about poor Ashley. She hoped the police could find enough on Dan Herdan to put him away for a long time.

The thought of Herdan made her think about getting a taxi. She should have phoned for one, but sometimes they took ages in coming, and at least the pub was situated where taxis went by on a regular basis.

She stepped outside, looking for one.

Then a figure stepped out from the shadows. Patricia gasped, holding her breath for a second. Then she saw who it was, and she smiled, putting a hand to her chest.

'You scared me,' she said, stepping forward to kiss her boyfriend.

'I wanted to surprise you.'

'Mission accomplished.'

He laughed, and kissed her on the lips. 'I thought about coming in, but I figured you might be sneaking around behind my back, and I wanted to catch you with your other boyfriend.'

The smile fell from her face for a moment. 'Tell me you're kidding.'

'I'm kidding, I'm kidding.' He beamed his smile at her, the one she fell in love with. 'Sorry, it's just my sense of humour.'

She hit him playfully on the arm. 'That's not funny. I don't want you kidding around like that anymore.'

He laughed. 'I'm sorry, my darling. I won't joke like that again.'

She smiled, and put her arm through his as they walked along, pulling him in closer. 'What excuse did you use to be out this late?'

'I'm my own boss now. I don't have to answer to anybody anymore.'

'I like the sound of that.'

She saw a taxi put its orange *For Hire* light on, farther up George IV Bridge, as if the driver had been reading her mind. She put her hand out, and the driver did a U-turn so he was on their side of the street.

'The Shore, please,' she said, as her boyfriend settled in beside her.

The cab took off, and headed down High Street, which was almost deserted at this time of night.

'How was the bar tonight?' the boyfriend said, making small talk in case the taxi driver wasn't really deaf.

'It was busy, surprisingly enough. A ton of students were in, but they were mostly well-behaved.'

They chatted until the taxi pulled in to Patricia's block of flats on The Shore itself. She liked living down here. The whole place had changed over the years, transforming like a chameleon. New flats were springing up all over the place; new restaurants were making the area a go-to place to dine. She loved the whole atmosphere.

They paid the cabbie, and went up to the top floor.

'Settle down and I'll get us a drink,' she said, watching the tall figure take off his scarf and sit down on the couch. She knew she was falling in love with him, and that it would devastate her if he broke up with her. Ashley would have told her to go easy if she'd known about him, but Patricia didn't want to introduce her boyfriend to any of her friends until she knew for sure their relationship was going to last.

'Beer okay?' she asked, from the small kitchen next to the living room.

'Beer is always okay.'

She brought them through, and they drank. Then Patricia put her bottle down on the table, and snuggled into him. 'You can take your jacket off, you know. Or are you not planning on staying?'

He laughed. Of course I am. I told you, life for us is going to be very different from now on.'

'Then why don't we take these beers through to the bedroom, and you can show me how much you love me?'

He stood up, still holding his bottle, and she grabbed hers. They went through to the bedroom, and after the bottles were put down, she roughly grabbed his jacket and slung it onto the floor.

She gasped as he stripped her and threw her onto the bed. Their lovemaking was going to be long, rough, sensual, and exciting.

It was going to be a night that Patricia Wilkinson was going to remember for the rest of her life.

Which was only going to last for the next two and a half hours.

His head hurt like a bitch. When he finally surfaced into a foggy recollection of what happened, the little nuclear bomb went off in his head. Years before, his doctor had diagnosed him with cluster headaches. On questioning the aged GP, the doctor had looked at him as if going through his mental medical encyclopaedia only to find the page he was looking for had been torn out.

'Old age,' the man had said. He had left the office with a *Don't talk pish* look on his face. He didn't even think of himself as middle-aged now, far less back then.

This was more than a cluster headache. This was the result of...

what? His eyelids flickered as tiny pieces of the cerebral movie reeled behind his eyes.

There had been words spoken to him. *'Just here's fine, mate. And if I make thirty, can you give me a receipt?'*

Jesus. Him. His passenger. The unremarkable man with the big moustache and unkempt hair. The big tipper. In his haste to get his receipt book, he'd taken his eye off the ball. The passenger had got out. By taking his foot off the brake, he had released the locks that kept the would-be runners in the back until they coughed up. But a big tip with a request for a receipt was always one to trust.

Not now it wasn't.

He had been outside of Edinburgh, to the west. His mind was grasping for details again. Somewhere quiet. Not some mental neighbourhood where a Stanley knife was just as likely to be produced than a tip, but a little village. No more than a row of houses. A scrapyard was just outside the perimeter of this village. Dark after hours, the trucks and crushers silent, the guard dogs hungry.

A red telephone box. One of the few left. Maybe a village riot had been threatened if the phone box was taken away, BT relenting and deciding to wear the cost of maintaining it. And by maintenance, they meant emptying the coin box. The smell of stale pish could linger for all they cared.

'I need to make a call,' the man had said. 'I'm calling my girlfriend, and I don't want her husband to get my mobile number. Know what I mean?' He had laughed.

'Oh, yes, I know exactly what you mean.'

The sound of his taxi's diesel seemed loud in the little village green. There was a small pub, long shut for the night. He couldn't think of the name. It wasn't a watering hole he'd ever been in or picked up from.

He had started writing the receipt when the fist shot through the open window. He realised now it had been a glove that was filled with shot. The punch had been to his temple. His eyes had spun in his head like reels in a slot machine, and then another bang. This one didn't seem so hard. Maybe the first one had made his brain go into *batten down the hatches, lads, it's gonna be a big one!* mode. Just to protect him. Whatever it was, the second punch had put his lights out.

Now he was here. Where was *here*? He didn't know. He was on his back, staring up at a dark, dirty ceiling way above his head. He tried sitting up, but that just made the pain worse. Something was holding him back anyway. He was tied to whatever it was he was lying on. He tried moving his hands, but he couldn't lift them. Same with his feet.

There was a dense heat in here. And noise. Some sort of machinery.

'Ah. There you are,' the man said, as he came into view. His face was dirty like some sort of homemade camouflage had been spread over it.

'Who are you?'

The man reached into a pocket and brought out a bushy moustache. Held it against his face. 'If I make it thirty, can you give me a receipt?' Then he laughed. 'Greedy bastard. You fell for it though. Thirty quid, including the tip! And you were fine about taking it.'

'Look, I don't want your money. I won't say a thing.' He was sweating now, his brow moist. The rest of his body felt slick, a thin sheen covering him.

'Is that what you think this is about? Money?'

He watched as the man walked round the end of the stretcher. He lifted his head up a bit, but the straps running over his chest let him move only so far. Then the man was coming up to his face again. He had reached into his pocket and brought out a knife.

'Do you recognise me now?' The moustache had been put away.

'No. Should I?'

The man laughed. 'He doesn't recognise me. You do disappoint me.'

'Why don't you introduce yourself. You can start by untying me, and we can shake hands.' *Or I can kick you square in the nuts.*

'No thanks. I appreciate the offer anyway. However, it doesn't matter if you recognise me or not. The outcome is still going to be the same. You're still going to die.'

'Now, look, there's no need for this. Whoever you are, we can sort this out.' He was struggling against the straps that held him in place. He knew there was going to be no *sorting this out*.

He started shouting and yelling as the man walked out of view. Then suddenly, he heard a loud *whump* noise.

'No, no, please, you can't do this. Please! I'll give you anything you want.'

'That's good, because I want you dead.' He pushed the trolley.

'Why can't we talk?'

'We did talk. A long time ago. Don't you remember?'

'Let's talk again. We can sit down like two reasonable men and have a chat. Maybe over a beer.'

'What makes you think I'd want a pint with you?'

'Coffee then. Or tea. I'll pay.' He could feel the stretcher moving, and he kept trying to sit up, straining against the leather straps.

'These straps were made to restrain somebody weighing a lot more than you. They'll keep you well tied to the basket stretcher. These plastic devices are great for slipping onto a gurney. And because they're plastic, they melt easily.'

The gurney stopped, and then he knew where he was.

'Oh God, no. Please.'

'Too late for begging.'

'Why can't we talk about this?'

'You know why.' The man leaned in closer. 'And you know why you're here.'

The man disappeared from sight for a few seconds. He heard a metallic clang, and then the heat hit him in a wave.

The man came back round, smiling. He was wearing thick gloves. 'Can't be too careful. You could get burnt.'

Then he recognised the man. In the few seconds before he died, he actually recognised him, and he knew there was no negotiating with him.

The sound of something being loosened, like the clips on the side of a cat carrier. And then he felt the body basket being moved forward. His head felt the heat first.

To an outsider, the screams would have sounded like an animal caught in a trap. The heat wasn't at its fullest, not reaching two thousand degrees until the door was fully closed. With the door open, the gas flames were small and hungry.

He continued to scream as the man pushed the stretcher into the confined space. He thought he could burst the straps, such was the ferocity of his movements, but all he did was stretch the tough leather.

His head was up, looking back at the face.

Then the door clanged shut.

The flames shot down from the top and up from below.

His screams didn't last long.

TWENTY-EIGHT

The morning sun was weak, and there was a ground frost.

Will Beam was in his study with a sheaf of papers in one hand, a pencil in the other. He could hear the two men grunting down in the basement of the rectory, and one of them cursed loudly.

'Ah, ya bastard. Watch my fucking fingers, Hamish!' Then a few seconds later. 'Sorry, Father.'

'God forgives you, my son. But he also wants you to get a move on.'

More grunting and groaning, and then the two men appeared, rubbing the dust off their hands.

'You both did a splendid job this morning. Now, clean up and I'll get the bacon on.'

Beam was about to go into the kitchen to get the frying pan going when the doorbell rang.

'You expecting anybody else, Father?' Hamish said. He was holding a hammer and looked like he was in the mood for smacking something other than nails with it, should Cathy Graham's killer come calling.

'No, I'm not.' He looked at both men. 'Can you stay here a moment, gentlemen?'

'Aye, we'll do that,' the other one said. 'If it's some nosey cu... person, we can tell them to go away.'

'There's no need to resort to that. I can deal with them. If it's just a parishioner I would just like you to stay and finish the job downstairs.'

The men exchanged a glance, both of them wondering what parishioner would come to the rectory when the church had a front door.

Beam walked to the door and opened it, letting the chilly morning air in. 'Detective Miller! What a surprise! What can I do for you?'

'This is Superintendent Purcell. We'd like to talk to you, Father.'

Beam turned to look into the hallway. Both the men had gone back downstairs. 'Come in. Please excuse the noise. I have two maintenance men in. They're just reinforcing the windows down in the basement, and making sure they have decent locks on them. Burglars, you know.'

'Technically known as *Housebreakers* in Scotland,' Purcell said.

'We won't keep you long, Father,' Miller said.

'Yes, yes, of course. Please forgive my manners. And I'm hoping you won't say no to coffee,' he said, as the two detectives walked past him into the hallway.

'If you're offering,' Miller said, following the priest into the kitchen.

'I'll get the kettle on right away.'

'Bit cold to be keeping the back door open, isn't it?' Purcell said.

'It's the cat.'

'He good at opening doors then?'

Beam laughed. 'I meant I'd opened it to let him in earlier, and it mustn't have shut properly. Wee rascal. The cat, not you.'

Purcell stepped forward, and looked out into the large back garden. 'Nice place you have here. I love the size of your garden.' The church itself had an L-shaped footprint, and there was a fence that bordered Drummond Community High School next door.

'Thank you. I wish I could say it was all my own work, but a contractor does it all.'

Miller was watching the priest. Then Beam turned to him. 'Please go through to the living room, and I'll bring the coffee through.'

Miller and Purcell sat where Andy Watt and Jimmy Gilmour had done only a couple of days before. This time, there were no biscuits brought through. Just the coffee.

'So, your detectives wouldn't give me any details about the murder with the Polaroid the other day, so now I'm guessing that the victim they've been talking about on the news, Ashley Gates, is the poor girl who was murdered and taken away. Am I right?' Beam looked at Miller, and took a drink of coffee.

'Father, you know we're not at liberty to talk about the case,' Miller said, sipping the coffee, which was surprisingly good.

'You want to see if I can remember anything else from that night, something that might be useful to you. A speech impediment maybe, or a glass eye. Maybe one hand bigger than the other, maybe if I just close my eye! And to think he used my letter opener to threaten me.'

'Father,' Purcell said in a calm voice. 'We know you went through a lot back then, and you had a knife against your face. Nobody thinks it was easy for you, but in our experience, sometimes a person will remember a little detail, months, sometimes years after an event, something that seems small, but can be quite significant. We're not here to scare you or to put pressure on you.'

Beam's rapid breathing began to slow. 'I'm sorry. I do get scared, but I put my faith in God, and he sees me through each day. If it wasn't for him looking after me that night, I would surely be dead.'

'We understand that, Father,' Miller said. 'However, there was a brutal murder, and we don't think he's going to stop. So if there's anything else you can remember from that night, it would help us a great deal.'

'You found photographs. Who had them? Don't tell me it was Monty Chase?'

Purcell didn't want to look at Miller, but he couldn't help it. It was as if the priest was psychic.

'By your silence, I'll take that as a yes. I heard about his death on the radio. Poor soul.'

'We wanted to ask you how well you knew Montague Chase.'

'He was a parishioner of mine. He used to stay along the road in the New Town and came here before I was given this church. He still came here even after he moved to Ravelston. We were friends too. I'd visit him at home, and we'd have a drink or two. I was there the night Cathy was murdered, if you remember? Jack, your father, interviewed him, I believe.'

'I read your file, Father Beam,' Purcell said. 'And we made a few calls before we came here. It seems that not only was the old judge a member of your flock, but so were Ashley Gates and her family.'

'Do you know anybody who would want to hurt Mr Chase, or tarnish him? Or Ashley and her family?'

Beam drank some more coffee, his hand shaking a little. 'No, I don't.'

'Are you okay, Father?' Purcell said.

'Just the fact that you're here could get me killed, but I prayed this morning, just like every morning, of course, but I got a sense of peace like never before. Maybe our good Lord sensed you were coming to see me today and wanted me to tell you.'

'Tell us what?' Miller said.

Beam was looking into his cup for a moment as if he didn't want to make eye contact. Then he looked at each detective in turn. 'He was here. On Sunday night, in the confessional. He threatened me.'

'What did he say?' Purcell asked.

'The confessional is sacrosanct, Inspector. You know I can't reveal what he said. And he knows it too. I didn't look at his face, just like I wouldn't look at anybody else's face in the confessional, and even if I wanted to, I wouldn't have. I was too scared.'

Miller guessed what the killer had said to the priest. He had more than likely told him to forget what he'd seen, or anything he *thought* he'd seen.

'I'm sorry, gentlemen, but I do have a lot on today. I wish I could have been more helpful.'

Miller sensed they weren't going to get much more out of him. The detectives stood. 'If you ever need us, please don't hesitate to call,' Miller said, putting a business card on the table.

Beam showed them out.

'It feels like we could just reach out and collar whoever is behind this,' Purcell said once they were back in the car.

Just before Purcell pulled away, Miller's phone rang. 'Hello?'

It was Beam. 'I forgot to ask you if you've ever seen an Al Pacino movie, Frank? I can't remember the name of this one, but one of my favourite scenes is where he plays a bad cop who's talking to a suspect.'

Miller looked puzzled. 'No, I haven't seen many Pacino films.'

'I remember this one as if it was only a few days ago. *This isn't over. If you look at me, I'll kill you. I'll do you just like I did them. Take a warning. Don't turn around. Keep your eyes down, and I'll leave you alone. You can't see me. Keep it that way. If you tell anybody, then I'll find you before they find me.* It was really scary. If I remember the name of the movie, I'll call you.' He disconnected the call.

Miller let the words sink in before putting his phone away.

'Everything okay, Frank?' Purcell asked.

He told Purcell what Beam had said. 'The church wouldn't be upset if Will Beam was only talking about movies, right?'

'Correct.'

'Then that's what he was talking about.' Except Miller knew that this particular movie had been played out in Will Beam's confessional only a couple of nights ago. And the priest was trying to help him.

TWENTY-NINE

Kate woke up feeling happy, and found herself whistling along to the tune on Forth One. Jimmy had gone home in the early hours of the morning, but they had made love again when he woke up. She felt like a teenager again.

Pouring a coffee, she sat down at her kitchen table, and looked out onto Holyrood Road. Just over the rooftops was Dumbiedykes. Where Jimmy was. God, she missed him already.

Kate, you're a doctor. A woman who cuts up corpses for a living. You're not supposed to feel this way. She couldn't help but smile. What way was a doctor supposed to feel? She certainly didn't want to go back to feeling like she used to. When her name was Arlene. Before the witness protection.

Her smile dropped for a moment.

She would have to tell Neil McGovern. Any new friends she made, any man she met, had to be run through the system. Jimmy would be okay. She didn't want to upset McGovern though, the man who had looked after her. Who had brought her north of the border.

Her phone rang. She turned the radio down, and answered it,

picking up the receiver from its base. She assumed it was Jimmy, calling her to tell her how great a night he'd had with her.

'Hello?'

'How are you doing, Arlene?'

Kate froze for a moment. Couldn't form an answer.

'Or should I say, Kate?'

She didn't know what to say. But she knew whose voice it was on the other end. Jared Flucker. If she said his name, she would be admitting who she was. 'I think you've got the wrong number.'

'Oh, I don't think so, Kate. I thought I would give you a call to see how you were doing. How's the new name working out for you?'

'I really don't know what you're talking about.'

'Your secret's safe with me. Maybe we can catch up with things over a coffee?' Silence on the phone but she could hear his breathing. 'I'll take that as a yes, shall I?'

She wanted to hang up, to disconnect her phone and leave the apartment, but it was like a dream she'd once had, where the house was on fire and she wanted to run, but her legs felt as if they were made of jelly and she couldn't move fast. It was like that now. She couldn't physically put the phone down, and she could feel her mouth going dry.

'Anyway, you might be wondering why I can call you. Well, thanks to your former boyfriend, and his dishonesty when it comes to evidence, I'm a free man. Along with four other men. It made the papers down here, but you obviously don't buy the red tops. So now I'm free.'

'Look, I don't want to be rude, but you're mistaken.'

'Oh, I don't think so. Brian was very forthcoming when they arrested him. Maybe you should call him and ask. Whoops. No, you can't. He's sitting in a remand cell just now. I'm not though. I have to say, I love the Scottish air. I think I'll have a stroll along Princes Street later. Good talking to you, Kate. See you soon.'

She hung up after the call disconnected.

Then she dialled a number she'd hoped she would never have to call.

———

Miller was sitting in his office, looking at paperwork, but not seeing anything. Beam's words were cutting through his mind. *If you look at me, I'll kill you.*

There was a knock at his door. 'Come!'

Andy Watt walked in. 'You okay, boss? You look like shit.'

'I'm all the better for seeing you, Andy.'

'My girlfriend says that too, but that's usually before I take her through to the bedroom.'

'I've not even had my lunch yet and you're turning my stomach.'

'How did your visit with the priest go? Get any teacakes?'

'Nope, no teacakes. He must have taken a shine to you, Andy.' *Keep your eyes down, and I'll leave you alone.*

'That's not what I came in to talk to you about.'

'What's going on?'

'There's a woman in reception, shouting the odds, not wanting to leave in a hurry. She says her sister is missing, and she wants to report it.'

'What's that got to do with us?'

'She wants to speak to you personally.'

'We don't do missing persons in MIT, Andy, you know that.'

'She says she knows who killed Ashley Gates.'

Miller stood up and grabbed his jacket off the back of his chair. 'Why didn't you say so? Bring her up, and take her into interview room one. I'll go and get Purcell.'

'Way ahead of you. She's already in there with a uniform watching over her. With a cup of tea. But no teacakes. Although, by the look of her, she should be standing over a cauldron, stirring it with her broomstick.'

Miller strode along the short corridor at the other end of the incident room, and knocked on Purcell's door.

'We have somebody whose sister is missing, and she has information about Ashley Gates.'

Purcell stood immediately. 'Let's go and see what she has to say.'

The interview room had a window that looked down into the Canongate over the rooftops. The woman's attention wasn't fixed on the view, but rather her fingernails. Her hands were clasped on the table in front of her, and she jumped when the two detectives entered the room.

'Thank God. I need to report my sister missing. I think he killed her,' she blurted out, about to stand.

'Calm down, Mrs...?' Purcell said, as he and Miller introduced themselves.

'Tate. Rosemary Tate.'

'Please, stay seated.' Miller putt a notepad down in front of him, though the recording devices were already rolling. They sat down opposite the almost hysterical woman.

'Let's start at the beginning, Mrs Tate,' Miller said. 'How do you know your sister is missing?'

'She was leaving her boyfriend, and she was going to come to my place. That was yesterday. I haven't heard from her since.'

'What's her name?'

'Jessica Thorn.'

Miller looked at her. 'Who do you think killed her?'

'Her boyfriend. Mitchell Robb.'

A look passed between the two detectives. *How many Mitchell Robbs could there be?*

'Why do you think he killed her?' Purcell said.

'He uses women. He's an egomaniac. He leaves women, not vice versa. That would make him look bad.'

'Maybe she just walked out, and decided not to come to your house. Is there anywhere else she would go?'

'No. I'm the only family she has. Besides, he was always sleeping with other women. He's a complete pig, never away from that bloody golf club of his.'

'The Royal up in Ravelston?' Miller said.

Purcell was all ears now. 'You told our sergeant that you knew who killed Ashley Gates.'

'Well, I can't prove it of course, but Robb was sleeping with her.'

'Do you know that for a fact?'

'Jess told me. Apparently, Robb didn't deny it either. If it has a pulse, he'll shag it.'

'It doesn't mean to say he's a killer, Mrs Tate. People have affairs all the time.'

'He's sleeping with a murder victim, and then my sister goes missing. It doesn't take a degree in rocket science to put it all together.'

Purcell sat up straighter in his chair. 'Give us your sister's details, and we'll go and have a word with Robb. Do you know where he works?'

'At the Western. When I last spoke to her, she said he had the next couple of days off, so he won't be working today, barring being called in for an emergency. He also has a taxi, so he might be out and about in that.'

'A taxi?' Purcell said. 'What kind of a doctor is he? A tree doctor?'

'He's a neurosurgeon. His father was a taxi driver, and he kept the license plate when the old man died. There's a long waiting list for one apparently. So he kept it, and he drives about. He's fully qualified. Passed the knowledge years ago, being the smart arse that he is. Jess said he used it to meet women, not to make money. It wouldn't surprise me.'

'We'll go and see if he's at home now,' Miller said, sliding the pad over to her.

She wrote on it, and slid the pad back across the table. 'I wish she'd stuck with that other guy she was going with before she met Robb.' She looked at Miller. 'Please find out what happened to my sister.'

157

THIRTY

'Nice place,' Purcell said, from the passenger seat as Miller turned into the driveway of the apartment block in Ravelston. Forensics were still going through Ashley Gates' house, and police vehicles were outside, as were a few journalists.

'I wouldn't mind a place here.' He pulled up to the front door.

'What do you think he's done with Ashley Gates? Whoever killed her.'

'Jeez, Percy, she could be anywhere.'

'He's one hell of a risk taker though. Kill a woman, and then take her out into the street to put the body into his car.'

'I was thinking about that. It must be some size of a car to get a body out, still wrapped in a rug, and into the boot before anybody comes along and sees you. Unless.'

'Unless what?'

'Unless it's a taxi.'

Purcell nodded. 'That would make sense. Or a van would make even more sense.'

'Not a van. Think about it; some nosy neighbour looks out, sees somebody loading a van in the wee hours of the morning. That's something they'll remember. Now, if they look out and see a taxi, they'll just close the curtains and go back to sleep. Taxis are always in the streets. They're practically invisible.'

'You're thinking her ex-boyfriend killed her. Dan Herdan.'

'After what Rosemary Tate said about Robb having a taxi, it got me wondering.'

'You might have a point there.'

'And now we know his girlfriend suspected he was messing about with Ashley Gates.'

They got out of the car into the brisk air. 'He's got some balls if he was sleeping with her after she broke up with his friend.' Purcell pressed the buzzer with Robb's name on it.

'Hello?' the voice answered through the speaker.

'Doctor Robb?' Miller said. 'It's the police. We'd like to speak to you.'

'Okay. Top floor.'

'It's *Mister* Robb, remember?' Purcell laughed. 'Surgeons are never called *Doctor*.'

'Fuck 'im.'

He buzzed them in, and they hit the lift button for the penthouse level. Robb was waiting for them with the door open.

'Come away in. I have the kettle on.'

Both detectives were ready to show their warrant cards, but Robb didn't ask to see them. He closed the door behind them, and showed them into the living room.

'Detectives Miller and Purcell,' he said. 'I remember both of you from last night at the golf club.'

'That's right.'

'Make yourself at home. I'm going to have a quick coffee before I head out. What do you take?'

'We're fine, thanks,' Purcell said. 'We just had one.'

He headed into the kitchen, both men staying in a position where they could see him if he came charging out with a cleaver.

He came back with nothing more dangerous than a coffee mug. 'Pull up a pew.'

Both men sat down on the couch while Robb sat on a chair, putting his mug on the coffee table.

Miller saw the doctor was dressed in jeans and a sweatshirt. 'Not working today?' he asked, knowing that Robb's sister-in-law had said that he wasn't.

'I have a taxi. I drive it about when I have a day off.'

'Really?' Purcell said. 'I think you're the only surgeon I've ever met who drives a taxi.'

Robb smiled, any hint of offence taken quickly dispelled. 'My father was still alive when I was going through university. He had his own taxi, so I got my license and drove in my spare time. I decided to keep his plate when he died. It really is quite refreshing, getting down to grass roots level.'

'The level of a policeman, you mean?' Purcell said.

'Exactly!'

Miller observed the other man, noting that he hadn't asked why they were here. 'We have a few questions for you, doctor.'

'Fire away.' He grabbed his coffee mug and cradled it.

'Where's your wife?' Purcell asked.

'Jess?' he smiled. 'We're not married. She's gone, Superintendent.'

'Gone where?' Miller said.

Robb kept his *smarmy bastard* look on, and shrugged his shoulders. 'Your guess is as good as mine. I had to do an overnight, Monday into Tuesday, and when I got home, she'd packed her things and gone.'

'You don't seem surprised.'

'I'm not. She'd been threatening it for ages.' He took a sip of coffee, and put the mug back onto the table, making sure it was on the coaster. 'Why are you asking?'

'We have her reported as a missing person.'

'Ah. The great Rosemary. She always was a nosy cow. But there's one thing puzzling me.'

'What's that?'

'She's at Rosemary's house. Jess told me she was going to stay with her sister until she got on her feet. So why has she reported her as missing?'

'It seems like she never made it there.'

Robb laughed, a brief chuff, like a bride might laugh on her wedding night when she found out that her new husband hadn't exactly been truthful about the size of his manhood.

'You know, they're both a pair of conniving bitches. Jess has probably gone to a hotel for a week or so, giving Rosemary the cue to go to the police and have them come round here and hassle me.'

'We're not hassling you, are we?' Purcell said. 'In fact, I don't think I've ever been in a less hassling mood in my life.'

'No, you're not hassling me, but that's what the sisters want to happen. They're just so sneaky.'

'Jess's sister seemed really upset, Doctor Robb. Not the kind of reaction we would have expected from somebody who's making up stories to the police. Unless she's a good actress.'

'Come with me, gentlemen.' He got up, and the two detectives followed.

In the bedroom, Robb opened a wardrobe. Half the clothes that had been hanging were gone. So were most of the shoes. 'I'm guessing she took what she could fit into the two suitcases that lived in the wardrobe in the spare bedroom. She loves her shoes though, so I'm sure she'll be back for all the rest of her crap whenever I'm back at work.'

'So you're officially telling us that she left of her own free will?' Miller said.

'You can see for yourself, Detective Miller. To be honest, when she told me she was leaving to go and stay with her sister, I felt happier than I had in a long time. We were arguing all the time.'

He led them back through to the living room.

'Were you having an affair with Ashley Gates?' Purcell asked, as they all sat down.

'Ashley? Good God, no. She was the ex-wife of a friend of mine. Why? Did Rosemary say I was?'

'We're not at liberty to say.'

'She must have. Cheeky cow.'

'So you had no dealings with Ashley?' Purcell said.

'You'll be aware that she lived just over the road from me. So yes, I did have dealings with her. I would see her going about, and if I was passing in my car, I'd stop and say hello to her. She was my friend's wife. Why wouldn't I speak to her?'

'Did Jess talk to her?'

Robb sipped his coffee. 'We went out as a foursome. Ashley was very friendly and outgoing. She had more personality than Jess. They were good friends though. They hit it off right away, but Jess couldn't keep her jealousy in check. To my knowledge, she never said anything to Ashley. They used to go out for coffee and do shopping trips. It was me Jess didn't trust, not Ashley.'

'When did she leave?' Purcell asked.

'When I got in yesterday morning, she was gone. As I said, I was on-call and had to go in to the hospital, and I was there all night. I didn't get in until around ten or so.'

'Can anybody verify that?' Miller said.

Robb smiled. 'Yes. One of your detectives, Jimmy Gilmour. He came in to be with his ex-wife when her uncle died. And I was still there when they came back in the morning to pick up the hospital death certificate.'

'Monty Chase was a patient of yours?'

'Yes, he was. But that's all I can say on the matter.' Robb stood. 'If there's nothing else, I'd like to get going.'

The detectives stood. 'We may need to talk to you again, Doctor Robb,' Purcell said.

'Anytime. And tell Rosemary her imagination's running away with her.'

'Is there anywhere Jess would go if she left you.'

'Well, she has left me. And no, I don't know who she would run off with.'

As Miller was walking towards the living room door, he noticed a photo in a frame on a little side table, partly hidden by a lamp.

'Is this your girlfriend?' Miller asked. He took his iPhone out, and hit the photo album button.

'Yes. That's her with Ashley at a party at the golf club.'

Miller had recognised Ashley Gates. He opened up the photo he'd taken of the photo in Ashley's house, the one somebody had drawn a noose on.

The noose was round Jessica Thorn's image.

THIRTY-ONE

Neil McGovern was in his office going through paperwork. As head of the Scottish branch of the government witness protection programme, his workload had increased. Nothing he couldn't handle, but he missed his days back in London sometimes, when he'd worked undercover.

Still, he was home every night, and his missus was happy about that.

There was a knock on his door, and he called for his secretary to come in.

'This report came for you, sir.'

'Thanks, Linda.' He took the paper from her as she retreated. Read through it, and picked up his phone.

'Frank? How's things?'

'Great, Neil. I'm just back at the station.'

'How about lunch?'

Frank looked at his watch, almost midday. 'Where were you thinking?'

'I like your style. Ask where before committing. However, I do need your help with something. And I thought you wouldn't mind accommodating the father of your wife-to-be.'

'Sure. Why not?'

'The North Bridge Brasserie in the Scotsman Hotel. Say, fifteen minutes?'

'Won't you need to reserve a table there?'

McGovern laughed. 'They'll have a table for us, Frank.' He hung up, actually looking forward to seeing the man who was going to make an honest woman of his daughter. If he hadn't liked Miller, then there was no way he would be marrying Kim, copper or no copper.

He grabbed his jacket, and walked out into the anteroom. 'Have Brian bring the car round, Linda, please. And don't rush back from lunch. I'm having a meeting.'

'Right away, sir.'

McGovern walked along the corridor. These offices occupied two levels of a corner of the new Scottish parliament building down in Holyrood, directly across the road from the palace. His invite to the Queen's garden party had been greatly appreciated, especially by his wife, Norma Banks, the procurator fiscal.

The black Range Rover was waiting for him when he entered the underground car park and the luxury SUV whisked him up to the North Bridge, where Frank Miller was waiting for him outside the side entrance to the hotel.

'Frank, glad you could make it.'

'Well, if it was McDonald's, I'm afraid another appointment would have come up.'

They walked in and went through to the restaurant where a young woman took their coats.

They both ordered soft drinks when the waiter came over.

'Kim was round talking with her mother about the wedding,' McGovern said. 'She's excited, Frank. Even more so than when she was preparing to marry Eric.'

'You know I haven't asked her yet?'

'My Kim loves you, and in her mind, it's just a matter of time. She's very patient, but she wants to spend the rest of her life with you.'

'I do want her to be my wife, Neil. I just want the timing to be right. To be special. I'm excited. On the inside. I have my *tough copper* look on just now, but I promise you I'll be smiling for the photographer.'

McGovern was reading the menu then he put it down, apparently having settled on a dish. 'I need you to be honest with me now, Frank. I know you were married, and you're a widower at thirty, but are you sure you're happy with my daughter?'

'Of course I am.' Miller put his own menu down. 'I love Kim. I love wee Emma as if she were my own daughter. I'll treat her as if she's flesh and blood. And hopefully we'll have our own child. Why? Did I give you the impression that I wasn't in this for the long haul?'

'Trust me, you wouldn't be sitting here right now if I thought that. No, as a parent, I worry about my child. She's twenty-nine, but she'll always be my little girl. I know Carol was pregnant when she died, and I just want to make sure that there's no doubts in your mind.'

Miller looked McGovern in the eyes. 'I was a good husband before, and I'll be a damn good husband again. I love Kim and Emma so much that I'd die for both of them. And if any fu—'

McGovern smiled and held up a hand, seeing the fire in Miller's eyes. 'That's all I wanted to hear. Now, what are you ordering?'

They were just going to order a main course, since it was a working lunch. 'I'll have the Black Isle organic beer battered haddock with the chunky chips. What about you?'

'Since the government is picking up the tab, I'll have the eight ounce fillet steak.'

McGovern nodded to the waiter that they were ready, and the young man came across and took their order. Their drinks arrived.

'So, are you going to tell me why we're here? It wasn't just to ask me about my intentions.'

'Frank! Always so suspicious. Relax.'

'Well, if the government's paying for this, then it's a business lunch, which you can put down on your expenses. Therefore, you didn't get me here to ask me if I was having cold feet about marrying your daughter. So why are we here?'

'You're good. I knew you wouldn't let me down.'

The waiter brought their lunch.

'Do you remember Jared Flucker? The man Kate helped put away.'

'Yes, you told me all about him. And Kate was called Arlene Donaldson before she went into witness protection.'

'Correct. Well, it seems he's out of prison now.'

Miller finished his mouthful before speaking. 'I thought he was put away for murder, and got twenty-five years.'

'He's a free man. He was let out of Bridgefield prison two weeks ago.' McGovern cut into the steak, and chewed on a piece. 'You know, this would be so much better with a nice glass of red.'

'So how come Flucker is out in the open now?'

'Where do I begin? What we thought was an open-and-shut case turned out to be anything but.'

'He was convicted of murdering a policeman.'

McGovern cut another piece of steak, and waved it about on the fork – something his wife hated, calling it *talking with his food* – as he answered. 'That's what he was charged with, but he denied it. He said he didn't push the copper down the stairs. He said he was running away, and never heard the copper chasing him. Turns out that part was true as well.'

'How did you find this out?'

'The Crown Prosecution Service in London should have called the office down there, and they would have called me. Somehow, the left hand thought the right hand had called, but it hadn't. How's your fish?'

'Excellent. I'll get Kim to make this one night,' Frank said. 'So how come Flucker was let go?'

'Because of Kate's – Arlene's – previous boyfriend, Brian Crane. He's a DCI in the Met. He's been up to a lot of capers though. Bent as a two-pound note. He hid it very well, especially from Kate. They split up after the case, so she doesn't know about him being arrested. She was taken away, and put into witness protection before anybody knew she was gone. We made it look like she disappeared.

'Anyway, Professional Standards got a tip-off, and they started looking into him. Not only was he bending the rules, he was taking bribes. That's what got him done. One of his sergeants was lifted as well, and he didn't want to take the fall for it, so he cut a deal with the CPS. Started telling them just how bent Crane really was.

'Then they got down to the business of how Crane had fitted up a few guys. One of them, Jared Flucker.'

'So Flucker didn't kill Kate's mother after all?'

'Supposedly. You see, a man was seen going into the old woman's house. The neighbours didn't get a good look at him, but Crane showed them photos of Flucker, and got them to admit that it could have been him. Then he persuaded them that Flucker might come back and slit their throats if they didn't give a positive ID. So they said, oh yes, that's him! And although Kate disturbed him, he said he'd just come into the house looking for her mother, him being a senior citizen bus driver.'

'Didn't they find evidence at the scene?'

'A cigarette butt with Flucker's DNA on it. That was the clincher in the jury's mind, I think. Solid evidence. Turns out Crane had put it there. When they were going over the crime scene, he slipped it out of his pocket with his gloves on, and then directed one of the forensics crew to it.'

'And this can be proved?'

'After his sergeant was hauled in and told them, another detective backed his story up. They hated him, but they feared him as well.'

'What about the copper who died?'

'Get this; Flucker was telling the truth that he slipped out of custody. Somebody dropped the ball, and he made a run for it. One of the uniforms only noticed afterwards. Crane was furious, and he started in on the young uniform, and then pushed him down the stairs and the poor lad died from a brain injury three days later.'

'And this was witnessed?'

'By the same two detectives. So after Crane's house was raided, they found all sorts of DNA evidence from other cases. The silly sod had kept it in a box in his attic. Like trophies.'

'I'm surprised the other two grassed him up.'

'They were looking at a long prison term for murder. They cut a deal, and didn't serve any time, but they were fired. Now Crane's the only one who's going to prison for murder. They're going to love him in Bellmarsh.'

Miller finished his fish. 'Please thank Her Majesty's Government for that lovely lunch, but there's obviously more to this story. That sort of stuff you would have come round to my flat to tell me.'

McGovern smiled, not being able to finish the steak. 'My eyes are always bigger than my belly.' He dabbed at his mouth, and put the napkin down. 'You're right, of course. You see, Kate got a phone call from Mr Flucker. He called her by her new name. He must have got her phone number, somehow, but he also knew she was in Edinburgh.'

'And you want to know how.'

'Exactly.'

'Couldn't somebody from your department have leaked that information?'

'Not worth the risk. If I thought somebody in my office had done that... well, I wouldn't be a happy camper.'

'What about Kate herself? Could she have told Flucker?'

'I doubt it.' He drank some more of the soft drink. 'Don't take this the wrong way, Frank, but could you have let something slip?'

'No. Not at all. Kim and I only ever discussed it with each other, and we agreed not to talk about it outside the flat.'

'I do have one suspect.'

'Who's that?'

'Connie Gilmour.'

'Jimmy's wife? How would she know?'

'Because her ex-husband is sleeping with Kate Murphy.'

'Jimmy is?' Miller looked incredulously at McGovern. 'Are you sure?'

'Yes I am. Maybe Connie Gilmour doesn't like the fact that her ex has moved on. I mean, she's very friendly with him, getting him to go to the hospital with her when her uncle was dying. Maybe Gilmour let it slip he's seeing Kate.'

'How would Jimmy have found out about Kate being Arlene Donaldson?'

'That's what I'd like you to find out, Frank. I want to go and talk to him at home. Sort of casual, like. I'd like you to be there, just as a buffer.'

Miller shook his head. 'I can't believe Jimmy wouldn't tell me.'

'I'd like to find out as soon as. He hinted that he's already here in Edinburgh. Kate has protection but it's minimally invasive.'

'And if Flucker is here, that means only one thing.'

'He's not here to catch up on old times.'

'Why would he do that if he wasn't guilty?'

'I didn't say he wasn't guilty. I said he denied it, and yes, he didn't kill the copper, and Crane planted evidence, but Crane was convinced of Flucker's guilt. Now that he's called Kate, so am I.'

'And if he really is up here in Edinburgh, then you think he's going to kill Kate.'

'I think he's going to try,' McGovern said. 'Unless you find out who tipped him off. Before you do that though, I'm going to have a word with Kate. If this is going to get serious with Gilmour that changes the whole game. He can't find out she isn't who she seems to be.'

'Kate's life is never going to be the same again, is it?'

'No.'

THIRTY-TWO

'Pull your finger out your arse, man!' Commander Lloyd Masters shouted into the microphone, his voice booming out over the loud-speakers on the firing range.

Jimmy Gilmour stood in the large booth overlooking the range. 'These guys are good,' he said.

'Not good enough. They need to get a ninety-seven per cent or higher. Those clowns are barely getting ninety.'

'So what happened to your assistant?'

'Broke his thumb skiing. Apparently, his ski pole hit something, and his thumb broke. That's all I bloody needed, what with the amount of re-certifications I have coming up.'

'I was talking to some old-school bloke today and he was glad our coppers aren't armed.'

'What's your opinion on that?' Masters asked, as he stood looking out on the range. Two more instructors stood outside with clipboards. This wasn't like the army. Most of the officers who were down on the range were being re-certified, but there were two women who were in training.

'You know, there's a lot of shooting in America, and I'd hate to get to the point where every wee scumbag has access to an illegal gun, but I think our heads are up our own arses if we don't think there's guns out there. We read about shootings all the time. So, in my humble opinion, if we're not going to give our cops guns, then the courts have to come into the twenty-first century and bang the fuckers away for life. And by life, I mean until they're put in a wooden box.'

Masters looked at him. 'I agree. I'm training these officers to get to a scene where there are guns being used. There are the armed response guys, but a lot of people don't realise we also have to mobilise other armed officers if there's something going down.'

'There's too much red tape as well. All this enquiry shite when an officer shoots somebody.'

'There has to be accountability, Jimmy.'

'Agreed. But the brass don't have to drag their fucking feet.' He looked at Masters. 'Sorry, sir.'

Masters laughed. 'No need to be sorry. I asked for your opinion.' He pressed the button for the microphone again. 'Number four! My granny can shoot better than that. And she's blind in one eye!'

Gilmour sat down in one of the chairs facing the window. 'I know Percy Purcell told you why I was being sent here, but to be honest, it all seems a bit surreal. Connie's uncle with photos of a dead woman.'

'It takes all sorts, Jimmy. Nobody knows what goes on behind closed doors.'

'I never got that vibe off him, though. I mean, I don't think he was a killer.'

'Neither did Harold Shipman's patients.'

Gilmour looked at the older man. 'I know what you're saying, but I think my mind's trying to block this out, since we had our little girl round there.'

'At least there's no evidence of him being a killer. I'm sure Frank Miller's working on the theory that somebody put them there.'

'I hope to God that's true. And now they just have to figure out who.'

Masters nodded. Stepped up to the microphone again. 'Those two ladies are shooting better than you, number five, and this is their first fucking day! Pull yourself together!'

He laughed when he stepped back. 'Sometimes I love my job.'

'You look like you've lost a pound and found a penny,' Kim said, when she entered Miller's office.

'My eyes feel much better now they're on you,' he said, throwing his pen down onto his desk. 'Close the door and come here and take advantage of me.'

'You wish. You look like you couldn't handle a kiss, never mind anything else.'

Miller looked past her, into the enquiry room beyond. 'Close the blinds, and I'll show you.'

'I bet you say that to all the girls.'

'Only the blondes.'

Kim raised her eyebrows.

'That I'm in love with.'

'That's better.' She smiled and sat down. 'How's your afternoon been so far?'

'I've been tracking down friends of Jessica Thorn, the woman who was living with the surgeon I told you about. They all say she was unhappy in her relationship, and was planning to leave him.'

'So you're thinking he maybe got angry and stopped her from leaving?'

'I don't think he did, to be honest. Jessica spoke to a friend of hers late on Monday night. We confirmed that he was at the hospital late Monday. In fact, Jimmy was there with Connie through the night, and Jimmy himself spoke to Robb. And Robb was in his office after nine on Tuesday morning, confirmed by his secretary.'

'So maybe she did leave. Decided to go away on her own for a while.'

173

'Maybe.'

'But you, being a detective, say that isn't what went down.'

'I'm keeping an open mind.'

The phone on Miller's desk rang. 'Hello?' He spoke to the caller for a few moments before hanging up. 'That was Maggie Parks. They found an interesting DVD in Monty Chase's collection. They were opening up the boxes looking for more photos when they found a home-made one. In the case for an old Bette Davis movie.'

'Did she say what was on it?'

'They copied it and sent it over.' He stood up, and they both left his office. 'Let's go and find a TV.'

Kate Murphy stretched her back in her chair. She was feeling tense, but nothing a glass of red with Jimmy wouldn't fix. She smiled at the thought of him. He was the best thing that had happened to her since Brian Crane. She had loved Brian, and had fallen head over heels, but the more she got to know him, the more she found out about him skating on thin ice.

But it was all a moot point. She had been whisked away into witness protection at short notice.

There was a knock on her door, and she jumped.

'Sorry, Kate,' Gus Weaver said. 'It's just that there's a woman in reception to see you.'

'Did she give a name?'

'Lauren, was all she said.'

'What does she look like?'

'Twenties. Brown hair. Skinny.'

'Jesus.'

'Do you know her?'

'Not exactly.'

'Do you want me to get rid of her?'

Kate shook her head. 'No, but I'd like you close by, to be a witness if it comes to that.'

'You think she's here to cause trouble?'

'Oh, yes. Before we go up, go and get Jake, please. Tell him if things get heated up there, to come in and tell me there's a phone call. Then make sure this woman leaves.'

'Right. He's just through by the fridges. I'll go and get him.'

A few minutes later, one of the other pathologists, Jake Dagger, poked his head round her office door, a huge grin on his face. 'Is there going to be a cat fight?'

'Ha bloody ha. However, if this is who I think it is, she might give you a kicking.'

'Me? What have I done?'

'I'll think of something on the way to reception.'

'Did I tell you how much I used to enjoy working with you?' Dagger looked at Weaver. 'Of course, I'll then blame you, Weaver.'

'Sod off. I'm not getting involved in all of this,' Weaver replied.

'Too late, my old son, you already are.' He clapped a hand on the older man's shoulder. 'Never mind, we can have a pint afterwards. If you're not in A&E that is.'

'Or on one of your bloody slabs. I used to be married, remember? My ex was a nutcase. She could fight like a woman possessed.' Weaver shook his head.

Dagger laughed. 'I'll be watching from a distance. I've got Frank Miller on speed dial.'

'I hate you, Dagger. Your time will come, my friend.'

Dagger laughed again. 'Go get 'em!'

'There's a special place in hell reserved for people like you.'

Kate walked up the corridor and through a door, Weaver close behind. 'If she seems like she's got a knife, then we cut it short, and we'll lock this door behind us.'

'God. I'm too old for fighting.'

The reception area was reserved for families who were waiting to identify a deceased loved one. Lauren was standing by the doorway when they arrived.

'So you're the whore who's shagging Jimmy.'

'You watch your mouth,' Weaver said, but Kate held up a hand.

'It's okay, Gus.' Then she looked at Lauren, and smiled. 'As introductions go, I've had better. However, if you've come here looking for a fight, you've come to the wrong place.'

'I came here because I wanted to tell you you're fucking welcome to him.'

'I'm not going to stand here and argue with you. Jimmy and I were just friends, and then you decided to dump him.'

'And you couldn't wait to move in.'

'We're seeing each other now, yes. Not that it's any of your business.'

'Tell him he's a wanker, and my new boyfriend is so much better in the sack than he ever was.'

'I'll be sure to tell him that.'

'Sarky fucking cow. I know what you're up to. I was in here waiting for Jimmy one day, and I saw the way you looked at him. Mentally undressing him.'

'I think you have too much imagination.'

'I think you need to be taught a lesson.'

'You need to go now.'

'I'll go when I please.'

'Listen, Lauren, Jimmy and I weren't messing about behind your back. You chose to leave him for somebody else. Did you really think he was going to stay home and watch TV every night?'

'I don't care. He blames me for finding somebody else, and here he is, shagging you. He's got a fucking cheek. Well, if I find out he's been going behind my back and seeing you, you'll both regret it.'

Lauren turned round, and stormed out of the reception area.

Kate turned to Weaver. 'You heard that threat, right?'

He smiled, and took his iPhone out. 'Me and my phone both did.'

He switched off the recorder on his phone, and put it back in his pocket.

'Thank you, Gus.'

Dagger came walking along the corridor, his own phone in his hand. 'I was about to hit the button.'

'Thanks, Jake. Anybody for a drink?'

'Thanks, but I think Jimmy will be wanting to see you alone.' He paused for a moment. 'You were going to tell us about you and Jimmy, weren't you?'

'Of course I was. When the time was right.'

'Good. We look out for each other, Kate.'

'Okay. A rain check though.'

'Count on it.'

THIRTY-THREE

Miller, Kim, Purcell, Andy Watt, Paddy Gibb, Hazel, and Angie Rivers were in the conference room with the psychologist, American Professor, Harvey Levitt, who Police Edinburgh employed now and again.

The TV had been wheeled on its stand to sit at the head of the conference table.

'Anybody going for the ice cream?' Watt said.

'Right, ladies and gentlemen,' Purcell said, looking flustered after he had trouble getting the DVD player to show on the TV, 'let's get this show on the road. Andy, get the blinds, will you?'

Watt trudged over and closed the blinds, darkening the room from the cold, wet daylight. Purcell pointed the remote at the TV, and played the DVD.

It was the inside of a house. Somebody was obviously holding the camcorder, and was ushering guests into the hallway. The date stamp on the bottom of the screen showed it had been filmed two years earlier.

'Dan! Patricia! Welcome to the party!'

'Sorry we're late, but I brought a special bottle to make up for it.'

'*Nonsense. We're just getting warmed up.*' *The free hand reached out and took the bottle anyway. The camera followed the couple into the kitchen where they took their coats off and put them on a chair.*

'*Go through to the living room. They're all waiting.*'

'Dan Herdan and Patricia Wilkinson,' Miller said.

Purcell paused the video. 'For those who don't know, Dan Herdan was recently dating Ashley Gates. They broke up, but he still has a thing for her. This was filmed before he split with Ashley, as you can see. It seems like Patricia Wilkinson was his girlfriend back then.' He looked at Watt. 'Did she tell you she had been seeing him back then?'

'She mentioned she dated him a while back, but she broke it off with him. He was the sort who wanted to go boxing when he had one too many. She didn't mention the parties.'

Purcell hit play again.

In the living room, they were greeted by a cheer as if they were castaways returning home after being rescued. There were hugs and kisses all round. The camera was sweeping round the room.

Purcell hit the pause button, highlighting a man's face. 'Don't be shy, ladies and gentlemen. Speak up if you see anybody you recognise.' He hit the play button again.

'*Dan, you old cock!*' a man said. The camera panned round, and the smiling face of Mitchell Robb was centre stage.

'Right, DI Miller and I spoke to this joker. His girlfriend is missing. He says she left him, but then her sister thinks he killed her. She also thinks he killed Ashley Gates, but there's no evidence, so there's nothing we can do except list the sister as a missing person.'

'She might be there with him, at this party,' Miller said, nodding to the TV. 'I took a photo of her photo with my phone.' He took his iPhone out, and brought up the picture as Purcell started the movie running again. 'There she is, Jessica Thorn.'

'And that's Robb's wife?' Andy Watt said.

Miller looked at him. 'His girlfriend, although they lived together like man and wife.'

'There's Ashley Gates,' Purcell said.

They watched Ashley on the arm of her ex-husband, Arthur King.

'*King Arthur!*' the cameraman said. King waved back.

Robb grinned like an idiot, and squeezed Jess's backside. She squealed in delight.

'*Who wants to party?*' the cameraman shouted. Somebody out of view put the music on as everyone cheered.

Purcell stopped the video. 'Does anybody recognise the cameraman's voice?'

'I do,' Miller said. 'It's Monty's nephew. I last saw him a few years back, but I would recognise his voice anywhere.'

The video started again. There were more people at the back, and the camera was just catching glimpses of them. Somebody was pouring drinks, and the two newcomers were handed one each.

'*And there she is, my beautiful girlfriend.*'

They heard a woman's giggle off camera, but her face wasn't shown.

The motion started again.

'*Right, Dan, get your keys in the bowl,*' Gabe said. A cheer went up as Herdan's keys landed with the rest of them.

'*I know you're all dying to go and have some fun, so let's get at it.*'

'See these dirty bastards, like kids in a sweet store,' Purcell said. 'Can somebody take a note of who gets paired with whom?'

'I will,' Kim said. She poised her pen above her notepad.

Ashley Gates walked forward, and picked up a set of keys. '*Oh, a Jaguar. I wonder who this belongs to?*' The camera swung towards Mitchell Robb, who was standing grinning. He stepped forward, took his car keys, and held Ashley's hand as they left the room.

'*Next in line. Come on ladies and gentlemen, don't be shy!*'

Jessica Thorn was next, and she beamed as she pulled out the keys to a Porsche. '*Well, well, the lovely Jessica has taken my keys!*' Gabe Chase said.

She stepped forward, and they could hear her kissing his cheek out of view.

'Now, I do believe it's Patricia's turn. Come on, Patty!' Another cheer went up.

'Well, well, I've picked the nice BMW,' she said, waving Arthur King's keys in the air.

'And I do believe that leaves you with the – so I've heard! – capable Mr Herdan!' The unidentified woman was addressed, and more cheers rang out.

The film ended, and the unidentified woman wasn't shown. Purcell fast-forwarded a bit to see if there was anything else added after this clip, but there was nothing.

Purcell ejected the DVD, and switched the TV off.

'Right, Kim, let's run over the names again.'

Kim looked down at her notes. 'Right, we have Ashley Gates paired off with Mitchell Robb. Robb's girlfriend Jessica with Gabe Chase. Patricia Wilkinson with Arthur King, and the unknown female with Dan Herdan.'

'Thanks, Kim,' Purcell said, standing up. 'Bunch of bloody deviants. But we need to ask them who that woman is.'

'I fancied the idea of a bit of rough sex, once,' Andy Watt said.

'There's got to be two of you in the room for it to count, Andy,' Miller said, and everyone burst out laughing.

Once they'd settled down, Purcell pointed to Levitt. 'Any thoughts, Doc?'

Levitt was sitting with his fingers steepled against his mouth, as if deep in thought, then he suddenly sat forward. 'You're wanting to know if I think any of those men killed Ashley Gates. My first impression is any of them could have. At first, it seems they're all quite happy to share one another's girlfriend or wife, but we now know Mitchell Robb's girlfriend left him, Ashley Gates divorced her husband, and then she split from Dan Herdan.

'As for them sharing partners, it seems to have had a detrimental effect on all their relationships. Sometimes what starts out as fun can become something else. Maybe one of the women was starting to like being with her part-time partner more than her husband.' The American opened the folder in front of him. 'In Frank's report, he says one of the office staff at Ashley's work told him Ashley played around. Was that the reason she and King divorced? Not according to King, but we don't know what went on behind closed doors. Maybe he was jealous that his wife liked fooling around on him.'

'It makes sense. Some wives have died for less,' Paddy Gibb said.

'If you want my opinion, Chief Inspector, it seems to me that the women enjoyed being with the other men, but something shifted in their little world. Was Cathy Graham part of that world two years ago? Was the priest? I have to say no, I don't think he was, but I could be wrong. It doesn't mean to say he was guilty just because a photo was found in his office. Like photos were placed in Monty Chase's home office. I don't think your killer is one of those men, but somebody wants you to think they are.'

Purcell sat forward, his hands clasped in front of him on the table. 'We're forgetting Michaela Savage. She wasn't in the film, but she was killed in the same way.'

Levitt looked thoughtful for a moment. 'I think she was in the mix somewhere. Maybe she was part of the group and just wasn't there that night. Or maybe she hadn't met them yet.'

'I couldn't find any connection between her and any of those people in that film,' Purcell said, 'but, we'll keep on looking. I have my team in Aberdeen working on it too.'

'There has to be one somewhere,' Miller said. 'Maybe she was the woman off camera?'

'We'll check that out. Right, folks, let's get some interviews done. Andy? Take Angie with you. Talk to Patricia Wilkinson about that DVD. Paddy, can you and Kim go and chat with Herdan again. I want to see what he says about that party. I want that woman's name. I'll take Frank with me, as he knows the ins and outs of this investigation. I want to talk to Mitchell Robb again. See what he has to say about the swingers club.'

Everybody stood up and left. Miller waited to talk to Purcell. 'If Ashley and Jessica have been murdered, then Patricia might be in danger too.'

'I hear you, Frank, but Jessica is only listed as missing. We don't know that she's been murdered. We'll put Patricia on her guard.'

'You and I both know that missing wives are potential victims, killed by their husbands.'

'I'm keeping that in mind, Frank. That's why we're going to blitz the bastards.'

THIRTY-FOUR

Music blared out through the radio in the loading bay of the City Mortuary and Malc Freeman was chatting to one of the mortuary attendants, Natalie Strozewski, or *Sticks* to her friends, while Freeman's driver was helping Charlie Warner.

'You still playing drums in your band?' he asked Sticks.

'Yes I am. You should come and watch us play in the Station bar in the Waldorf.'

'Maybe I will.'

Kate Murphy walked in. 'Hello, Romeo. I hope you're not corrupting that young lady.'

'As if. Sticks was just inviting me round to watch her band play.'

'As long as you behave with her.'

'I honestly don't know where you get the impression that I treat a lady with anything other than respect.' He was grinning when he said it.

'I've seen you in the pub, remember?'

'Ah, yes. But I will be on my best behaviour.'

'Or you'll have us to answer to. Her friends.'

Freeman held up both hands. 'Don't shoot.'

'Maybe I'll just arrest you,' Jimmy Gilmour said from behind Freeman's back.

'Now that you put it like that, maybe I'm too busy to go and see Sticks play. Goodbye, sergeant.'

He left Kate alone with Gilmour.

Gilmour walked around Kate's desk, and gave her a kiss. 'God, I needed that.'

'I missed you too. Hard day?'

He put his jacket on a coat hook. 'Not so bad. It took me back to my army days. But they finished early so I got to knock off a few hours early.'

'And you thought you'd spend it with me? How lovely. Except I still have to work until around five.'

'I have an idea; why don't I pick some stuff up for us then I'll do the cooking? At your place, if you like.'

'I do like.'

'Great.' He made to take his jacket back when she stopped him.

'Listen. There are a couple of things that I need to talk to you about. Sit down for a minute.'

He sat on the chair opposite her. 'Go on.'

'First of all, Lauren paid me a visit today. She was all strung out, accusing me of taking you away from her.'

'What? That's bloody ridiculous. She and I were finished before you and I even considered seeing each other.'

'*I* know that, *you* know that, but *she* doesn't know that.'

'I don't believe that woman. First she messes about behind my back, and now it's my fault.' He shook his head. 'She's supposed to clear out today, so I hope to God she's away.'

'We haven't seen the last of her. She said we'll regret it.'

'She'll regret it by the time I'm finished with her.'

'Don't do anything daft, Jimmy. Just let her stew in her own juices.'

He took a deep breath and relaxed. 'You're right. She's not worth bothering about.'

Kate's phone rang. She answered it, and looked at Jimmy before handing the receiver over. 'It's Frank Miller.'

He took it. 'Hello, sir.'

'Jimmy, I need to have a word with you in private, and Lloyd up at the range said you were finished for the day and where you were heading. Can I come round and see you after dinner?'

'Sir, why don't I come up to your place?'

'What I want to talk about is just for our ears.'

'Okay. What time?'

'How about eight o'clock?'

'I'll make sure I'm in.'

He handed the receiver back to Kate, and she hung it up. 'Are we still on for dinner?'

'Yes, but dessert will have to wait. Miller wants to come round to my flat to talk.'

She smiled. 'I guess you'll just have to come back down to me, Jimmy Gilmour. The kind of dessert I have, you don't want to miss.'

THIRTY-FIVE

Once again, Miller found himself driving up to the front door of the expensive flats in Ravelston.

'Do you think he would look so unperturbed if he'd offed his girl-friend?' Purcell said, from the passenger seat.

'It depends how badly he wanted to see the back of her.'

They stepped out into a late afternoon that was dying on its feet, getting colder by the minute.

Miller pressed the buzzer for Robb's door.

'Have you spoken to Gilmour about his temporary assignment?' Purcell asked.

'Not yet. I'm going round to see him tonight. We're having a beer.'

'Jimmy's a good guy. He just needs to rein it in a wee bit at times.'

'Agreed.'

'Hello?' The voice from the speaker came at them.

'Mr Robb, it's DI Miller and Superintendent Purcell. We need to have a few words again.'

'Right.'

Miller could have sworn he heard a muted *Fuck's sake* as Robb hung up the receiver, but couldn't be sure.

They were buzzed in.

The front door was open, but nobody was waiting for them, which would make any police officer nervous. Miller nudged the door with his foot. 'Doctor Robb?' he called, walking in slowly.

'Come in!' They heard a voice from farther in the apartment.

When they walked into the living room, Robb was pacing about as if he was nervous about something.

'We want to talk about the other women you've been sleeping with,' Purcell said.

'How dare you. I've never been so insulted—'

'Save it, Doc,' Miller said, 'we know all about the swinging parties.'

'I don't know what you're talking about,' Robb said, going over to a dresser and pouring himself a large whisky.

'Do you want us to show you the DVD that Gabriel Chase made. The one where you and Ashley Gates go through to a room?'

Robb took a sip of his drink, and then put the glass down. 'Oh, that. I told Gabe not to film the fucking thing, but, oh no, he wanted to shove it in his uncle's face. *Look what we were doing at your place when you were on holiday.* Stupid prick.'

'How many did he film?'

'One or two, I can't remember. We're usually gassed up by the time he gets the camcorder rolling.'

Robb sat on a chair with his whisky, cradling it as if it was a grenade. 'We weren't doing anything wrong,' he said, then looked at both detectives.

'Nobody says you were, doctor,' Miller said. 'Look at it from our perspective; one of your group has been murdered, and one, your girlfriend, is missing.' He didn't mention Michaela Savage or the fact that she was dead.

Purcell sat back. 'Do you think any of your group could be a killer?'

Robb looked at them. 'No. Absolutely not.'

'What about Monty Chase?' Miller asked.

'Old Monty? I don't think so.'

'Any idea why Monty would have photos of Cathy Graham in his house, almost identical to the one we found in Will Beam's office two years ago?'

'Who's Cathy Graham?'

'The woman who was murdered in Father Beam's church.'

'Oh, right. I have no idea at all.'

'What about Arthur King? Do you think he could have killed his wife?'

Robb looked at Miller. Laughed. 'Are you kidding? Arthur likes sleeping with women more than he likes breathing. He wouldn't do anything to ruin that.'

'Who was Gabriel Chase's partner when he filmed your session back in June?'

'Her? I don't know. I hadn't seen her before.'

'And since then?'

Robb shook his head. 'I don't know who she is.'

Purcell looked at him. 'It seems as if you all liked sex.'

'Don't you?'

'With my girlfriend. I don't need to sleep with the wives of my friends.'

'Then you don't understand the concept of swinging, my friend. Everybody likes to have that buzz in a relationship. Us more than others. We just spice things up a bit. It's a safe environment, and we all know each other.'

'So why would somebody want to kill the women in your group?'

'God knows. But just because two of them are dead doesn't meant to say there's a maniac on the loose.'

'Who said *two* of them are dead? Your girlfriend is just missing, isn't she?'

Robb sat up straight. 'That's what I meant. I don't have the answer.'

There was a group of students in the Philosopher when Watt and Angie Rivers entered. A few more afternoon drinkers keeping the place alive until the evening rush.

'Ever been in here before, Angie?' Watt asked.

'No.'

'Obviously, I know you're just down from Aberdeen, but I thought you might have been here before.'

'To be honest, I haven't spent much time in Edinburgh.'

'You'll soon get to know all the watering holes, especially after we get involved. Stabbings, beatings, you name it, one pub, or the other goes like a funfair at the weekends.'

'Same shit, different location.'

Watt walked up to the barman, and asked to speak to Patricia Wilkinson.

'She's not here.'

'Do you know where she is?'

'On her day off. We have different days off on rotation. Her being the manager, she's here most weekends.'

'Can you get me her details, son? We need to speak to her.'

'Sure.' He had a word with the young girl he was working with, and came back a few minutes later with a piece of paper. 'I knew her number, but I had to look up her address.'

Watt thanked him, and they left. Ten minutes later, they were down at The Shore, pulling up outside Patricia Wilkinson's flat.

The wind was sharp, coming off the North Sea. There was no answer from the buzzer. Watt pressed a few more. Finally, somebody answered, and they were let in. They took the lift to the top floor.

'No answer on the phone, and no reply at her house.' He knocked hard on her door, but still nothing.

'She's maybe away shopping,' Angie said.

'You're a woman. How many times do you leave the house without your phone? My daughters are always posting shite on Facebook, and doing some bloody thing called Snapchat, though God knows what the hell *that's* all about.'

'It's called the twenty-first century, Andy. And to answer your question, I never leave home without my phone or a spare condom.'

'What?'

'Just testing to see if you're paying attention.'

'I'm paying attention. I just think I smell gas, that's all.'

'Wha—'

Before she could finish her sentence, Watt had the door kicked in. It banged back against the wall. 'Get on your Airwave, Ange, and tell control we forced entry before somebody calls the cops.'

'The real cops, you mean.'

'Exactly.' They walked into the hall. 'Miss Wilkinson? Police. Come out if you're in here, please.'

'She's either shitting herself on the toilet, or she's hiding in the wardrobe after hearing us break in.'

'It's not breaking in, it's reasonable cause. You did go to Tullial-lan, didn't you?'

'Well, I think so, Mr Watt, sir,' she said, in a voice that was slow.

'You're definitely management material with a voice like that. Now just watch my back in case she's a nutcase, and she's not hiding in the wardrobe, but she's in the hall closet with an axe.'

'Devil takes the hindmost, eh?'

But there was nobody in the flat. It was empty. There was no sign of Patricia Wilkinson at all, except for one small thing, the Polaroid photo sitting on the gas fire.

THIRTY-SIX

Kim Smith pressed buttons on the coffee machine. 'You want one, Paddy?'

'Black, thanks, Kim.' Gibb sloped off to his office, and hung his jacket up as Kim came in with two cups. He took his and sat down.

'You okay, Paddy?'

'I'm fine.'

'You seem a bit despondent. Is it because Percy's here now?'

'No, not at all. Sit down for a minute.'

Kim sat opposite, and sipped at her own coffee. It was acceptable only because it was so cold outside. 'So what's up?'

'You know Andy met a woman in a club a few weeks ago? Well, I met somebody as well.'

'You didn't.'

'Jesus, don't say it like that. You make me feel like a perv.'

Kim laughed. 'Sorry. I'm listening.'

Gibb leaned forward on his desk, as the door was still open, though the incident room was half-empty. 'Well, we've been seeing each other for a couple of weeks now. I wasn't going to shout it about the office after the hard time I gave Watt, but she's really nice.'

'That's great, Paddy! I'm glad for you.'

'The thing is, she has her own business, but it's an online business and she's thinking of upping sticks and going to live in Spain in the new year. And she wants me to go with her.'

'After only two weeks?'

'God, Kim, I can't see enough of her. I see her every day. I can't believe how well we hit it off. She's spectacular. I know it's a rush, but I retire next month. Then after Christmas is over, we can go and live in the sun.'

'That's brilliant. I mean, if you want my advice, take it easy. Get to know her a bit better. Then you can decide if you want to make the move.'

He sat back. 'She would have a lot to wrap up here. So I have time to think about it.'

'You have doubts though.'

'I do. I mean, one of my daughters is married with two kids, one isn't married, and has one on the way. I'd miss the kids.'

Kim suddenly felt sorry for the man. 'I can't imagine what it would be like to leave kids or grandkids behind. I don't want to put you off though. It's your life, and you still have plenty of time left to enjoy yourself. It's a tough one. At the end of the day, you have to think what you'd be happiest doing.'

He drank some more coffee, and looked out of his window. 'Would I miss this cold weather? That's the real question.'

She smiled as she got up and went back to her own little office. Her main office as an investigator with the procurator fiscal was in the PF offices that were part of the Sheriff Court building in Chamber's Street, but she was more often here than there.

She sat down behind the little desk, careful not to spill her coffee on the file she had thrown down there. Flipping through it, she looked at the copies of the Polaroids of Cathy Graham. Swinging was not a thing she would be into at all, though she wasn't a prude. She didn't want to share Frank with anybody, and she was only his. She had old-fashioned values, not something her ex-husband had.

She thought about the murder of Cathy Graham. Ashley Gates had been murdered in the same way, yet they didn't know each other. So what was the connection? Their killer knew what it was. So far, Monty Chase was the only connection they could see, and he couldn't have killed Ashley.

She drank her coffee, and waited for Frank. Started wondering about whether he really did want to get married.

Miller had received a call when he and Purcell had been getting back into the car. It was control requesting they attend a locus in Leith, down on The Shore.

'Oh shit. Patricia Wilkinson's address.'

The rush hour traffic was already hotting up as Fifers headed for the Forth Road Bridge. Miller doubted the new one would help reduce the traffic flow, as the commuters still had to get out of the city centre.

When they reached The Shore, the forensics van was pulling up beside the patrol cars with their blazing blue lights. The section between Sandport Place and Commercial Street had been closed off. A uniform waved Miller through, and he parked behind the forensics van.

Andy Watt was waiting at the front door of the flat.

'What's up, Andy?'

'Same situation as before, but there's a slight difference this time. See for yourself.'

He and Purcell brushed past the suited forensics crew. DI Maggie Parks' second-in-command, DS Peter Fukuto, was in the living room.

'*Fuck you too* here says there's no sign of blood.'

The DS turned to Watt. 'It's pronounced Foo-koo-toe.'

'That's what I said.'

'Have you been introduced to Detective Superintendent

Purcell?' Miller asked.

'No, sir. Pleased to meet you, Superintendent.'

'So what have you got here?' Purcell asked.

'There's a photo on the gas fire. It shows a woman we believe to be Patricia Wilkinson, who was identified by Sergeant Watt. Inspector Parks gave a debriefing for my team in case we were called out, and she said at her crime scene, there was a lot of blood. There doesn't seem to be any here. Not even minuscule drops. If somebody cleans up, they always miss a little bit. I'm getting one of my team to spray with luminol just to be sure.'

'Get the uniforms knocking on doors, not just in here, but on other doors in the street. In those businesses down there, especially the pubs. See if anybody saw her in the last few days,' Miller said.

'So, she's one of their pervy group, and we think she might have been targeted, but why the change in MO? Usually these loose-screw merchants like to refine their killing,' Purcell said, bending to take a closer look at Patricia's dead-looking face staring back at him.

'We'll track her next of kin. Andy? Get back onto the bar staff where she works, and see if there's anything in her file.'

One of the forensics team came in with a case.

'That's the luminol now. We'll have to bag everything and need to have the room cleared.'

Everybody left the living room.

Back out on the street, Miller blew his breath into the cold afternoon air. Dusk was rapidly approaching, turning over the city to the night crawlers.

'You know this is something personal now, don't you, Percy?'

Purcell pulled up the collar on his jacket. 'There was never any doubt, but that would mean he's changed his MO. He took her away without leaving any evidence, and now he's killed Patricia, but he didn't cut her throat.'

'He's playing games. I've seen it before. I wouldn't be surprised if he sent us a fucking letter next, taunting us.'

Purcell was looking farther along the road, where Robert Molloy's floating restaurant was moored. The *Blue Martini*.

'Do you think Suzy is going to like being down here?'

'Hey, wherever this bad boy is, she'll love. Besides, her new position will see her in uniform.'

'She's going to miss being a detective.'

'Not as much as you'd think. She just likes being a police officer, and this is the next step up the ladder for her, and she'll go far. ACC one day, or even the big chief. You never know.'

'Good luck to her. Remember to tell her not to be a stranger. Kim and her little gang will welcome her into the fold no problem.'

'I appreciate that.'

They heard a shout from the stairway door, and walked over. It was Fukuto. 'There's no blood at all. Not in the bathroom, or anywhere else in the flat. I'm not a pathologist, but I've seen my fair share of dead people, and if I were to hazard a guess, I'd say she looks as if she was either strangled, or her neck was snapped. And there doesn't seem to be much bruising round the neck, so I'd put a ten spot on broken neck.'

'Thanks, Peter.'

They walked back to Miller's car. 'There's not much else we can do here until forensics process the flat. And anything they have, we won't get until tomorrow.'

'That's fine. You can drop me off at the hotel. I want to check that my dad has taken his meds.' *And I want to see my dog on Facetime.*

THIRTY-SEVEN

Miller had loaded the dishwasher while Kim did some homework with Emma, which consisted of doing something with crayons. Jack was out with Samantha at one of their favourite Italian restaurants

Kim's father, Neil McGovern, had spoken to him on the phone before dinner, reminding him that they shouldn't mention that Kate Murphy was living a new life under a new name. Miller had said he knew how to handle Gilmour, but the truth was Jimmy was more prone to outbursts since his divorce. Miller reckoned the sergeant was taking it hard, and that his life needed to get back on an even keel.

'I've left her watching cartoons since her homework's done,' Kim said, coming back into the living room and sitting beside him on the couch.

'She's a wee doll. I'm lucky to have her in my life.'

'You're so sweet, Miller.'

'I know. And smart. And a terrific lover.'

'Well, two out of three ain't bad.' She laughed, and poked him in the ribs.

He grunted, and pulled away from her.

She laughed again, and took the remote control.

'Just remember, there's not a gold band on your finger,' Miller said.

'What are you trying to say?'

He stood up, and laughed. 'Just that I might have to wear a pair of socks in bed tonight, in case I get...?' He looked at her with raised eyebrows.

'If you say *cold feet*, Miller, I swear—'

The buzzer rang from street level. 'Sorry. Got to go. That'll be your dad.' He laughed again. 'I won't be long.'

'This isn't over,' she said, standing up. She walked over, and put her arms round his neck. 'I love you.'

'I maybe love you too.'

'Oh, get out of here,' she said.

Kate Murphy fussed with her hair, wanting it to be just right for Jimmy. She felt like a schoolgirl going out on a first date. What's wrong with you? she thought, as she looked in the mirror again. He was only coming round for a few drinks after he'd met with Frank Miller.

It had been a long time since she had made an effort for a man. *For Brian Crane, you mean.* Yes, him.

Crane had been good fun, always ready for a laugh. He had been tough, but with her, he had been gentle. Now he was going to prison, where his chances of staying in one piece were slim.

She felt a pang of sadness now that he wasn't in her life, but considering what he'd been doing, maybe that was a good thing. Still, she remembered the last secret night they'd had together before Neil McGovern whisked her away.

Then her phone rang.

'Hello?'

'Kate. Good evening.'

Jared Flucker. 'What do you want, Flucker?'

198

'After all we've been through together, Kate, you can call me Jared. It would be nice to be on first name terms, don't you think?'

'Not really. I don't know who gave you this number, but you need to go away.'

'I'd like for you and me to get together. Maybe have a coffee. Sit and chat for a little while.'

'After you killed my mother, you want to sit and talk to me? I don't think so.'

'All I'm asking you is to think about it. Then you'll find out the truth. I always said I was innocent, didn't I? And now they've freed me because they know it's the truth. You will too.'

'I don't think so.'

'I have to say, you must get an impressive view of Arthur's Seat from your living room window. I'm sure I would like it too.'

Kate hung up as if the receiver had just stung her, and peeked out between the curtains, wondering if Flucker was standing in the street below, looking up at her window. But there was nobody there. She wished Jimmy would hurry up and get here. Until he did, she called Neil McGovern.

'It's Kate, Neil.'

'Has he called again?'

'Yes. He wants to meet for a coffee.'

'Don't accept his offer under any circumstances.'

'I won't.' She took a deep breath, in through the nose, out through the mouth. 'It's just that, he doesn't seem to be acting like a serial killer would.'

'How would you expect a serial killer to act, Kate?'

Even now, hearing him call her Kate instead of her real name, Arlene, sounded strange. 'I don't know, Neil. I dealt with people who did horrible things to other people down in London, and even up here, but when it comes to Jared Flucker, I don't know what to think. I can't seem to get my thoughts straight.'

'Don't worry. Just because I put you into witness protection, doesn't mean to say my job ended there. I've always got your back, Kate.'

'Thank you.'

'Even Frank and my daughter are only a few minutes away. However, if things get too bad, I can have you put in our safe house in Juniper Green.'

'No, I don't want that. Once again, that would mean he's won. I won't let the bastard win. I just wanted to talk with you as you said to call you if anything happened.'

'You did the right thing. Are you going out tonight?'

'No. My friend is coming round.'

'Just be careful who you open the door to.'

'I will. Goodnight, Neil.'

She hung up, and had one more quick look out through the curtains. There was nobody creeping about in the darkness.

The Range Rover was waiting downstairs for Miller when he left his building. Rush hour was over, and the buses that sailed by on the North Bridge were half empty. People trudged by, huddled in their coats like turtles.

The big, black car had heated rear seats and Neil McGovern was sitting in the back, waiting for him.

'I'm a bit late, Frank. I had an interesting call from Kate Murphy.'

'Nothing that would make Norma cut it off, I hope.'

'Just the thought of that brings tears to my eyes, me old cock. No pun intended.' He smiled, and faced forward. 'Whenever you're ready,' he said to the driver.

The car swung round in a U-turn when there was a break in the traffic.

'How's my granddaughter?'

'Let me tell you, Neil, she is six going on thirty at times. I couldn't love her more.'

'Glad to hear it, Frank. I have to say, I wasn't best pleased when my Kim came to me and told me that Eric had been sleeping around on her. I almost had him dropped into Kabul. Without a parachute. But Kim begged me not to do anything to him. He's Emma's father after all, but as far as I'm concerned, you're a better father than he's ever been.'

'That means a lot.'

'Don't get too excited, me old chum. The same goes for you; you make my Kim cry, you make me cry.' He smiled at Miller in the darkness of the car. 'And believe me, no man wants to make me cry.'

Despite the heated seat, a chill ran down Miller's spine. He'd been threatened before, but there was something very real about this man.

'I always carry a packet of paper hankies, just in case.'

McGovern laughed. 'That's it; show face to the future father-in-law. You've got a pair, I'll say that, my friend. Unlike this little twat we're going to see.'

The car headed down High Street, then hung a right down St Mary's Street.

'Jimmy's alright,' Miller said.

'And your loyalty to your team is admirable, Frank, but let me put it to you this way; there's no way in hell he'd be marrying my Kim.'

'Kabul, right?'

'Damn straight. I mean, don't get me wrong, he's a nice enough lad, but there's something about him that I can't quite get to grips with.'

'You had him checked out, didn't you?'

Into Holyrood Road now. 'Of course I did. Right back to when he left high school and joined the army.'

'He's a good member of the team, Neil.'

'I'm not doubting that,' he replied, as the car turned into the Dumbiedykes estate before pulling into the side of the road. 'Keep the engine running, we won't be long.'

'Yes, sir,' the driver said.

They stepped out into the cold. The estate was well lit, but it still seemed like a different world.

In Miller's experience, you could always tell what a place was like by the state of the cars parked outside the houses. Here, there were a lot of yesteryear models. Old vans with rusted wings, and probably only half an exhaust system.

'Jimmy Gilmour lived near Trinity, and he threw it all away for what?' McGovern said, as they walked up the stairs to Gilmour's stair entry door. 'A piece of skirt. Jesus, she must have been good, that's all I'm saying.'

'It happens to the best of us,' Miller said, as he opened the stair door and they climbed to the second floor. The stairway smelled of piss, and their footsteps echoed on the concrete steps.

'And now she's split with him.' McGovern stopped outside Gilmour's door, and lowered his voice. 'She wasn't worth it after all.' He knocked on the door, and it was answered a few minutes later.

'Come in,' Jimmy said, stepping back and looking surprised that McGovern was there.

They walked through to the living room where a drink was offered but refused as they sat down.

'So to what do I owe the pleasure?' Gilmour said, taking a drink from his own glass of whisky.

'It's about Kate,' Miller said.

'Kate who?'

McGovern laughed, but there was no humour in his voice. 'Is this how it's going to be, Jimmy? You denying you're going out with Kate Murphy?'

Gilmour looked down for a moment then straight at McGovern. 'Look, we're keeping this to ourselves for the moment. I've just split with my girlfriend, and I didn't want to antagonise her before she left. Why? I don't think it's anybody's business who I'm seeing outside the force. If I was shacking up with another officer, then fine, I would disclose it. But I'm not, so I don't see the problem.'

Miller sensed the change come over McGovern, and wanted to

step in before any threats were thrown about. 'Nobody's saying you can't do what you like with your life, Jimmy, but Kate is a close friend of Neil's. They were friends in London before she came up here. He doesn't want to see her hurt.'

'I'm not going to hurt her.'

'Listen, my friend,' McGovern said, leaning forward, 'I know you were in the army, and you're probably a good fighter, but that doesn't worry me. Men I work with are more than capable of dealing with you. So here's the thing – you're going to treat her like a lady, or you'll have a choice to make; you either get stationed in Shetland, or you go and work somewhere else, without any pension or benefits.'

There was a flash of anger in Gilmour's eyes. 'You come into my home and start threatening me? Who do you think you are? I like Kate a lot, and I have no desire to mess her about.'

'So you'd finished with Lauren before you started seeing Kate?'

'That's none of your business.' Gilmour jumped up, spilling his drink as he dropped his glass onto the carpet. 'You need to get out.'

McGovern stayed where he was, and looked at Gilmour. 'Sit down.'

Gilmour remained standing.

'Now, sergeant.'

Gilmour took a deep breath and sat back down.

'You said you were keeping a low profile about your relationship, Jimmy,' Miller said, 'but could you have told anybody inadvertently about it?'

'No. Nobody. Why?'

'As Frank said, Kate and I used to be friends. We worked on several cases together. I don't want to see her hurt.'

'Are you sure you didn't tell Lauren about Kate?' Miller said.

'I'm sure, Frank.' There was still anger in his voice.

'It's just that she visited Kate at the mortuary and made a threat against her. She knows all about the two of you.'

'I know. Kate told me this afternoon.' Gilmour's tone changed in an instant.

'Needless to say, Kate was shaken up.'

'Has she finished with me? Is that why you two are here?'

'No, nothing like that, but she doesn't have many friends here in the city. She's worried, that's all.'

'That fucking cow. I'm glad she's fucked off with her new boyfriend. Whoever the hell he is.'

McGovern nodded to Miller, and they stood up. Put their coats back on. 'She thinks a lot of you,' McGovern said. 'Just treat her nicely. Think of me as her uncle Neil. You don't want to upset Uncle Neil, son. Or the next time somebody has a conversation with you, it won't be over tea and biscuits.'

Oh there it is. Miller couldn't look at Gilmour as McGovern issued his *not-quite-so-veiled* threat. 'I'll see you around, Jimmy,' he said, following McGovern out to the stairs. Gilmour closed his front door softly behind them.

'Jesus, Neil. Threatening him?'

'I'm not fucking about, Frank. I don't care if he's a copper or not. Even if he quits the force and decides to hang around, I can still have him removed from Edinburgh altogether. Her Majesty has some nice little hotel rooms in England. And if that doesn't work, well, you join the dots.'

Miller noticed the man wasn't smiling. 'I don't think Jimmy will give you any grief.'

Finally, McGovern smiled as they left the relative warmth of the stair into the cold. 'He doesn't know she's in the programme, but I still have her under my wing. If I don't want him going out with her, then trust me, he'll leave her alone.' They climbed back into the Range Rover.

'Do you think he knows about her being a witness? That somehow Lauren found out and tipped off Flucker?'

They got into the warmth of the car and belted up as it drove off. 'No, I don't think he does know. Which means he couldn't have told Lauren.' He looked at Miller in the darkness of the car. 'You know, with the proper training, he could join my team.'

'Hey, we're already a man down with Bruce Hagan being off.'

'I thought you had a new team member?'

'We do. But until she gets used to our ways down here, she's still in training.'

'Same job, different location. How hard can it be?'

Miller thought about Angie Rivers shouting at Stanley Gates. 'Hard enough.'

THIRTY-EIGHT

Martin's restaurant was in Rose Street Lane, tucked round the corner from Rose Street itself. It had become one of Samantha's favourite restaurants since she split from her ex-husband, Ralph. A place where they had never dined together.

At first glance, a passer-by wouldn't see the restaurant; the street was basically an alley behind the buildings that fronted Rose Street, but the business was an oasis for people wanting to eat in a classy environment, off the beaten track.

Jack parked the Audi across from the entrance, and came round to open the passenger door for Samantha, grinning at her.

'Steak again tonight, darling?' she said.

'Of course. Am I becoming that predictable?'

'Of course you are. I can set my watch by how long it takes for you to make love to me.'

'You jest, woman. Wars have been fought in shorter time.'

She laughed as he closed the door, and they made their way into the stylish establishment. It was a different maître d'.

'Pierre not here tonight?' Jack said, as their coats were taken.

'No, sir. Pierre doesn't work here anymore.'

'Really? He seemed happy here.'

'We're under new management, sir.' The man smiled at him. 'The food is just as good, if not better. Please, allow me to show you to your table.'

The dining room was through a door from the little vestibule, and the place was almost full. There was an elevated part to the restaurant at the back, and Jack knew there was a private room there. He saw somebody go through the curtains that concealed the room.

They were seated at a table, and their drinks order was taken while they looked at the menu.

'Oh, I wonder if I'll have the steak for a change?'

'Have what you want. I'm picking up the cheque tonight,' Samantha said.

'Indeed you're not. I might just be on a copper's pension, but I can afford to treat a lady right. Besides, I've done a few jobs for Neil McGovern lately, and he pays handsomely. Just a few babysitting jobs and the like. He doesn't want them called security jobs, but that's what they are. So no, my love, this is on me.'

She reached over and put a hand on his. 'You know, I know some female authors who're married to men who can't handle the fact they have a wife who earns more than they do. Even though we're not married, I'm glad you're not one of those guys.'

Jack still loved hearing Samantha's American accent, though she said she never noticed his now.

'You're always buying us lunch when we're out, so it balances out at the end of the day.'

Their waiter came over with their drinks, and another came over with a bottle of champagne and two glasses.

'I didn't order champagne,' Jack said. Then he looked at Samantha. 'Unless you want...?'

'We didn't order it,' she said.

'Compliments of the new owner, sir, madam,' he said, putting the bottle and glasses on the table.

Jack looked round and saw the curtain to the back room had been opened and tied back. Robert Molloy was sitting smiling at Jack, raising a glass to him. Molloy was what Jack would have referred to as a gangster, but the man himself said he was merely a businessman.

'Excuse me, honey,' Jack said, as the waiter poured the champagne. He walked up the stairs and into the back room.

'Jack! Come and have a glass with me,' Molloy said.

'Don't tell me you own this place now.'

'I thought it was about time I branched out into the restaurant business. Sit down, you're making the place look untidy.'

Despite himself, Jack sat down. A waiter rushed over, and poured a fresh glass of the bubbly for Jack.

'So you bought our favourite restaurant? Things will never be the same again.'

'Of course they won't. You have a special price in my establishment.' He lifted his glass again, and smiled, as Samantha looked round at the two of them.

'When did you buy this place? I didn't even know it was for sale.'

'It wasn't, but I made the previous owner a very generous offer.'

'Sell up, or you'll be wearing concrete wellies?'

'That's crude, Jack.' He drank some more champagne. 'I won't keep you long. It would be rude to keep the lady waiting. I would invite you to join me, but I'm expecting company. I have a new woman in my life, just like you, Jack. Maybe we could do a foursome one night.'

'I don't think so, Molloy.' Jack drained his champagne.

'Think about it. We could have a good laugh.'

'I could keep you on your toes after talking with Frank, you mean.'

'Jack, you don't have to be so sceptical. You're not a copper anymore.'

'Thanks for the drink.'

Molloy smiled. 'I've been keeping an eye on the news. Watching the story about Monty Chase. Old bugger.'

'So have a lot of people.'

'He was a friend of mine, Jack. Yes, I know you find that hard to believe, a man with my reputation being friends with a judge, but it's true. A group of us get together to smoke our fancy cigars, drink the finest brandy, port, champagne, you name it. Play a little poker. Shoot the breeze. Have a little fun. So I hear things. And I hear that your son found some photos in Monty's place.'

'I can't comment on that.'

'Come on, Jack. You know me better than that. I know you're above reproach. No, I was just upset to read about Monty's passing. Since he was one of our group.'

'So you play poker upstairs with your cronies.'

'I didn't say I played up there.'

'You didn't have to. This wasn't always a private room. And that door over there leads to a back corridor. One way to the storeroom, the other way to the manager's flat above here. I was there with Pierre one night. Me and a few of the boys. So what better place to have your pals round than in a flat above a restaurant that's tucked away in a little lane? No surveillance would be able to sit close by without being spotted.'

'You're being a little paranoid, Jack.'

'No I'm not. And that little private hire company you bought? Now there's a little satellite office in the pedestrian plaza round the other side from here. So there's always one or two of your cars sitting about. An early warning system, I would call it. That's how you knew I was in here without you even having to open that curtain.'

'I bow to your superiority, my friend.'

'I used to be a bloody good detective, Molloy.'

'I'm not arguing with that. However, now that you're here, I just wanted to ask, after finding the pictures, whether there was anything suspicious about that.'

'If you mean, do I think he killed Cathy Graham, no, I don't.'

'I know Gabriel is his nephew. He's a right little tosser. But I don't think he's got it in him to kill a woman. However, a couple of years ago, Monty wasn't his usual self. After our game of poker, I asked him if everything was alright. He said no, he was concerned.'

'About what?' Jack poured himself some more champagne. 'Don't worry, Samantha's driving us home.'

'Anyway, Monty said he was worried about a young man his cleaner was dating. Her name was Janet, if I remember correctly, and Monty wasn't happy at all. Apparently, Janet liked this guy a lot, but there was something shifty about him.'

'Did he tell you the boyfriend's name?'

'No. But if Frank finds out then that might point him in the right direction.'

'Okay. I'll pass that on to him.'

'Tell Frank he can come here anytime.'

Jack stood up. 'I think my son's started being a vegetarian. Thanks for the tip.' He strolled back to their table, and by the time he got there and turned round, the curtain had been put back in place, as if the show was over.

'What was all that about?' Samantha asked.

'That's just somebody I used to know.'

The waiter came over and took their order.

'I enjoyed being a part of your family the other night. Tony seems like such a nice guy.'

'He is. I don't think Frank remembers him so much as they were both only teenagers when Tony's family died.'

'I thought it was just his dad who died?'

Jack suddenly looked sad. 'No. A year after Archie died, Tony went on a weekend trip with the Boy Scouts. He came back on the Sunday, and his mother and sister weren't home. They'd been planning a girls' weekend of their own at the granny's house. So Tony called his granny's neighbour, the one who looked in on the old woman. She had a key so she let herself in. She found them all dead in their beds.'

'Good God. What happened?'

'It was a faulty boiler. It hadn't been serviced for a while, and they all died of carbon monoxide poisoning. Tony was devastated. He was only around sixteen at the time. Lost his whole family in the space of a year.'

'That's terrible. But look how he turned out.'

'I know. He would have been a credit to the force.'

'It's a wonder he didn't follow in his father's footsteps.'

'He's happy with what he's doing.'

'Not everybody's cut out for being a cop.' She reached over with her glass. 'Now be a gentleman and pour me a glass of Robert Molloy's champagne.'

'How did...?'

'I'm a crime writer, Jack. I know people.'

He couldn't argue with that.

THIRTY-NINE

Jared Flucker looked in the mirror, and smiled. His teeth weren't bad, just needing a bit of attention. Never mind, his lawyer said the money they'd get in a settlement would be more than enough to get him veneers.

His hair had been cut by a hairdresser who charged more money than he usually earned in a week, but it was worth it, as was the black hair dye, followed by some styling gel. He was looking good. His daily fitness regime had helped him lose a few pounds as well. Cutting out sugar, watching the calories, and exercising. That was the key.

He'd started working out in prison. He'd thought that was all a load of clichéd bollocks created by TV writers, but he'd soon learned it wasn't so. If you didn't want your head rammed down a toilet while some sod made like it was your wedding night, you worked out and learned how to fight.

Flucker had learned pretty fast. He'd been put on a special wing reserved for kiddie fiddlers, and men like him who'd killed old women. Except he hadn't killed an old woman. Try telling those bastards that, though. They didn't want to know. If it was in *The Sun*, it was gospel. He'd been there only one day when one of those wankers had lamped him one in the showers. And that was from a guy who had "married" a thirteen-year-old. He'd been warned about him, but no matter how vigilant you were, all it took was you letting down your guard for a second.

The nutter had punched him in the face and given him a black eye. Luckily, there was another guy there who hated this pervert more than he hated Flucker, and he'd dealt with him.

Flucker had started working out hard after that. The next time Mr Pervy Bastard had tried it on, Flucker had broken his nose and kicked him in the balls. Then he'd leaned down and whispered to him, 'If you ever come near me again, I'll cut your fucking dick off with a toothbrush.' Of course, the cleaning implement would have to be sharpened, but that wasn't a problem when you had time to kill.

Now, he had six-pack abs and looked much better than he had ever looked in his life. And it was all thanks to prison. He knew Kate wouldn't be impressed by his new look, but that wasn't the point.

He didn't want to talk to her about his new and improved self.

He had something far more important to say.

Kate cleared away the pizza box, and sat down on the couch as Gilmour brought in two beers from the kitchen.

'Cheers, m'dear,' he said, after he'd taken off the caps. They clinked bottles.

'I can't have too many. I have work tomorrow. You do too, and you're playing with guns.'

'Hey, at least your customers are already dead.'

'And yours will be too if you get hammered.'

'Just the one.' He put his bottle down on the coffee table in front of them.

'Isn't this the bit in the movies when the guy sneaks his arm around the woman's shoulders and slides in closer?'

'Not in *The Shining* it isn't.'

'You romantic fool.' She pulled him in closer and kissed him, running her fingers through his hair before coming up for air. Then Kate moved away from him slightly.

'Look, Jimmy, I hope I haven't given you the impression that I'm easy or anything. It's just that when I slept with you, it had been a long time since I'd been with a man.'

Gilmour held up his hands. 'Relax, Kate. I didn't think any such thing. I'm not here just to get you into bed. This sounds corny as hell, but I respect you.'

'Just hold me for a little bit, Jimmy.'

He put both his arms around her, and held her tight. They sat that way for a while, listening to the background music that was playing. Lighthouse Family. *Sun in the Night.*

Outside, the man stood looking up at the light behind the curtains, imagining what the woman was doing. He'd watched the man go in earlier. What to do?

He'd wait. There was plenty of time. He was in no rush now.

He turned away and started walking up Holyrood Road, hands in pockets, head down.

Just another soul wandering the dark streets.

FORTY

There was a morning briefing scheduled for eight thirty but Percy Purcell was up early anyway. He had called his father's house on his iPad, and Lou had been the one to answer when he had expected Suzy.

'You know I'm starting to hate this fucking machine?' Lou said.

'Dad. Where's your teeth? I've not even had my breakfast yet.'

'What? Was the room service late with your French cakes and caviar?'

'Get a grip of yourself. You know I don't eat cakes. And the caviar was off. Tasted fishy.'

'It is fish.'

'I know. I was being facetious. But where's Bear?' He took a sip of his coffee as the big German Shepherd bounded up on the couch as if on cue. 'There's my boy! You didn't pee in the house again, did you?'

Lou got up and left.

The dog chuffed and ran away, and Purcell could hear a commotion in the background, followed by voices.

Lou came back, dentures in place. 'I never have my teeth in

before seven o'clock. I'm going to skelp your bloody arse when you get back for waking me up. Oh, wait. I forgot. You're not coming back.'

'Don't get all maudlin on me now.'

Lou smiled. 'You wish. I've already rented out your room.'

'Well, I hope he's in a mariachi band, you old sod.'

'She. It's a young woman, and we hit it off. In fact, we started dating.'

'Away and don't talk pish. You must have been eating cheese close to bedtime again and had one of your hard-on dreams.'

'Hey, enough of that talk. There's a lassie in the next room getting the kettle on. More than you used to bloody well do. You and that poncy coffee maker.'

'I'm sure Keurig won't be using that in the new adverts.'

'Well, they should. It's just for ponces like you.'

'How's the place without me? Missing me, old man?'

'Like I'd miss a dose of... oh, thanks, hen. I'll make it tonight. I don't want you running after me all the time.'

'That's okay, Lou,' Suzy said, out of view.

Lou took a sip from the cup.

'I could have got that for him,' another female voice said.

'That's okay. You want one too?' he heard Suzy say.

'Thanks, love. You're a sweetheart.'

After the volume of the voices diminished, Purcell shook his head at his father. 'Tell me you've hired a new cleaner, and this is her early shift.'

'If that's how you want to deal with it.'

'Is that you praying to the little blue God now? Up all night.'

'Listen, son, when you get to my time of life, you just have to grab it by the horns. Elizabeth and I had a good time last night, and she decided to stay over. She and Suzy get on like a house on fire.'

'So you're saying Elizabeth woke up to find old age creeping up on her.'

'You're a dirty wee sod. Yes, we spent the night together, but

216

nothing happened.' More coffee. 'Anyway, why am I explaining to you?'

Bear came back into view with a rubber chicken and waited for Lou to take it.

'God, it's too early for this. You've got the whole bloody house up now, and he'll be going off his head until I take him out. Wait 'til you're having a lie in at the weekend. We'll see how you appreciate being woken up at three o'clock in the morning.'

'Three o'clock? Why were you up at that time?'

'At my age, that's what time my bladder gets me up.'

'Jesus, that's the last thing I need to know about. See, if I had you in an interview room right now, I'd be asking the uniform to leave so I could give you a slap.'

'Away. You couldn't slap a wet fish.' Lou stood up. 'Just you wait. Three o'clock Saturday morning. I'll tell the front desk in your hotel that it's an emergency.'

'I'll tell them to ignore you. That you're in an asylum. Which might be true by the time I get home to pick up my stuff.'

'And what if I've dropped down dead and you ignored the call? You'd feel bad.'

'No, I wouldn't. I would be on the Breitling website picking out my new watch. Spending my inheritance.'

'I've got news for you; I'm spending it for you.'

'What on? Tits 'n' beer?'

'I'm cutting you out of the will. I'm leaving my millions to Bear.'

'He'll share with his dad.'

'He won't even piss on your leg by the time he's tasted the high life. Right, I'm away. Mind and behave yourself.'

'As always. And I'm a big boy now, Lou.'

'Of course you are. Did you iron your own shirt this morning?'

'Listen, I would have if that wasn't a service the hotel offered. I'm too busy to be bothered with that stuff.'

'Sexist pig. I'll put Suzy straight before she moves down there.'

'Are you going to iron *your* shirt this morning?'

'I'll be too exhausted later to do that. I'm going to wash down Mr Blue with my morning coffee.'

'Christ, there's just some things you can't un-imagine. Go away, you manky old sod.'

Lou laughed, and the dog followed him to wherever he was going. Suzy sat down. 'I was up anyway, Percy. Just out the shower.'

'I like this dirty talk. Get to the good bits.'

'Well, I got dressed after that, and then had just put the kettle on when your Facetime rang.'

'You've never worked vice, have you? We're going to have to practise this a bit more.'

'Next time I'll be Slutty Suzy, just for you.'

'That's my girl.'

They both laughed. 'So how's the enquiry going?'

'We've hit a dead end, Percy. Nobody saw anything. She worked up here, but there's no record of her ever being threatened. No assaults, nothing. Michaela Savage led an unremarkable life. Except for one thing.'

'What's that?'

'Somebody had a restraining order taken out against her. In Edinburgh.'

'Who?'

'A man called Mitchell Robb. He's a surgeon.'

'I know. I interviewed him.'

'In connection with Michaela?'

'No. His girlfriend. She's disappeared. And now it's starting to ring even more alarm bells. Why was the order issued?'

'She was stalking him. She was obsessed with him. He said she was like a she-devil. Then Michaela lost it, and told him she was going to break his face. Quite a temper on her, apparently.'

'And the court order was issued by?' Purcell had a feeling he knew the answer.

'Montague Chase. Robb had his lawyer deal with it. A man called Arthur King.'

'They all closed ranks. Sounds like Michaela had them running scared.'

'Do you think one of them killed her?'

'I don't know, but it's not a coincidence that two women from their little swinging group are dead, and one is missing, presumed dead.'

'Was the Patricia Wilkinson crime scene like the others?'

'That's the strange thing, Suze; this was different. It didn't look like a crime scene at all, except for the Polaroid that was left on the gas fire, showing her dead. We're going to have a forensic photographer look at it again, see what he makes of it.'

'I'll let you know if anything else develops here. If you'll pardon the pun. How's the flat hunting going?'

'I'll get onto it today.'

'I guessed you'd be busy, so I've already made phone calls.' She was smiling when she disconnected.

FORTY-ONE

Miller awake earlier than Purcell. Emma getting ready for school dictated what time they got up. Kim liked to take her daughter down the road to her primary school whenever she could, but when she couldn't, there were always others ready to help out. Samantha Willis for a start.

Today was normal though, and Kim was able to do it herself.

'Where you off to so early?' she asked Miller, as he handed her a cup of coffee. 'Your other girlfriend got a day off?'

'No, she's working the back shift, so I'll be able to fit in a quickie before work.'

'A quickie's the norm for you, Miller. And I'm not the jealous type, but—'

'I know, I know, you'd rearrange bits of my anatomy.'

'You learn quickly.'

'You've told me often enough.'

She laughed. Then gave him a kiss. 'Did you ever worry that Carol might cheat on you?'

Miller drank some of his coffee, and had a sudden ice-cold feeling inside. He thought about his dead wife now and again, usually good memories, but now Kim bringing this up made him feel cold inside.

'No. Not one time. We sat down before we got married and I told her, all I ask is you don't mess me about. If you don't love me anymore, just tell me, and let's move on. Don't go behind my back and lie to me.'

Kim put her coffee mug down, and put her arms around him. 'God, I didn't want that to be a heavy question. It was more out of curiosity. I wasn't suggesting for one minute that Carol would have cheated on you.'

'I know. But I will say the same thing to you too. Just don't lie to me. If you want to go, go.'

'Listen, Frank, I just want a stable relationship, a man I love to come home to. I don't need outside excitement.'

'Maybe we'll sit down when the time comes, just you and me, away from everybody else, before we get married, and have a time where we can get things off our chest.'

'Or we could just learn as we go along, Frank. Live the dream, but get to know things about ourselves as we grow old together.'

'Or we could do that.' He kissed her. 'I have to go. I want to talk to the officers who've been sitting outside Dan Herdan's house all night.'

She pulled away from him. 'You think he's involved in all of this?'

'I'm not ruling him out. He was closely involved with those dead women.'

'You think one of them is the killer?'

'I think it's a possibility. They're the ones with the motive.'

'Okay. I'll see you in the office later.'

Miller called, and asked Andy Watt to meet him at his car round in Cockburn Street.

'Taking a sicky from work? Sounds good to me, boss,' Watt said, getting in and putting the seat heaters on.

'If I was, I think I would spend it with different company, Andy.'

'So you'd have a bit of skirt in here instead?'

'I don't think *bit of skirt* is the right thing to say these days.'

'What is though?' He pulled a sandwich from his pocket as Miller drove into Waverley Bridge.

'Don't be dropping crumbs in here.'

'It's a chicken sandwich made from Warburton's bread. It's soft. It doesn't fall apart.' He took a bite, and wiped the crumbs from his lap onto the floor then looked at Miller. 'What? You've got mats, haven't you?'

'So, how's this thing with your girlfriend?' he asked, as they headed out to the west of the city towards Carrick Knowe, going against the traffic flow.

'It's going great.'

'What's her business again?'

'She has a flower shop in Bruntsfield. And she lives round the corner from there, too.'

'And she still likes a man in uniform. So to speak.'

'I don't eat like a pig when I'm out with her.'

'Only in my car.'

'Correct.' He wiped his fingers, and looked around for somewhere to drop his trash.

'Don't even think about it.'

They pulled in behind the unmarked car in Carrick Knowe Drive. The houses were four in a block, with an upper and a lower house on each side.

'Want to bet they'll be sleeping?' Watt said, getting out of the car into the cold. Wet leaves were still banked up against the kerb. As Miller locked the Audi, Watt knocked on the passenger window of the unmarked vehicle. 'Wakey, wakey.'

The window rolled down, and a young DS looked back at him. 'Tell me you've brought the coffees and bacon rolls?'

'Away, man. I've already had mine and I couldn't look at another one.'

Miller joined them. Looked across at Herdan's house, and the front garden that had been totally paved over to make it into a parking space. His old Mercedes was there, but there was no sign of the taxi.

'Has he come in and left again?' he asked, as he bent down and leaned in to talk to the driver.

'No, sir. There's been no sign of him. At six, I contacted the taxi firm's control room, but they said he hadn't logged on. Which could mean he was operating as a street taxi, and not accepting radio jobs. But that doesn't make sense they said. First of all, it's not allowed by the company, and secondly, he would have probably got more jobs from the radio.'

'So where the hell is he, I wonder?' Frank stood up, and looked at Watt. 'Maybe we should knock on a few doors.'

'Why don't we just boot his door in?'

'As much as I'd love to, we have no reason to force entry.'

'I was talking hypothetically.'

'No, you weren't.'

'I'll start with the one upstairs from him.' He walked over the road as Miller told the other two officers to start knocking on doors.

Miller got a hit on the second try. An old man answered.

'Sorry to disturb you, but I was wondering if I could ask you a few questions.' Miller said, showing his warrant card.

'It wasn't me. It was his idea.' He pointed at Watt. 'He made me do it. I didn't want to, but he said we would make a fortune.'

Miller looked at Watt before looking back at the man. He felt sorry for him. 'Thanks for your time, sir.'

'Who is it, Dad?' they heard a female voice ask behind the old man. Then a woman appeared, gently guiding the man to one side. 'I've told you not to answer the door'

She was a woman who would be more attractive had she chosen to take more care of herself, but as it was, she had a shabby dress on and her hair was unkempt.

'Have you seen Mr Herdan this morning?'

'If you come in for a cup of tea, I'll tell you anything you want to know.'

'Make mine black,' Watt said, barging past the old man. Miller followed him in as the woman closed the door and led them through to the living room.

The woman busied herself in the kitchen, the morning radio playing softly beside her. The old man tapped his fingers along one arm of his old armchair, not wanting to do it too hard in case the stuffing came out. There was a rent in the material, partly hidden by a cloth that hung awkwardly over the end.

The woman came back into the room carrying a tray of cups and a teapot. Miller noticed there were only three cups.

'Where's mine?' the old man asked, suddenly sitting up.

'You've had one. You'll get another one in a little while.'

'She hits me, you know.'

'Dad, for God's sake.' She looked at Miller, her face turning red. 'He's got the onset of dementia. He doesn't know what he's saying half the time. I swear to Christ he'll have me in prison by the time they screw the bloody lid down.'

She poured the teas, and added milk for herself before sitting down on the other chair. Watt drank some of his, and balanced his notebook on his knee.

'I'm Clarissa Dixon, by the way,' she said, pre-empting Watt's first question. 'My father and I have lived next to Dan Herdan for a long time. My mother died when I was a teenager.' She gave her father a look as if thinking the wrong one was taken first.

Miller took a sip of the tea, which was remarkably good. Clarissa probably got a lot of practise. 'Can you tell me what Mr Herdan was like as a neighbour?'

'Oh, he's such a nice man,' Clarissa said, her eyes going somewhere distant. A beach maybe, where Dan Herdan was taking off his clothes in preparation for a lovemaking session.

'Did you ever see anybody coming and going into his house?' Watt said, bringing her back to the here and now.

Her mood changed. 'Just those tarts he seemed fond of. Always giggling and squealing as if he was nipping their arse or something. And those dresses! You could almost see next week's washing.'

'So there were quite a few?' Miller said.

'Oh, yes. I could have been one of them. He asked me out for a drink one night, but old pissy pants there threw a fit. Then he feigned a heart attack, and I cancelled. Dan never asked me out again.'

'Hey, I can hear you,' her dad said.

Miller looked at the top of the gas fire, and imagined a Polaroid photo of Clarissa Dixon sitting there. Maybe she had dodged a bullet.

'Well,' she continued, still on her tirade. 'Bloody old moan.'

'You can always get help with him,' Watt said.

'Again, I'm in the same room,' the old man chirped.

'When did you last see Herdan?' Miller said, anxious to get away from this woman who was obviously about to lose her patience. He'd make sure to call social services and have somebody come round to check on her.

'Can I have a cup of tea?' the old man asked.

'No, you can't. It makes you pee.'

'I saw him,' her father said, grinning.

'When was this?'

The smile fell away. 'Well, my bladder isn't what it used to be, young man, and I'll thank you to respect that fact. Cheeky young bugger. I can't help having to get up for a pee in the middle of the night.'

'That's if he can bothered to get up,' Clarissa said. 'Sometimes he just lets go. Pssshhh.' She used her hands to indicate that the whole bed was covered.

'So you saw him in the night?'

'Let me think.' More tapping the chair. 'It was a couple of nights ago. Can I have a cup of tea?'

'A couple of nights ago?' Miller said.

'I just said so, didn't I? I remember because I woke up with a stiffy. I'd been having a dream, you see? Or was I awake at that point? I can't quite remember, but it was definitely about a girl. Mable, the girl I met at the Palais a few nights ago...'

'Sixty years ago,' Clarissa interrupted.

'...and we were in her bedroom, about to dance or something...'

'Dad, get to the point where you saw Dan.'

Oh, right. Well, I can't quite remember what I was doing up at that time.' He looked around vacantly.

'You got up for a pee,' Watt reminded him.

'Did I?' He looked at his daughter. 'How does he know?'

'You told him, Dad. Now get on with it, and then I'll get you a cup of tea.'

'Oh, right.' He brightened up at that. 'Well, there I was, just finishing having a pee when I decided I wanted a cup of tea. I went through to the kitchen and there he was. That boy Herdan, going through his kitchen door with a huge thing over his shoulder.'

'Thing?'

'You know, one of those things.' He pointed to the floor.

'A carpet?' Clarissa said.

'Yes, a carpet.'

'Why didn't you tell me you'd seen this?'

'You never asked.'

Miller sat up. 'So you didn't see this, Miss Dixon?'

'No, I didn't, but he's always parading about throughout the night. No wonder I look knackered every morning.'

'Do you know what time this was?' Watt asked.

'No. But it was dark.'

'I put him to bed around eight thirty, then I go to bed around nine. And then we're up at seven again. Fourteen hours of being in a holiday camp.' She shook her head. 'I'd have served less time if I'd thrown him under a bus.'

Miller would get Watt on the phone to the emergency number at social services as soon as they left the house. *Immediate action required.*

'Do you know if his taxi was parked here?'

'I can't remember.'

'When did you last see Herdan?'

Clarissa focused her attention on the detective again. 'Last weekend, I think. He just said hello in passing. He's been busy lately.'

'Did you see anybody else coming and going?'

'No. He doesn't have many people round, except for those tarts. And once he's done using them, they leave. I don't know what they see in him.'

'Maybe he's got a big tadger,' the old man said.

'Dad! It's all about stiffies and tadgers with you, isn't it? No wonder my mother used to walk about like a half-shut knife.'

Miller stood up, followed by Watt. 'Thank you for your time. You've been most helpful.'

'You haven't finished your tea,' Clarissa said, hoping the policemen would stay longer, have more tea, have some breakfast, spend the night, take her away from all this...

'Thanks again.'

She followed him out along the hall, leaving her father eyeing up Miller's unfinished tea. 'Listen, Clarissa,' he said in a soft, conspiratorial voice as he handed her his card, 'my grandfather was like your dad. Nobody knows how hard it is. I can make a phone call and get you some help in here. There are people who can look after your dad while you have a wee break. Give you a chance to recharge your batteries.'

'Would they do that for me?'

'Of course they would. I'll make a call now. I'll tell them you're a priority.'

'Thank you, Frank. Maybe you could pop round and see my dad sometime.'

'I will. I promise.'

Miller stood looking at Herdan's door. 'He saw him walking into his house with a carpet over his shoulder. And we're looking for a murderer who takes his victims away in a carpet.'

'Say no more,' Watt said, stepping forward and kicking the door in.

FORTY-TWO

Mitchell Robb had showered and shaved, and was sitting at his dining table after getting dressed. The first coffee of the morning was like crack. He didn't know what he'd do without the dark brown liquid that set him on the right track every morning.

His copy of *The Caledonian* newspaper was spread out before him. This was one of his late mornings, where he could go into his office, sit at his desk, and play with some paperwork before preparing for his patient this afternoon. It wasn't a full-blown brain surgery, just some easy-peasy procedure.

His front lobby buzzer rang.

Aw, who the fuck is this? Hoping it wasn't the copper again, he went through to the hall, wishing the handset was in the living room.

'Hello?'

'It's me.'

Shite. He recognised the voice, and instead of feeling joy that she was here, he felt anger inside. 'What do you want?'

'What do you mean, what do I want?'

Sensing she was about to have an outburst, he buzzed her in. The last thing he wanted was her standing downstairs, shouting into his entry phone while one of the suited minions was leaving to cross over to his garage. No doubt to jump into one of those Japanese machines that were just overpriced Toyotas.

What the fuck did she want at this time of the morning? *You're about to find out, old son. Not only have you been shagging her, but now she's round your gaff.* Bollocks. He'd not even finished his coffee or got past the TV section in his paper. He was gearing himself up for reading Monty's obituary. He couldn't believe the old sod was dead. Not in an *Oh, I'll never see him again* way, but in a *Thank God the old bastard's croaked it* way.

There was a gentle knock on the door and he strode down the hall, ready to tell her to go away, he was working, he would call her...

'I'm in trouble,' Lauren Stevens said, walking past him into the hall.

He followed her into the living room. She wore an overcoat over her nurse's uniform, and he had to admit, the rosy glow on her cheeks made her more attractive. She pulled out a packet of cigarettes, and lit one up, tilting her head slightly back as she blew a plume of filthy, acrid lung cancer into his clean living room. *That* wasn't attractive.

'What do you mean, you're in trouble?'

'I threatened the pathologist.'

'What pathologist?' he said, taking the saucer from under his coffee cup, and giving it to her to use – for the first and last time – as an ashtray.

'Try and keep up here, Mitch. Do you think you could do that? That would be fucking spectacular if you could.'

'Now look—'

'No, you fucking look. I'm talking about that dumb fuck my boyfriend is now sleeping with. You know, the police officer boyfriend. The one who's screwing that cow in the city mortuary.'

'You threatened her? Why? What did you say to her?'

'Get me a coffee, Mitch.'

No please or thank you. Hang on while I put the kettle on and get the jar of instant, you rancid cow.

She undid her jacket, keeping the cigarette balanced between her lips, and he watched it bob up and down as he left for the kitchen. Suddenly, nothing between her lips seemed attractive.

Putting the kettle on would take too long, so he poured her a small coffee by running the hot tap over some coffee granules in an old mug. When he went back into the living room, she was sitting on his couch, knees tight, elbows resting on them, smoking her cigarette as if it was the last one on earth.

'Here,' he said, handing her the mug, the handle towards her.

'Ta.' She sipped at the hot liquid. Screwed up her face.

Ta? What the hell have you done, Mitch, my lad? Get shot of her.

'So, what did you say to her?' He hated asking, but if he didn't she would go off at a tangent and be here even longer.

'I can't remember word for word, because I was so angry, but I basically told her that she'd better watch herself.'

'Why would you do that?' He sat back at the table, Monty's obituary taking second place.

'Oh, well, you know, I just happened to be a bit jealous. I saw him outside with her one day, and they looked all cosy with each other. When I went inside to embarrass him, they were in an embrace with their tongues down each other's throats.'

'So you wanted to leave your boyfriend, but you didn't want anybody else to have him, is that it?'

'Basically.' She sucked on the cigarette, and blew the smoke out in his direction before stubbing it out on the saucer. 'Look, I know I have you now, and I love you more than anything, but I just wanted him to hurt. And now it feels as if he couldn't care less.'

I know the feeling he wanted to say, but he knew he was skating on thin ice. When he had met Lauren, she had been upfront with him, telling him all about Jimmy Gilmour, the big, bad detective, and that had added to the thrill. He actually believed it added to his orgasm, knowing he was screwing a woman whose boyfriend could probably beat him into a pulp and drink him for breakfast.

Now, all he felt was a tinge of fear creeping up his neck. To say that Lauren was a loose cannon was putting it mildly. Hell, yes, she was one of the best lays he'd ever had, but everything had a price. Once he'd done the business with her, it was time to do up the zipper and head off home. He didn't want her sitting, smoking, and blowing her bad breath at him while he read his paper every morning.

'So, let's sit and think about this; what's the worst that could happen?'

'She'll tell Jimmy, and he'll either have me arrested, or he'll start grilling me or something. I don't know, Mitch. I don't know what to do.'

'Listen, he'll understand that you were under duress.'

'Will he now? When were you going to tell me you'd minored in psychology?'

'I'm just trying to help you here.'

'You're not doing a very good job.'

Was this a good time to tell her to fuck off or not? Decisions, decisions.

Lauren sniffed as if she had a cold, took out another cigarette, and lit it. 'Well, you know what?'

You've decided you're going to become a nun and leave? After a quickie of course. One for the road. 'What?'

'I'm going to stand up to him. I'm going to tell him that I'm going to be living with a surgeon now, somebody who's a lot better than he is. I don't know why I'm up to high doh. Fuck 'im. I'll just tell him. And I'll admit that I've been seeing you.'

Robb started mentally juggling between a rock and a hard place.

'Look, Lauren, we really need to talk.'

She stopped her hand from reaching her mouth with the cigarette. 'Talk? As in, *It isn't you, it's me* kind of talk?'

'Basically, yes.' He stood behind the dining table; putting her out of reach should she entertain the thought of stabbing him.

'You're dumping me?' She stubbed her cigarette out, and looked at him. Anger he could have dealt with, but it was the calm look she gave him that made him wish he'd chosen his brown trousers that morning.

'I wouldn't use that crude term, but I do think we should spend less time with each other.'

'Oh, do you now? Did you think of this as you were shagging somebody else?'

'No, it's not like that.'

'It's fucking exactly like that.'

He started to feel his hackles rise. 'You know what? Screwing you was a mistake. Marrying you would be an even bigger one. You're good in bed, but you have a mouth like a docker, and your breath stinks of cigarettes all the time. God almighty, what was I thinking?' He sneered at her, preparing to run round the table.

Lauren stood up. Walked to the edge of the table opposite Robb, as if she really was going to start chasing him. 'That's fine. I'll go now, and you'll never see me again.'

'Look, I'm sorry I raised my voice, but it's for the best—'

'Shut up. I said I'm going. But two things before I go; if I find out you were fucking somebody else behind my back, I'll come back when you least expect it and cut your knob off with a pair of scissors. And I promise you one thing; you'll live to regret taking advantage of me. Having your way with me then dumping me. You haven't heard the last of this, Doctor Robb. And if you see me coming towards you in the hospital, walk the other way.'

That went without saying.

She stormed past him and closed the door softly behind her.

He turned away from the table, went down the hallway to the spare bedroom door, and knocked.

'You can come out now. She's gone.'

FORTY-THREE

Patricia Wilkinson had the unmistakeable look of death about her. Her face was pale, as if the life had literally drained from it. She was dressed in jeans, and a polo shirt had been pulled over her head. Then her killer had taken the time to brush her hair before laying her down on the bed.

The smell of her death pervaded the bedroom like a disease, and Miller involuntarily put a gloved hand up to his nose and mouth.

'It's Patricia Wilkinson,' he said to Watt. 'I recognise her from the DVD.'

'I see that. We didn't get to her in time, Frank.'

'We tried.' He looked back at the face of the young woman who'd had so much in life to look forward to. This was the part of the job he hated; any life taken by the hand of a stranger was diabolical, but Miller always hated it when a female was murdered. It wasn't a sexist thing, but he knew some men preyed on women who couldn't – or wouldn't – fight back.

He took a step back.

Watt called it in while Miller walked through the house, slower this time. The rolled-up carpet was at the side of the bed in the other bedroom. It didn't look like Herdan had been staying here for a while. Some mail had piled up behind the door.

In the bathroom, his toothbrush was in a holder. Miller ran his thumb over it. Dry. No sign of water on the razor in the bathroom cabinet.

There were no dirty dishes in the kitchen, just a coffee mug, washed and set upside down on a small drainer next to the sink.

Nothing else was out of place.

'He's a slippery bastard,' Watt said, as Miller came back into the room. 'I've called it in. The cavalry's on their way.'

'Good. By the time they're finished, I want forensics leaving this place looking like a building site.'

'She's a fucking mad cow, you know that?' Gabriel Chase poured himself another coffee in the kitchen. 'She's trouble for you, Mitch.'

'I know that. The last thing I expected was for her to come round here. I was going to take her somewhere public and dump her.'

'You shouldn't have told her where you live.'

'I realise that now.'

'You should have given her a false name.'

'She's a nurse at the hospital. How could I give her a false name?'

'You're right,' Chase said. 'Lesson learned though.'

'Damn straight.'

'What did you see in her?'

'You mean, apart from the fact she's twenty-four and never says no?'

Chase laughed. 'I'm sure she meant it when she said you haven't heard the last of her.'

'I couldn't care fucking less. I've used her, and now it's time to move on. I never once said we were exclusive.'

'I'm sure that'll look good on your headstone.'

'It's true. I never said I was only going out with her.'

'Are you mental? That's not what she thinks.' Chase added milk from the fridge, sniffing the carton before he poured. 'This is all going to fuck. Ever since they found the photos of Cathy in my uncle's house.'

'Ever since somebody killed Ashley,' Robb said, standing looking out of his living room window. Patrol cars were still outside Ashley's house, with a van behind them. The TV news sharks were gone, with nothing more to glean from the bones of the crime scene. He turned back to Chase.

'They'll find you eventually.'

Chase smiled as he came into the living room. 'I'm a lawyer, remember. And if they take me in for questioning, then I'll have one of my friends run rings round Miller and his cronies. They have nothing on us.'

'It's not a matter of *if*, it's *when* they come for you. God, they've already been round here talking about Jess.'

'Isn't it about time you told them about her?'

'Are you kidding me? There's no way I'm going to give them anything. If they want answers, then they need to find them. I'm giving them nothing.'

'So now you have two things to worry about.'

Robb slumped down on a couch, feeling the air expel out of the leather cushion. 'I think we've got a lot more to worry about. Like who killed Ashley.'

'And Jess.'

'Jesus, Gabriel, do you really think Dan went off his head and killed them?'

'You don't seem too upset about Jess being dead.'

'We were finished. We'd started to hate each other. That's why Miller will think I killed her.'

'But you didn't kill her, Mitch.'

'Miller isn't going to believe that. Maybe I should have just called him and dealt with the consequences.'

'No time for ifs and buts, my friend. We need to dig our way out of this.' Chase drank more coffee. 'To be honest, I can't see Dan doing this.'

'I can.' Robb stared at his friend. 'Look at us, successful, loaded, suave, good-looking. Look at him; a bloody taxi driver, ugly as sin. And a temper to boot.'

'If he hit me, I'd pay somebody to give him a kicking.'

'You don't know people who would do that sort of thing.'

'When you have money, you can buy anything.'

'I forgot; you're going to be loaded when you sell old Monty's gaff.'

'I have to split it with that daft cow.'

Robb laughed. 'I think she's probably thinking the same thing about you, but not using that particular c-word.'

'I wanted to spend more time with the old bastard, but he just lectured me. *All this drinking and going with floozies. I ask you, fucking floozies.* He was so out of touch with reality. I just couldn't drag myself to go round there anymore. Maybe him having a stroke was the best thing that could have happened.'

Robb sat up straight. 'You can't mean that.'

'I do. He was an old bastard.'

'You'll be an old bastard too, when you're sitting on the bench with your fancy wig.'

Chase laughed out loud. 'Oh, I don't think so, Mitchell. Dressing up like some old seventeenth century ponce. No, I'm going to take half the old codger's money, invest most of it, and have a good time with the rest.'

'Good luck to you. I'm going to retire to Spain where the weather's great, and I can play golf every day.'

'Sounds good. You and Arthur King make a good couple.'

'Piss off.' Robb laughed then his face took on a serious note. 'Ashley and I made a good couple. Maybe we should try to find Dan ourselves. I want to show him why it's not a good idea to fuck me around.'

'Don't let him get to you, Mitch.'

'Let him get to me? Fuck. If he murdered Ashley, we'll be dealing with the bastard, make no mistake.'

'Why kill the women though?'

'He's after me, Gabe. He killed Ashley. Then he killed Jess, although the police don't know that yet. He's getting back at me. He never liked me.'

'That doesn't answer my question.'

Robb shook his head. 'You know why. He's a member of the golf club, and then I started talking about driving a taxi, and that's how we got involved with him, remember?'

'I remember that night very well. Didn't I tell you not to invite him into the group? His sort don't fit in.'

'What *sort?*'

'Working class. The kind who get their hands dirty instead of using their minds to make money.'

'Poor Gabe. Born well after his time. I'm sure Dickens would have featured you in one of his novels.'

'You may well mock, my friend, but hasn't this come back round to bite you in the arse? I don't know why you wanted to keep your dad's old taxi going anyway.'

Robb laughed. 'I hate the fucking thing, but how many women have I picked up in that shagging chariot? Once they see my smile, and listen to my spiel, they're all over me.'

'I heard that about taxi drivers, getting a blowjob down on Silver-knowes promenade in lieu of payment.'

'Please. Like I need to do that. However, you're right. I need to get rid of the damn thing. Make a new start.'

'Now that Lauren's got on her high horse, you'd be wise to make a new start in Mexico.'

'Maybe Dan will take care of her as well, since he hates me that much.'

'That's tempting fate, old son. But better her than you.'

Kate Murphy pulled her facemask down, and turned away from the dead woman. 'It looks to me as if she's been dead a couple of days.'

'Does it look as if she was killed in her flat after all?' Purcell asked. 'Then moved here?'

'It does. You can see from the lividity in her hand that she died somewhere else, most likely her flat, on her back. There's no sign of where the blood has pooled on her front, so it will be on her back.'

'Not that I'm after your job, Doc,' Watt said, from the other side of the bed, 'but that was what I thought when I first saw her.'

Kate looked at him. 'You're welcome to swap jobs, Andy. I'd like to sit about all day, drinking coffee.'

'Hey, it's not all about drinking coffee, I'll have you know. We have doughnuts too.'

Purcell spoke to Kate. 'Is there any indication of the cause of death?'

Kate moved around the body, her hands feeling through the dead woman's hair, round the back of her head. 'It feels like her neck is broken.' She stepped back. 'Has the room been photographed and videotaped?'

Miller went in search of Maggie Parks, and came back a few minutes later. 'They're done photographing the room, but they still need to go through it again.'

'I just want to check something.' Kate stepped forward, and gently lifted Patricia by putting her hands under the girl's shoulders. Patricia's head leaned sideways at an awkward angle. Kate then put her back again. 'I won't make an official pronouncement yet, but it would seem her neck is indeed broken.'

Purcell nodded. 'Thanks, Kate.' He led the other two detectives outside. 'Are more uniforms going door-to-door?'

'They are,' Miller said. 'We were doing that when we got a tip-off about Herdan bringing in a carpet a couple of nights ago.'

'Good. Keep them at it. Somebody might have seen him carrying the carpet from his taxi into here.'

'I called the taxi office earlier,' Watt said. 'He was last logged-on Tuesday night, around ten thirty. Then he logged off, and they haven't heard from him since. However, as long as you pay your radio fee every week, they couldn't give a toss whether you log on or not. It's no skin off their nose. It just means more work for the other drivers.'

'He's definitely trying to avoid us,' Purcell said. 'Get his licence number circulated, Andy. I want everybody looking out for him. The bastard must be keeping that black cab somewhere.'

Miller's mobile phone rang, and he excused himself. A few minutes later, he returned.

'That was the lab on the phone. They found a black jacket button under Patricia's bed. It doesn't belong to any of her clothing, and it wasn't covered in dust like the other stuff under there.'

'Let's go in and have a look. Andy, go and supervise the uniforms. Have them spread wider. Somebody might have been out walking a dog and saw something. Knock on as many doors as you can.'

'Yes, sir.' Before he left, Kate caught him by the arm.

'Andy, I'm sorry I snapped. I'm just going through some stuff right now.'

Watt smiled. 'Don't worry about it. I was married. I have two daughters. I lived in a house with three women.' He winked at her, and walked away.

'This doesn't make sense, Percy,' Miller said. 'Why does he put Patricia on show, when he hasn't done that with Cathy or Ashley? And leaving her in his own home?'

'Maybe he brought them all here before dumping them wherever it was he dumped them. But this time he was delayed for some reason.'

'You don't believe that.'

'Of course not, but sometimes when you bat ideas about, a light bulb will come on.'

'And the lack of blood. Patricia has a broken neck. Different MO.'

'So what changed?'

'He's playing games with us, trying to throw us off. It doesn't change the fact that she was a member of a small group of friends, and now somebody is murdering them. We should be worried that he might start killing the men now.'

'You're going to give me a bloody ulcer, Miller.'

FORTY-FOUR

'Jesus, and apple pies too?' Tony Matheson said, as Sergeant Roger Robertson got back into the passenger seat. 'And you'll honk the bloody car out as well.'

Robertson stuffed some cheeseburger into his mouth. 'You know, you can actually buy food in there instead of just using their lavvy.'

'I only needed a pee, Roger, not plaque added to my veins.'

Robertson laughed, stuffing more burger into his mouth.

Matheson drove the patrol car from the McDonald's on Gyle-muir Road in Corstorphine, on the west side of Edinburgh. Since Scotland had become one unified police force, the number of patrolling police officers had been cut. Which meant they relied more and more on the services of the special constables, who were all volunteers.

Matheson worked out of High Street, alternating between foot patrol and mobile duties, but they could be asked to cover at any station in the city. He had been assigned to Corstorphine for a few weeks now, and had been with Robertson every shift that Robertson had been on.

They'd just turned onto Glasgow Road when the call came

through. Control, requesting any available units to attend a locus not far from where they were. A report of a woman screaming for help.

'We can take this one,' Matheson said.

'Cool your jets there, Tony, we're on a break.'

'This shift is a break, sarge.'

Robertson puffed air, throwing bits of burger about the car as he reached for the radio. 'Roger, Tango Alpha Two One. ETA five minutes.'

'Roger,' control answered, logging their response.

'Roger, Roger,' Matheson said, laughing as he switched on the blues and twos, putting his foot down.

'Not too fast. I want to enjoy this.'

'Hey, if you don't eat it, you might add a few years to your life.'

'See, it's alright for a bloke like you, Tony. I used to be fit, but stopping for coffee and snacks all the time really busted my gut.'

'I just like to keep fit, Roger. Heart disease can strike anybody.' He navigated round a few cars as he approached the lights at the Maybury junction, then turned right, past the casino and up Mayberry Road.

'Are you trying to make me feel better, Tony? Bloody heart disease. It's all a farce if you ask me. You see it on the TV, and then you think you'll have to eat sensibly. So you buy all that health food and at the end of the day, you die anyway, and the only person who's better off is the shopkeeper. If you ask me, it's all a conspiracy.'

Matheson shook his head. 'You won't be saying that when they cut you open on the slab, and it takes a crane to lift your heart out because there's so much fat clogging up your arteries.'

'I wouldn't be saying anything, would I? I'd be dead.'

'You've got an answer for everything, haven't you, sarge?'

'I do that, son.'

He held onto the *Oh, shit* handle above the window as Matheson turned the car into Craig's Road, and then immediately into Cammo Walk. This street was a narrow country lane. Matheson drove it expertly, his lights cutting through the dark as if they were on some rally.

'Jesus, there go some of my fucking fries,' Robertson complained, as Matheson floored it.

Then they came to the entrance to the Campbell Estate. Once a privately owned house and estate, it had fallen into disrepair back in the fifties. Now it was open to the public.

Matheson stopped just inside the perimeter, past the old stone entrance pillars. Robertson got on the radio requesting more details.

'Informant reports a scream coming from the old estate. Backup on the way.'

'Jesus. You ever been in here before?'

'No.'

'We chased a load of devil worshippers out of here one Halloween. Wee bastards, messing about with stuff they don't understand.'

What once had been a small mansion with a stable block and several buildings set in lush countryside was now just a pile of ruins.

'This is a real old place. It was originally part of the old Campbell estate, which was huge. Then they spilt the land up. Fucking place gives me the heebie-jeebies.'

'Especially after dark. Look at that,' Matheson said, as the head-lights from the car picked out part of the mansion in the distance.

'I hope it's not somebody taking the piss,' Robertson said, climbing out of the car. He stood looking around. 'Which way, left or right?'

'Fucked if I know, sarge. But why don't we leave the car here and split up. If there's somebody in here, he won't be able to drive out.'

'Good idea. Lock her up, but leave the lights on.'

Matheson locked the car, and they both took their flashlights out. Robertson was mumbling about his fries getting cold as he walked away in the opposite direction, his torch beam bobbing about in the dark.

What a piece of shite this was. It was probably only some of those toffee-nosed kids arsing about. Why the hell would somebody waste police time, sending them out on a wild goose chase? Well, he was buggered if he was going to waste much time hunting down some phantom victim when he could be sitting in a nice warm car, eating his fries.

Then he heard it. Somebody running through the woods farther in from the track. Behind the old house. The unmistakable sound of feet running through fallen leaves.

'Tony!' he said, in a shouted whisper. 'Tony!' No answer. Jesus. He ran as fast as he could towards the noise.

Miller was dressed casually now. Black jeans with a dark sweater under a dark jacket.

'You look like you're on your way to a biker fight,' Purcell said, as he came into the hotel bar.

'You look like you're on your way to a Liberace appreciation club.'

'Shut up, Miller.' Purcell looked down at his jacket, as if there were puffy sleeves sticking out. 'What's wrong with this jacket, anyway?'

'Nothing.'

'Come on. It's meant to make me look hard.'

'It does.'

'Lying bastard.'

Miller finished off the Coke he was drinking, and stood up. 'I feel like we're on the pull,' he said, as they crossed over to his car. The Grassmarket was fairly quiet, but there were always people going out drinking, even on a weeknight. The castle sat over to their left, lit up, looking as if it was tired after all its hard work hosting the annual Festival Tattoo.

'I wouldn't go saying that too loud,' Purcell said, as he got in the passenger side. 'Especially in front of the women.'

'I'm not that brave.'

Like many places in the world, Edinburgh took on a different character after dark. The Grassmarket was well lit, but it was like walking past a man who might or might not be a mugger. You give him the benefit of the doubt, but you know in your heart that if you have to protect yourself, you're all in. He's going down, and going down hard.

He pulled away, and headed through the Cowgate, driving past the City Mortuary, then up St Mary's Street.

'That reminds me,' Purcell said, 'did Kate Murphy call you before you clocked off?'

'She did, but her preliminary didn't change from earlier. It still looks as if Patricia Wilkinson's neck was broken. She's scheduled the PM for tomorrow morning.'

'I think I'll get a new motor when I come down here. Suzy says I'm a Jag sort of man, but that makes me feel old. Maybe a black Beemer.'

'Or a Mini.'

'Sod off, Miller.'

It only took ten minutes to drive down to the New Town. Miller parked in Bellevue Crescent and they walked across the road to the church.

Inside, it was warm. A woman sat on one of the pews a few rows down, her head bowed. A man sat in the row behind her, not looking at anybody. Miller took a pew on the left, Purcell one on the right, a few rows apart.

Miller bowed his head and looked at his watch. Five minutes to go.

FORTY-FIVE

'Sierra Charlie Seven Six, at locus now.'

The patrol car stopped next to the one Tony Matheson had been driving. 'Where are the daft bastards?' Officer Clemens said. He too thought they'd been sent on a wild goose chase. Another call had come in about a woman screaming, and they had been sent as backup for the first patrol that had responded.

'What a waste of time,' Perky Perkins said from the passenger side. Clemens turned right. 'Who in their right mind would want to walk about here?'

'A lot of people bring their dogs here.'

'I could think of a lot of better things to be doing with my time.' They passed the old, decrepit ruin of the main house. Clemens turned onto a track on his left.

'Over there,' Perky said, but Clemens was already driving towards it.

They both saw it at the same time, a form lying on the ground. Minus his head.

'Call it in, mate,' Clemens said, as he stopped the car and jumped out. He stopped at what he thought was a pile of rags at first, but then his flashlight caught the blood. Pinky shouted. 'Perky, get over here!'

Perkins ran over. 'Christ, what's that?'

'Look at the stripes. It's Roger.'

Perkins ran to the bushes at the side and threw up.

They heard the sirens coming from a distance. An ambulance and more backup. 'Where the hell's Matheson?' Clemens said out loud, looking around, but he could only see bushes and trees in the dark.

'Tony!' Perky shouted. No answer.

'Go and have a look for him, Perky. He might be lying injured somewhere just like Roger.'

'Give me a minute. The others shouldn't be far behind.' Then he threw up again.

It was dead on nine o'clock when the front door to the church opened again. The wind tried rushing in but its advance was quickly quashed.

Footsteps echoed round the large interior as the figure made its way round to the left, keeping out of the way of the security camera, then he reached the confessional.

Stepped inside.

Miller looked over at Purcell, who nodded to him. Together, they got up and walked over to the confessional and stood outside.

The man inside wasn't being quiet as he spoke.

'I told you I'd be back, didn't I? I said I would come back and kill you if you spoke to them. Now you're going to get what's coming to you. I'll fucking kill you right now.'

The priest's face was just barely visible in the gloom of the confessional box. 'Is that right? Well, why don't you step out and we'll talk about it now?'

The man jumped up, and practically exploded out of the confessional.

'Police! Show me your hands!' Miller shouted, but the man's face showed pure panic, and they only had a split-second to control him. He and Purcell grabbed him as Andy Watt got up from a pew and rushed towards them.

Kim, who hadn't shown her face so far, was also up and running towards them.

Miller grabbed hold of the man as he turned to run, and then they were all over him.

'Please don't hurt me! He told me to say this!'

Miller handcuffed the man's hands behind his back, and they hauled him to his feet.

'What are you talking about?' Purcell said.

'The man outside. He gave me money to come in here to say these words.'

'What man?'

'The taxi driver.'

Miller looked at Kim, and she got the message.

'Come on, Andy, let's go.' They ran outside while Miller marched the man through to the priest's office in the back of the church.

Will Beam came out of the confessional looking ashen.

'Do you recognise that man, Will?' he asked.

'Yes, I do. I have a soup kitchen here at the weekends. He's one of my regulars. Bob, he calls himself.'

'You can go and wait in your rectory now if you want.'

'No, I'll stay with Bob. I want to be there for him.' They walked to the office behind Miller.

The man's clothes were shabby, and there was a stench coming off him. It was clear he was homeless.

'Look, I'm sorry, but I'm cold and hungry, and he offered me fifty pounds to come in here and say some shit to the priest. He just wanted me to speak the words, that's all.' He looked up as Beam entered. 'I wasn't threatening you, Father. I'm just hungry. I know you feed us at the weekend. I'm sorry.'

'It's okay, my son.' Beam looked at Miller. 'You can uncuff him, detective.'

Miller took the cuffs off. 'What's your name?'

'Bob. Smith.'

'Tell us about this taxi driver,' Purcell said.

The man was sitting in the chair at the priest's desk, as if he was a parishioner talking about a fundraiser. He wasn't going anywhere without getting past the policemen, and that wasn't happening.

'I was walking along Green Street when he stopped. He offered me some money. Said he was playing a trick on the priest. He's a friend of his, and wanted to play a prank on him.' He looked sheepishly at Beam. 'Sorry. He had me when he flashed some cash. He said he'd have more when I came out of the church.'

'Don't you worry about that,' Beam said.

Kim came back in with Watt. 'There are no taxis outside,' she said.

'I didn't think there would be,' Miller said. Then to Bob. 'Can you describe the driver?'

'Dark hair. White shirt. I didn't get a good look at his face.'

'What about any numbers in the cab, like an operator's licence number?'

'I don't have reading glasses, so I can't make anything out like that.'

'So, what happens now?' Beam asked.

Purcell took the priest aside. 'I don't think he's going to come after you. To be honest, if he thought you would go to the police, then he would have taken care of you already.'

'Now he knows I did go to the police.'

'He also knows you didn't see his face. Maybe he was just testing you. You're not on his radar. It was just empty threats. If he wanted to kill you, he's had plenty of opportunity.'

'How do you know he won't come back?'

'Because he gave you a time when he was supposedly coming round tonight. That's why

you called Frank. Our boy wouldn't make an appointment to come and kill you.'

The priest didn't look convinced. 'You think he gave me a time so he could sit and watch if the police would come?'

'That's exactly what he did. I don't think he'll come back now because he won't know if we have people working undercover or not.'

'What will happen to Bob?'

'We'll let him look at some photos in our ID books, but I don't think our cabbie is stupid. If he thought he could be identified, he wouldn't have done it this way.'

'Will somebody help him get to a shelter?'

'We'll make sure he does.'

FORTY-SIX

The small hotel room was making him feel like a caged tiger. It was something he should have been used to after spending so much time in prison, but ever since he'd got out, the sweet taste of fresh air was addictive.

You could always go home. He'd entertained the thought many times, but no, he was here in Edinburgh, and he was going to stay. At least until he'd finished what he'd come here to do.

His *Mission*. There was no other way to think of it. At the end of it, there was a fifty per cent chance that he would be dead, but it was better than sitting back doing nothing.

He would go for a walk later. It was always good to feel the cold air on his face. To taste the *freedom*. He might as well enjoy it while he could, because the other option to dying was ending up back in prison. Not a great choice, but if he sat back, then there was a hundred per cent he was going to die. There were no ifs, ands, or buts.

Better to go out fighting. Prison was a better option than being in a box.

He stripped off down to his boxers, and went through his routine before showering. All the time thinking about one person.

———

Miller was parked in the car park, outside the station. Bob had been left inside where they would look after him.

'How's the Apex Hotel?' Miller said, nodding to the building.

'Bloody wonderful, actually. I've often wondered what it would be like living long-term in a hotel. No bills to worry about, except your mobile phone, but you don't have to clean, you can go down-stairs to eat your dinner whenever you like.'

'No washing dishes.'

'I bet you don't wash the fucking dishes anyway.'

'I'm a modern man, Percy, I do my fair share.'

'I'm going to get a dishwasher in my place.'

'We have one. I help load it.'

'I hope you don't get a hernia, lifting all those plates.'

Miller saw Kim coming out of the back door, talking on her mobile phone. 'How's the flat-hunting going?'

Purcell made a sighing noise. 'Who has time for that? Suzy said she'd send me an email with some places that I could check out, but once I get in my room and get Netflix on, I'm zoned out for the rest of the day.'

'She'll have your nuts in a hand basket,' he said, as the back door opened.

Kim climbed in, closing it behind her. The phone was still in her hand, but the call had been ended. 'What has he done now, Frank?'

'It's what he *hasn't* done that's going to get him demoted from *flavour of the month*.'

'Suzy wants you to do something for her, and yet here you are, arsing about with us?' Kim said.

'He bloody well roped me into this, or I would have been making phone calls,' he said, pointing to Miller. 'It's a conspiracy with you two. I'll be right on the phone to her dropping you both in it, make no mistake.'

Kim patted him on the shoulder. 'I was talking to her just now.' She held up her phone and wiggled it about.

'Well, that's just magic. I hope you took the blame for this.'

'Yeah, alright. I might be blonde, but my head's not zipped up the back.'

'I knew I couldn't trust you. Bonnie and bloody Clyde. There's a report going in tomorrow, I hope you realise that.'

Kim laughed. 'I don't work for you, remember?'

'Oh shit. I knew there was a flaw in my plan.'

'Right,' Miller said, 'what did we make of that?'

Kim looked at Purcell. 'I think Percy's right, our killer was just confirming what he already suspected, that Beam would call us. That's why he gave a specific time.'

'Agreed. I don't think he'll waste time and energy on killing Beam, but I want extra patrols going by there regularly. The uniforms at Gayfield Square can swing by on their way to and from the station.'

Miller's phone rang in his pocket, and he took it out and answered it. When he hung up, his face looked grim.

'Fasten your seatbelts. We got a shout. Kim, you need to attend as well.' He told her where they were going.

'I'll see you over there.' She got out of the car and ran over to her own.

Miller couldn't get his car onto the Campbell Estate for all of the other emergency vehicles, so he parked next to a patrol car. Kim parked hers behind his.

'You sure Samantha's okay with looking after Emma?' Miller said, a worried look on his face.

'She's fine, Frank. Jack's with her too. But thanks for worrying.'

'She's my daughter, now, too.'

The entrance to the estate was blocked with cars, their blue flashing lights making the place look like a Halloween display.

Inside, beyond the stone pillars, they were greeted by a uniform. 'It's down that way, sir, past the ruins of the old house.'

Purcell nodded, and they carried on down. An ambulance stood with its lights flashing. Behind it was the mortuary van. Jake Dagger was dressed in his forensic suit.

Paddy Gibb came across to them. 'I got a call to come here, sir. Two uniforms involved in an incident.'

'Okay, Paddy,' said Purcell. 'Give us the skinny on what happened.'

'We have an officer down.'

'Is it bad?'

'He's dead.'

Purcell turned to Dagger. 'Can you tell the cause of death?'

'His head was ruptured by a vehicle being driven over it.'

'Fuck. Show me.'

They followed the pathologist round the track, and saw the forensics tent up. Arc lights lit up the scene.

'God almighty, what happened here?' he said.

'It's bad, Frank,' Dagger said.

Miller looked over at two uniforms being questioned by other members of Miller's team. Everybody had been called out. Even Hazel Carter, who wobbled towards them.

'Sir, these two officers were the second unit to arrive at the scene. This is what they found when they got here.' She tried not to look down at the pile of puke, but as soon as her eyes saw it, her stomach turned. 'Oh God, I'm sorry.' She turned away into the bushes and threw up.

Kim went to her, and put her arm around her as Hazel bent over and let fly again.

'Frank, I'll see you at home. You can update me. I'm taking Hazel home. And when I find out which clown called her out...'

'It's fine, Kim. My name was on the on-call list. I could have refused, but I wanted to come.'

'You have an excuse not to be here. Consider yourself reprimanded. Now let's get you home, and we can have a cup of tea.' She turned to the rest of the detectives standing looking. 'Nobody's got a problem with that, have they?'

They all mumbled that they didn't and turned away. Miller was proud of Kim in that moment. His first wife Carol wouldn't have taken crap off anybody either, and he was glad that Kim was the same way.

'She's a keeper,' Gibb said. 'You better think about putting a ring on her finger before somebody else snaps her up.'

'We only started living with each other a few months ago, Paddy. Give us time.'

'Aye, stop busting his balls, Gibb, and get us inside this fucking tent before the wind blows your wig off.'

Purcell walked into the large forensics tent.

'Jesus, I don't even have a combover,' Gibb retorted as they followed Purcell into the tent, where a number of people were working round the dead police officer. Professor Leo Chester, the head pathologist, was in there. Dagger followed in behind Miller.

'It's Sergeant Roger Robertson. He and his patrol partner were down here first,' Gibb said.

'Hello, Superintendent,' Chester said. 'Good to see you again. I believe you're down here in our fair city for good this time.'

'Somebody's got to keep these reprobates in order.'

'My thoughts exactly,' the older man said, smiling. Then he got down to business. 'This poor man looks like he was run over by a car. The wheel went over his head, ending his life.'

Miller had seen some horrendous things in his career but this had to be one of the worst.

'Could it have been a taxi?'

'It could have. I'm sure forensics will be doing tyre impressions.'

'Why were they here?' Purcell said.

'There was a treble nine call about a female screaming in here. The caller didn't leave a name, but a patrol car was sent out anyway.'

'Did control get a number for the caller?'

Gibb shook his head. 'There's a number, but when Andy Watt called it, it was dead.'

'Where is Watt?' Purcell asked.

'They're still looking for the special who was with Roger.'

'A special?' Miller said. 'Do we have a name?'

'Tony Matheson.'

'Tony? Jesus.'

'We can't find him. We're bringing more officers in. He might be injured and wandering around the field outside the perimeter of the estate.'

Miller looked back at the forensics tent. 'Or the killer might have taken Tony with him.'

Then Angie Rivers gave a shout. Miller ran over to her.

'I just found this on the side of the track.' She held up a yellow business card.

Miller took it, and looked at it with his flashlight.

'It's an Edinburgh Cabs business card. The company Dan Herdan drives for.'

FORTY-SEVEN

The drive from Barnton to Barberton Mains took barely fifteen minutes. Bruce Hagan was sitting watching TV when Kim brought Hazel in. He gingerly got up off the couch when he saw his girlfriend had brought company home.

'Kim! Is everything alright with Hazel?'

'She's fine. She was just sick. It was a messy crime scene.'

'I might be pregnant, but I'm not deaf.' Hazel looked at the side of his head, his longer hair covering the spot where his right ear used to be. 'Sorry, love. Bad choice of words.'

'Ach, don't you worry about that. Come away in and get your feet up.' He didn't have his glove on, and Kim couldn't help but look at the part of his hand where three of his fingers used to be. Now, he only had the index finger and thumb on the one hand. 'It could have been worse,' he said ,when he saw Kim looking, 'he might have cut my willy off.'

'Bruce!' Hazel said. 'Not in front of ladies.'

Despite herself, Kim laughed. 'I'm sorry, Bruce. I didn't mean to stare.'

'Is everything okay?' he asked again, his mood going from jovial to serious in a heartbeat.

'Yes, I'm fine. I was just sick at a crime scene, that's all,' Hazel said.

'Right. I'll get the kettle on.'

The two women agreed that would be just the ticket. 'See what I mean? He's laughing and joking one minute, then moody the next.'

'Is he still going to see Jill White?'

'He is. She's a brilliant psychologist. I'm glad she didn't leave Edinburgh. Bruce has the scars from where his fingers were cut off, and where his ear was. They're talking about trying to stitch on a prosthetic ear. But it's the nightmares he has that are driving me mental. He wakes up screaming almost every night, even though the doctor's given him stuff to sleep. He's scaring Jane. I'm exhausted, Kim.'

'It'll get better, Hazel. You love each other, that's the main thing. If you lean on each other, you can work miracles.'

'I think I could handle it better if I wasn't in this state. Talking of which, I think he or she is determined to kick my bladder right out of me.' She got up, heading for the bathroom.

Kim opened the door that led into the kitchen, and didn't see Bruce at the kettle. Or anywhere else in the kitchen. The back door that led out into the back garden was ajar.

The security light was on in the back. She stepped out onto the patio, feeling the cold hit her after the warmth of the house. Noticed the side door to the garage was open. She walked over to it, and stepped inside.

The detached building was in darkness, with just the barest glimmer of light hitting the Ford Focus inside. 'Bruce? You okay?'

There was no answer, but she saw a shadow crouched in one corner. Bruce was hunched down, his face buried into his legs, his arms folded over them, like a little schoolboy who was being punished.

Kim could hear him crying, though barely saw his shoulders heaving.

She walked over and crouched down beside him, putting an arm around his shoulders. He suddenly turned to her, and put his arms around her, putting his face into her shoulder.

'Kim, I don't know how to handle this. Every night I dream I'm in a coffin. Only this time, you don't open the lid.'

'I can't even begin to imagine what you're going through, and I won't lie and say I understand, but I want you to know that we're all here for you. Me, Frank, Jack, and Percy, believe it or not. Hazel loves you so much. She's here for you too.'

His sobbing subsided, and he pulled away from her. She could see his eyes were wet as her own eyes started to adjust to the dark of the garage.

'I come in here and cry all the time.'

'Nobody would blame you for that.'

'I wish I'd never come back here. I wanted to go the extra mile, and I guess I really did. I can't blame anybody for this except myself. I wish I could turn back the clock and make a different decision that night.'

'We've all done things we wish we hadn't. We can't turn back time, but we can learn from our mistakes, and then we'll know how to deal with situations in the future. But if it's any consolation, you helped bring that guy down.'

'It's not. I know that sounds selfish, but it's messing with my head all the time now. I'm seeing Jill White, and she's brilliant, but even she can't get inside my head enough to stop the nightmares.' He put a hand on hers. 'I keep thinking they're coming back for me.'

'They never will.'

'I wish I could believe that. You know, if it wasn't for my daughter in there, I'd slit my wrists.'

'Does Jill know this?'

'Yes. Believe me, if it wasn't for her, I'd have done it already. She's keeping me on the straight and narrow.'

Kim felt her insides spinning. 'Jill will help you get through this, Bruce. You need to tell her how you feel. Do you want me to call her tonight?'

'No. I see her on Monday, I'll talk to her then. Don't worry, I'm not going to do anything stupid. That was a few weeks ago, and I've had plenty of opportunities to do it, but she said to tell my GP about it, so I did, and he prescribed some medicine for me.'

'If you ever want to talk to me alone, somewhere away from home, you can call me. I mean it. We can sit and drink coffee, and we'll just chat. No pressure.'

He wiped his eyes with the backs of his hands. 'Thanks, Kim. I really appreciate that. Hazel's sick to the back teeth of me, and it would be nice to get out of the house without going to some medical establishment or other.'

'Hazel's not sick of you. She loves you, Bruce, but she's also carrying your baby and looking after your little girl.'

'I know. I'm a selfish bastard. I don't mean to be, but it just comes over me at times.'

'Come on,' she said, standing up. 'Let's get you inside, and we'll have that cup of tea.'

When they got back in, Hazel had gone to bed.

'She does that sometimes. Just gets up and goes upstairs to bed.'

'She's tired.'

'I know.'

'Do you take your meds every night?'

'Yes. I take some before I go to bed.'

'I'll get going. You sure you're going to be alright?'

'I'll be fine. But why did you come here with Hazel tonight? Is she alright?'

'She was just sick at the crime scene.'

'Right.'

'How did she get down there? Did she take her car?'

'No. That's her Focus in the garage. Andy Watt picked her up. He lives round here apparently.'

'Okay. Tell her I said goodnight, and I'll see her tomorrow, but only if she's feeling fine. If she's not, she can call Paddy Gibb.'

They said their goodbyes, and she left in her car.

FORTY-EIGHT

He was lying on the plastic body basket, just like the others before him. His head felt like a hammer had been taken to it. He felt the straps bite into his wrists and ankles, restricting his movement. He'd been left here for... how long? It felt like an eternity.

He was dressed in clothes that weren't his. He tried lifting his head, but there was a leather strap round that too.

He heard footsteps approaching, scuffing on a concrete floor. *Where in God's name am I?* 'Who are you?' he shouted, and his voice reverberated round the large room. Sweat ran from his armpits, down his sides. It coated his brow.

The man came into view. He was wearing a surgeon's scrubs and cap with most of his face covered by a mouth mask. He laughed behind the mask, his eyes gleaming like ball bearings.

'What's all the noise? Aren't you having fun?'

'Untie me right now. I demand you undo these straps!'

More laughter. 'Demand? Well, that's not very nice. Do you speak to everybody like that? Of course you do. You're an arrogant prick.'

He licked his lips, feeling the place getting hotter. Maybe it was just his stress levels increasing, making him feel as if he were walking on the sun. 'Look, I'm sorry. I didn't mean to shout. Please. Please let me go. I won't say anything. This can just be between you and me.'

'That is so clichéd. Begging for your life, promising the earth. However, I'm not an unreasonable man. Let's play a game. You tell me something, and maybe I'll think about letting you go.'

'Okay, anything.'

'Tell me I'm better than you.'

'What?'

The man sighed behind the mask, letting out a deep breath. 'I thought the rules were simple. He suddenly stepped round from the end of the stretcher, and grabbed the man by the face, making him do a duck face with his mouth.

'One more fucking chance, or you're going to annoy me. Do we have an understanding here?'

The man nodded his head.

'You look like a duck.' He let the man's face go. 'Make a duck face on your own.'

The man was about to say *What?* but caught himself in time. He made a face like a duck.

'Good. Now tell me I'm better than you.'

'You're better than me.'

'I knew it! I fucking well knew it!' He was standing by the man's side now, looking down at his face. 'I've known it all this time. You're just a piece of shit, and I'm better than you.'

'Of course you are.'

'Did I ask you to add anything else? Did I?'

'No.'

'No what?'

'No, sir.'

'That's better. You should really learn some manners; you know that? Manners cost nothing.'

'I know. I'm sorry.'

'Tell me again how better we are than you.'

We? 'You're better than me.'

'Both of us are better than you, not just me.'

'You're both better than me.'

'I love it. I knew it, didn't I just say that? I've known it all this time. Let me go and get my knife so I can cut those straps off.'

'Why don't you just undo them?' But the surgeon had walked out of sight. Then the gurney was moving. He could feel the heat getting stronger.

Then he knew what was happening. 'No! No! Please! Don't do this! Nooo!'

The surgeon laughed. 'This is a fun ride! Enjoy it. It's your last one!'

'I lied! You're not better than me, you fucking piece of shit!'

The surgeon screamed with rage. The body basket slid off the stretcher like a train sliding along a wet track, and the man's screams were feral-like in their intensity, before the steel door clanged shut and the flames brought death.

The surgeon pushed the trolley out of the way, and walked along to the next one where the woman lay on her back, tied to the body basket, just as the man had been. He'd gagged her, because she wouldn't stop screaming.

'He's gone into the fire now. He shouldn't take that long to burn. Then you're next.' He looked at the body being consumed by the flames.

'Goodbye, Roger.'

FORTY-NINE

'How's Hazel?' Miller said, buttering toast for Emma.

'She's totally stressed out. Bruce is getting help, but he feels he's a burden.'

'I'll go and see him soon.'

'He would appreciate that.'

Emma smiled at Miller as he put her toast in front of her. 'Frank, do cats eat toast?' she said, pulling a corner off and holding it down for Charlie to sniff. The cat licked the butter off.

'Not really, but they like the butter.'

'What about popcorn?'

He ruffled her hair. 'We'll have to ask him next time we have some.'

He made coffee for himself and Kim. 'I'm going over to see Anne this morning.'

'Anne?' Kim drank some of the hot liquid, feeling it go down her gullet.

'Anne Robertson, Roger's wife. She was told last night about her husband dying, and she's a basket case. I want to see if there's anything I can do. Jack was a good friend of Roger's.'

'Are you taking the new girl with you?'

'I think this is too sensitive for her to handle. She'll be a good member of the team, but I don't think subtlety's her strongest attribute.'

Miller picked up his mug and finished his coffee. 'I'm driving out there with Percy. Jack's coming too. Gibb called me earlier. He went round last night with a Family Liaison Officer, but she was just devastated. She had to be sedated. The FLO is there this morning, and their son came round with his wife, but we need to talk to her.'

'Did you hear from Jimmy Gilmour last night?'

'No. His phone was switched off. Nobody knows where he was.'

Kim raised her eyebrows. 'You really don't need to be a detective to figure out where he was.'

'Kate Murphy wasn't answering her phone either. She wasn't on call, so maybe she was just kicking back, having a bubble bath.'

'Yeah, that's what she was doing.'

'You're her friend, you ask her what she was up to.'

'Oh, I will, but it will be over a glass of wine so she can spill all the details.'

Miller got a text from Purcell saying he was waiting downstairs. 'You ready, Dad?'

Jack came out of the bathroom. 'I'll just get my jacket, and then I'm ready. See you, Kim. Bye, my wee darlin',' he said to Emma.

'Bye, Grandpa Jack.'

Miller kissed Kim. 'I'll see you later.' He kissed Emma on the cheek then he and Kim walked out to the front door where Jack was waiting.

'Norma's going to want a report on this ASAP, Frank.'

'Tell her she'll get it.'

'More importantly, you need to find Tony Matheson,' Jack said, worried. 'They've just started their daylight search, but I think somebody's taken him, for whatever reason.'

'Why didn't he just kill him? He'd already run over Roger, so he has nothing to lose.'

'I wish I had the answer.'

Downstairs in the car, Purcell was listening to the radio. 'Gibb just called me. He's down at the Campbell Estate. Every man and his dog is out looking for Matheson. It was on the radio, too. *Cop killer* they're calling him. Hi, Jack.'

'Hi, Percy. How's things going?'

'I'll be happier when we get Herdan.'

They headed west, eventually connecting with Slateford Road until they approached Hutchison Crossway.

A patrol car sat across the road, preventing the myriad TV news vans from getting closer to Anne Robertson's flat. When the uniform saw the blue flashers on Purcell's car, he stepped aside, and Purcell squeezed the car past. He showed his warrant card, and they were directed farther down the road.

Inside the cramped flat, Miller noticed how simply furnished it was. There were police officers inside, as well as outside.

The FLO was a young woman who Miller had seen about the High Street station. Give us a minute, will you?' he said, as he, Purcell, and Jack went into the living room where Anne was sitting crying her eyes out. There was no sign of the son or his wife.

'Anne. I hope you don't mind me coming round to see you,' Jack said, and this seemed to snap the woman out of her almost-hypnotic state.

'Oh, Jack,' she said, standing up and throwing her arms around him. After a few minutes of sobbing, she stepped back.

'Come on, let's get you a cup of tea,' he said, as the FLO came in from the kitchen with a tray.

'Anne, this is my son, DI Frank Miller, and the new head of MIT, Superintendent Purcell.'

'Percy,' he said, shaking her hand.

They sat down, and Jack poured the tea.

Miller took a sip, and put the cup down on the coffee table. 'Mrs Robertson, we need to ask you some questions.'

'Call me Anne, son.'

'Anne. We have a suspect right now, but he's still out there. As a policeman's wife, you'll understand that we can't talk about that just now. But we need to know if Roger ever had threats from anybody.'

The woman took a sip of her tea, and put the cup down, keeping her hanky in one hand. 'No. Roger hardly arrested anybody. He never got into fights. Didn't argue with anybody. In fact, sometimes it was hard to believe he was a copper at all.'

'As far as you're aware, nobody wanted to harm him?'

She shook her head, and dabbed at her eyes again. 'Nobody.'

'Did he get any phone calls where you didn't know who had called him?' Purcell asked.

'No, nothing. He was always popular at the station. Even that laddie, Tony, went out for a few pints with him. Tony's a special. He gets sent to different stations, and he and Roger struck up a friendship. He's missing now, isn't he?'

'Yes. We're doing all we can to find him.'

'He liked Tony. Especially since he knew his dad so well.'

'Archie Matheson was a good guy,' Jack said.

'Roger was gutted the day Archie slipped off that roof and fell. Especially as he was the one who was holding onto Archie. He spoke of it often. If he'd only been a bit stronger. If only he'd got there a few seconds sooner, then maybe Archie would still be here. As it was, he couldn't hold on until help got there.' She looked at Jack. 'You and the others were chasing that guy and you got him, but only after Archie had fallen.'

'I know. It was a hard day for us all, but Roger took a dive and got to Archie. That's not something all of us could have done. He put his own life on the line for the sake of a colleague.'

'I do need to ask you about any identifying features Roger may have had,' Miller said.

'He has a scar on his right leg. It was from a burn he got when he was a teenager. It's a little round mark like a bit of his skin melted.'

'Any tattoos?'

'No. He was funny that way. He said tattoos spoiled somebody's look.' She looked at Jack. 'He was old-fashioned that way.'

Jack smiled. 'I remember. He would never swear in front of a woman. Always held a door open for a woman. He was a great guy.'

She sniffed again. 'When can I see him?'

'We can talk about that later, Anne,' Purcell said. 'However, we have to get going just now. Thanks for seeing us, and I'm sorry for your loss.'

'Nice meeting you, Superintendent.'

'I'll stay here a wee while,' Jack said. 'I have nothing to do today. I'll keep Anne company.'

'That's good of you, Jack,' Anne said.

Outside, the wind blew the fallen leaves around. The sky was overcast, darker in the west.

Miller's phone rang. He spoke briefly, and then hung up.

'We're wanted down at the mortuary, Percy. Something's not right.'

FIFTY

'Hi, Frank,' Leo Chester said, as Gus Weaver let him and Purcell into the loading bay entrance.

'Morning, Professor.'

'Good to see you again, Doc,' Purcell said.

'Would anybody like a coffee?' Jake Dagger asked.

'I'd like us to get started, or I'll be pissing like a horse.' Purcell shrugged out of his jacket. 'Where can I hang this?'

'In Kate's office will be fine,' Dagger said. 'She's not in yet. She's due to start later.'

When they were all dressed, wearing the surgical scrubs, Chester took them upstairs to the PM suite where the remains of Roger Robertson were laid out on the stainless steel table.

Robertson's privates had been covered with a cloth, sparing his blushes, even in death.

Miller cleared his throat. He'd never been sick at a crime scene or at a PM, but there was a first time for everything. Above the neck, Robertson was missing. 'We've just been speaking with Sergeant Robertson's widow, and she told us he has a little round scar on his right leg, lower down. It's a little burn mark.'

Chester looked puzzled. 'I didn't see anything like that, but I'll double check. First though, I want you to observe the body. And you're working on the assumption that he was hit by a taxi, because of the business card found at the scene. Correct?'

'Correct,' Miller said.

They gazed at the torso, the Y-shaped incision neatly stitched.

'Did the taxi driving over his head kill him?' Purcell said.

'Oh, yes. His heart was in great shape, his lungs ditto. Liver was fine. It was definitely the taxi that killed him. But not in the way you thought it had. We all assumed he'd been knocked down first, then run over, am I correct?'

Miller and Purcell both nodded.

'He wasn't knocked down by the vehicle. First of all, when somebody is hit by a vehicle, they invariably have broken bones on their lower extremities, namely their legs and pelvic region, depending on how high the vehicle is. I would have expected both, at least one leg broken and his pelvis, because of the height of the front of the taxi. He has nothing. No bruising, no cuts, no breaks. I didn't see this last night because he was still wearing his uniform.'

'So you're saying the taxi wasn't going fast enough to cause any damage?' Miller said.

'I'm saying the taxi didn't hit him at all. He was placed on the ground, and the taxi wheel driven over his head.'

'In order for him to have lain there, and not get out of the way of the taxi, he would have had to have been unconscious or near unconscious,' Purcell said. 'This man didn't move when he was down. So, in order to knock him out, it would have taken reasonable force. Maybe a sucker punch caught him unawares, enough to put him down. I find it unlikely that a police officer would have been taken unaware like that.'

'He could have snuck up on him in the dark,' Miller said.

'Possibly. But if you look at the crime scene photos, you'll see heavy brush on either side of the track where he was found. It would be impossible to come through there without making a noise.'

'So maybe Herdan drove his cab close to Roger, and when Herdan got out, he lamped Roger one.'

Chester looked at the men in the room. 'The skull is too badly crushed to be sure, but perhaps he was struck on the head with something hard enough to render him unconscious. Whoever it was, he got close enough to Roger to hit him, without Roger hitting him back.'

It had been a long time since Jimmy Gilmour had enjoyed sex so much that he switched his phone off. Much against Kate's wishes. He had a child after all. What if there was an emergency? Gilmour had switched it off anyway.

He had taken the day off, knowing she was going in late. Now, a weak sun was coming in through the window as they lay side by side, sweating.

'So, what are you going to do without me today?' she said.

'I'm going home to box that cow's stuff up, and then when she comes round with a van, it won't take her long to get out.'

'Do you have any regrets?'

'Yes. That I didn't end it a long time ago. I know she's cheating on me, but I didn't realise it at first. This has been going on for months. Now I wonder if she really was doing night shifts at the hospital.'

'Well, it's over now, Jimmy. You have me, and I promise you one thing; I'll never cheat on you.'

He smiled, and kissed her. 'Once Lauren is gone, I want to make it official.'

'Fine by me.' She kissed him back. 'I need to shower then you can make me some breakfast. Scrambled eggs, lightly browned toast, and coffee.'

Gilmour sat up. 'As much as I'd love to, I have a lot to be getting on with. Sorry, honey. Rain check?'

'Do I have a choice?'

'I'll make it up to you.'

He dressed quickly, and kissed her goodbye. The morning was cold, but it felt invigorating to him. He walked up Holyrood Road and into Dumbiedykes, reaching his flat five minutes later. When he got inside, Lauren was waiting for him.

'What are you doing here?'

'I live here, remember?'

'Not anymore. I'm going to box your shit up, and you can take it with you. Your clothes can go in a bin bag.'

Lauren started crying, and stood up. 'Oh, Jimmy, I made a mistake. I still love you.' She put her arms round his neck. He gently pushed them away.

'I'm, sorry, Lauren, I'm going out with somebody else. Oh, wait; you already know that.'

'I'm sorry about that. I was off my head. I didn't mean to. I realise now I only did it out of jealousy.'

'You should have thought about that before you went storming into the mortuary.'

'I know, I know. I made a mistake.'

'I've moved on, just like you chose to.'

'Doesn't everybody deserve a second chance?'

'Everybody does. But the time for your second chance expired a long time ago.'

'So you're saying there's no hope for us?' Lauren had a pleading look on her face.

'I've just come in from spending the night with another woman. What do you think? Anyway, has your boyfriend kicked you out?'

'No.'

'Liar.'

'I'm not a liar. I chose to leave after I found out something about him.'

Don't ask. Don't ask. 'What?' *Fuck.*

'I found out he killed his girlfriend.'

FIFTY-ONE

Purcell stood at the front of the incident room. It was standing room only.

'Right everybody, listen up; I want to go through the events of last night. Paddy? Give us what you've got.'

He stepped aside, and Gibb walked over to the whiteboard. 'We know that Robertson and Matheson answered a call about a woman screaming in the Campbell Estate. Whether this was a false alarm, or a deliberate ruse to get a patrol car there, we don't know.

'We don't know what happened when they got there, but we think Robertson was killed, and Matheson either taken somewhere and killed, or just abducted. We searched the estate this morning, but found no sign of him.'

'Do we think it was random, or were they targeted?' Angie Rivers asked.

'Herdan is sending us a message; back off,' Miller said.

'It does seem a bit personal, if you ask me,' Watt said. 'I mean, if it was random, then what would happen if two young fit blokes turned up, built like brick shithouses? Unless he's extremely hard, then he might have got a run for his money, and it would have been a different outcome. But it makes sense that he could overpower Robertson.'

'I agree with Andy,' Hazel said. 'But how would he know it would be Robertson who turned up?'

'I knew it would happen one day!' Watt said. 'My detecting skills have finally rubbed off.'

'If I didn't feel so unwell, I'd have a comeback for that.'

'You're welcome.'

'But as I was saying,' Hazel continued, 'he must have known what area Robertson would be in, surely?'

'That's true. Robertson worked out of Corstorphine. The Campbell Estate is in their catchment area. If he knew information about Robertson, he could have lured him there. Then, he took Matheson after leaving the body behind.' Miller looked thoughtful. 'That's some logistics. We need to find Herdan, and find out what connection he has to Robertson.'

As the detectives filed back to their desks, the phone in Purcell's office rang.

'Get onto your better half, Frank. That was Jimmy Gilmour. We're going to need a warrant, and we need it now.'

It was called *Rapid Response*. Unmarked vans pulled in front of the building, and a forced entry was made. The stairs were guarded, and Lloyd Masters and other members of the team rode the lift with Miller and Purcell, wearing stab vests over their jackets.

At the front door to the apartment, an officer with a ram smashed the wooden door, and it exploded inwards.

'What the hell...?' Mitchell Robb shouted as he came racing out of the living room.

'Show me your fucking hands!' the lead firearms officer shouted.

When he hesitated, two officers rushed forward, and dropped Robb to the ground. Another door opened, and the two marksmen stayed down, as the first one gave a command for the second person not to move.

Gabriel Chase stood stock still.

Miller and Purcell walked in, Miller going straight for Chase, while Purcell arrested Robb. Hazel was behind them

'Mitchell Robb, I'm arresting you on suspicion of murdering Jessica Thorn, and Police Officer Roger Robertson.'

'What? No! I didn't murder anybody. Tell him, Gabe!'

But Chase was also being read his rights as he was arrested for aiding and abetting.

'Robb, where do you normally keep your taxi?'

'Down in one of my garages. I have two. One for my Jag, the other for my taxi. Why?'

'Give me your keys.'

'Do you have a warrant to search his property?' Chase said.

'Of course we fucking do,' Miller said. 'And one for stripping your place apart, and your friend's house. And by strip, I mean we're going to pull the fucking place apart looking for our colleague.'

The smirk left Chase's face. 'We don't know anything about your colleague.'

'I didn't kill Jess!' Robb said, as he was dragged to his feet. Purcell reached over and took the keys from Robb's pocket. 'Which is your garage?'

Robb told him. 'Frank, take some guys down with you.'

Miller left with Hazel, and they found Robb's garage. He opened it, and saw a Jaguar sports car. Opened the next one.

There was a taxi in there, facing nose out. Miller shone his flashlight into the darkened space, the light bouncing off the windscreen. Then he saw it, and stopped.

Somebody was inside.

FIFTY-TWO

Miller walked slowly round the side of the taxi, still keeping his light shining on the figure sitting on the back seat, slumped to one side.

'Jesus Christ, it's Tony,' Miller said, hauling the door open. He felt for a pulse. It was there.

Hazel got on her phone. 'Control, this is DS Hazel Carter. I need Medic One at a locus in Ravelston. We have an officer down. It's the special who's been missing since last night. We found him alive, but unresponsive.'

An immediate response would be put out for Medic 1, basically a hospital on wheels, dispatched to the most serious incidents. A trauma doctor would be on board, along with specialised nurses.

'Hazel, go and get some help.'

Hazel rushed away, making her way round the end of the garage block. As she went she felt a trickle of wetness running down her leg, and put a hand down to touch herself. There was blood on her hand. 'Oh Jesus, no,' she said, panic gripping her.

Officers were putting Robb and Chase into separate cars. Her head was spinning, and she wanted to shout out. Percy was there. She put her hand up, and then suddenly the ground was rushing up to smack her in the face. Then... nothing.

Purcell was overseeing the two suspects getting into the cars when he caught movement out of the corner of his eye; Hazel, raising a hand towards him, and then she fell sideways.

'Fuck me,' he said, and started sprinting across the gravel car park, followed by two armed officers. 'Hazel, can you hear me?' Nothing. Then he saw the blood on her hand. 'You two, go round and see what Miller's doing.'

The two men immediately assumed their combat stance as they rounded the garage block, and disappeared from Purcell's view.

'You two! Get over here!' he shouted to two uniforms, but one was already running, a female. 'Get on your Airwave. We have an officer down. I want this fucking place locked down until we know what's going on. But get those two scumbags away to the station. Move it, man!'

The uniform got on his radio, while the female officer took her hi-vis jacket off, and put it under Hazel's head. She then started feeling for vital signs.

'I was an army medic,' she said.

'Go to it,' Purcell said, standing back.

The officer felt around Hazel's crotch area with a gloved hand. It came back bloody.

'How far gone is she?'

'What?'

'She's obviously pregnant. How far along is she?'

'Oh, shit, erm... about five months, I think. Do you think she's going to lose her baby?'

'I'm not a doctor. Get on your radio, sir, and tell them we need an ambulance for the Smellie Maternity Emergency Unit.'

'Got it.' He turned away and made the call.

'Right,' the female said, 'let's get her lifted into the warmth. This cold ground isn't doing her or the baby any good.'

Purcell reached down, and lifted Hazel up, his body pumped full of adrenaline; his back he knew, would be paying for it later.

The two cars with the prisoners approached, and Purcell managed to lift a hand to stop the lead one. He carried Hazel round to the side. The driver wound his window down.

'Get the back window wound down.'

The driver obliged, and Purcell looked at Mitchell Robb sitting in the back. 'You know something? If she dies, you're going to be fucking praying they put you away, because if they don't, I'll see you on my own one night. You snivelling little bastard.'

'You can't threaten me like that. I'm a doctor. You heard that,' he said to the two officers in the front.

'I heard fuck all,' the driver said, winding the window up and driving away, lights and sirens on. The second car followed.

Lloyd Masters came out of the stair. 'Help that fucking man!' he snapped. Two firearms officers gently took Hazel into the warmth of the stairway, and laid her down.

'What happened here, Percy?'

'She just collapsed. Over by the garages. I sent two of your men round to see what's happening. They haven't come back.'

The female officer was attending to Hazel as Masters went running with more officers while others stood guard.

Miller was checking Matheson over when Masters arrived. One of Matheson's sleeves was rolled up, and he looked pale. He still hadn't regained consciousness.

'How is he, Frank?'

'He's got a steady pulse. I can't get him round though.'

They heard the approach of Medic 1, and an officer directed it round the back of the garages. Another ambulance followed closely behind.

'I've got it now, pal. Go and see to your team member,' Masters said.

Miller left the garage and ran back to the stairway. Purcell was on his knees with Hazel's head in his lap. He looked up at Miller. 'Her heartbeat's strong, but this young lady thinks it's got something to do with Hazel's baby. She's a medic.'

'There's not much else we can do but make her comfortable,' the young woman said.

Miller was impressed by the way she kept cool under pressure. 'You're heading for CID, I hope.'

She smiled back at him. 'I am indeed.'

'What's your name?'

'Stephanie Walker. Steffi to my friends.'

'Good to meet you, Steffi,' Purcell said. 'When the time's right, make sure you speak with me.'

She smiled again, and looked him in the eyes. 'In fact, I have an interview with you on Monday about being an acting DC, sir.'

Purcell looked at Miller. Then back at Steffi. 'I'm liking what I've seen so far. I have a feeling this will only be a formality on Monday. I'll be looking at the files this weekend.'

The ambulance crew pulled up, taking over and loading Hazel into the ambulance. More patrol cars attended, and were ready to escort the ambulances.

'Jesus, what a morning,' Purcell said.

'It's been one of our busier ones, I have to admit.' He watched Steffi walk over to her patrol partner, and they climbed into the car after she had put her hi-vis jacket back on. 'You like her, don't you?'

'I do. She just jumped right into action without waiting for me to say anything. And she wasn't fazed by the presence of a superior officer. It must be the combat training.'

'So she's in with a chance?'

'Unless we have a member of royalty ahead of her, I would say so.'

FIFTY-THREE

Several things happened at once. Hazel was admitted to the Smellie Maternity Hospital, and Tony Matheson was taken to the Accident and Emergency department at the Royal Infirmary. Gabriel Chase was taken to interview room 1. And Mitchell Robb was taken to interview room 5.

Angie Rivers was despatched to the Royal to be there when Matheson came round.

Miller was sitting in with Robb, while Purcell had taken Chase. He mumbled something about wanting to *fuck with a lawyer's head*. Both men had representation.

Miller was accompanied by Paddy Gibb, who was leading the interview.

After all the formalities were taken care of, Gibb sat back in his chair.

'Tell us where your girlfriend is, Mr Robb.'

'I don't know where she is. She left me.'

'She just got up and left?'

'We'd been arguing a lot recently, and she said she was leaving me. I thought it was an idle threat, but when I went home one day, she was gone.'

'We have reason to believe she's dead,' Miller said.

'Do you now?' He managed to keep a disinterested expression on his face.

'We have a witness who heard you talking with Gabriel Chase about it.'

Robb laughed. 'Lauren. What a vindictive cow.'

'That's just hearsay, Inspector,' the lawyer said.

'It's also something we have to investigate. Now, do you want to alter your answer?'

'There's nothing to alter.'

Miller tapped his pen against the writing pad. 'You know Chase is a lawyer. He's in there with another lawyer. You also know what a bunch of sharks they are.' He looked at Robb's lawyer.

The lawyer sat stony-faced, like he couldn't argue with that fact.

'So they're probably in there concocting a story between them, throwing you under the bus. There's no way he'll take the blame for you if it was something you did.'

'Oh, I get it. You're the good cop. The bad cop is in there giving it big style with Gabe, and then he'll come in here and give me all this shit about how Gabe did nothing, and now he's free and clear. Yes, I've seen the TV shows.'

Miller's phone buzzed with an incoming text. He looked at the screen. Typed something back. Then there was a knock on the door. Miller suspended the interview, walked over, and opened it. It was Steffi Walker, holding a sheet of paper.

'Sorry to disturb you, sir. This is urgent.'

'No problem.' Miller read it, and handed it back to her.

Robb looked towards the corridor as Purcell came into view. Gabe was standing with his lawyer, smiling.

'I'm sorry for detaining you any longer than was necessary, Mr Chase, but we had to be sure.'

'Understandable. There are no hard feelings, Superintendent.'

Purcell shook hands with Chase who looked in at Robb and smiled.

'You're free to go now, Mr Chase.'

'Thank you.' Chase walked away with his lawyer, escorted by a uniform. Miller closed the door, and kept his voice low as the others disappeared out of sight.

'How did that go, Percy?'

'You can see the end result for yourself. Chase was eager to blab once we let him know that Robb was putting all the blame on him. He told us everything, without implicating himself of course. I'll send the report to Norma Banks, and she'll be the one who decides if he's going to be re-arrested or not, but I think she'll have a fight on her hands. So my guess is, she'll accept the fact that he had nothing to do with it as long as we nail that bastard in there.'

'We still have to establish if Herdan killed Robb's girlfriend or not.'

'That's what we're working on, but he's still up to his neck in it.'

'That was a good idea, getting Steffi to come with that notice just as you were releasing Chase. Timing is everything, eh?'

'That's what Suzy says. Go get 'im.' He clapped Miller on the shoulder, and walked away.

Miller went back in and sat down. 'Sorry about that, Dr Robb. Now, where were we?' He started the recording again.

'I believe my client was patiently explaining his innocence.'

'You know, when you go to trial, how you co-operate will all be taken into account.'

'Please,' Robb's lawyer said. 'My client already explained that anybody could have taken his taxi and put that officer in the back.'

'Yet, not everybody could have given him flunitrazepam.'

'Rohypnol? Any fool can get their hands on a date rape drug, Inspector.'

'Not anybody,' Gibb said. 'Just deviants like you.'

The lawyer was about to chastise Gibb when Robb put a hand

up. 'It's okay. They think that because I'm a doctor I can easily get my hands on that stuff. Isn't that right, detective?'

'Yes. We think you gave some to Tony Matheson to subdue him. The hospital lab confirmed he had it in his system. Forensics also found bags of it in your apartment.'

'But—'

'We think that you took one of Herdan's taxi cards and left it at the scene. You placed Roger on the track, and ran over his head. Then drove it back to your house with our other officer in the back. We reckon you struck him to daze him, and then somehow made him swallow the Rohypnol.'

'That's fantasy!' Robb said, starting to rise to his feet.

'Sit down,' Gibb said.

Robb settled back down.

'We also have the reports back from our own lab,' Miller said. 'The blood that was lifted from Ashley Gates' house was found to have traces of Rohypnol in it.'

'I didn't give her that shit.' There was no smile now.

'She was your lover on the side, wasn't she?'

'Yes, but—'

'Forensics also found traces of blood down the drain in your bathroom. That's the thing about blood, Dr Robb; you can never quite get rid of all traces. No matter how much bleach you pour down the drain, or how much you clean. We also have DNA from Jess's mother and sister. We'll compare the DNA with the blood we found down your drain. Will it be your girlfriend's?'

'Okay, I didn't kill her. I swear. I found her dead.'

His lawyer started to protest, but Robb held up a hand. 'No. I have to tell them. I swear to God, when I got home, there was a Polaroid of Jess sitting on the mantelpiece. She was lying dead on the rug. I don't know if I disturbed him, or what he was going to do, but she was dead. And knowing Ashley was dead too, I knew I would get the blame for both.'

'You should have called us,' Gibb said.

'I know that now, but it just got out of control. I called Gabriel, and he actually said to call the police, but I didn't listen. I took Jess through to the bathroom, and cut her up.'

'What did you do with her remains?' Miller asked.

'There's a furnace room in the hospital where they burn medical waste and the like. They have big, wheeled bins filled with bags, and they sit there until the furnace guy puts them into the furnace. Look, I'm not proud of what I did, but I panicked. I put her into medical bags, and left them in amongst the other plastic bags.'

'Why would Tony Matheson be in your taxi?'

'I don't know.'

'Would Herdan have been able to get the keys to it?'

'If he killed Jess he would.'

'How come?'

'I haven't been able to find Jess's keys. Whoever killed her could have taken them. They sit in a bowl in the hall. He could have let himself in, and just taken the taxi without me knowing. The garage key was on her keyring too.'

'Where were you last night around eight?'

'At home. Alone.' Robb looked right at Miller, his eyes pleading. 'I didn't kill any copper. And I didn't take the other one and leave him in my taxi. Herdan must have taken my taxi when I wasn't here and used it. I don't go out in it very often. I only use the bloody thing to pick up women. I'm not doing it to make money. Obviously. So whoever it is you're looking for, it isn't me.'

Somehow, Miller thought the surgeon was telling the truth.

FIFTY-FOUR

'Where do Robertson and Matheson fit into all of this?' Hazel Carter said.

'We don't know yet,' Miller answered. 'But there's a connection we're trying to work out.'

'We let Gabriel Chase go, because we don't think he had anything to do with the murders,' Purcell said. 'He's only guilty of not reporting a crime. He didn't help Robb dispose of his girlfriend, and he fully co-operated with us.'

'We also think Robb didn't kill the other women, Ashley Gates, and Patricia Wilkinson. Or Cathy Graham,' Miller said.

'I still don't see the connection between Herdan and Cathy Graham,' Watt said.

'We don't know why Herdan went off his head and killed the women. But then, sometimes we never know why. They just go off their head. I mean, it's not as if he was rejected by the women. We all saw that from the mucky DVD they made.' Purcell drank more of his coffee.

Miller leaned forward, resting his elbows on a desk. 'Why only one DVD? I mean, don't you think they would want to record more than one session? Unless... somebody only wanted us to find one.'

Purcell looked across at a young DC who was manning the phones.

'Sir, a call for you from the lab.'

Purcell took it, and came back a few minutes later. 'I have the initial report from forensics. There's nothing in Herdan's house that sticks out. There's no evidence that he had any of the women there after he killed them.'

'He's going to a lot of trouble to drop Robb in it,' Miller said.

Purcell stood up. 'Paddy. You co-ordinate things here. I'm taking Frank to talk to Tony Matheson at the hospital. See if he's any clearer on what happened.'

'Don't bother,' Angie Rivers said, as she walked into the incident room.

'Why not? He's not dead, is he?'

'No, far from it. I was there with a bunch of uniforms. Apart from a splitting headache, he's right as rain. So well, in fact, that he signed himself out. Tony Matheson hopped into a taxi and went home.'

'Well, that's something, anyway,' Watt said.

'We should still go and talk to him.'

A female uniform walked into the incident room, and looked over at Miller. She had a sheaf of papers in her hand. Steffi Walker.

Miller walked over to her, and took them. 'Thanks, Steffi. Just a wee bit of practise before you join CID on Monday,' he said, taking her aside.

'I'm not counting my chickens, sir.'

'I can't say anything, but what I can tell you is, detectives drink in Logie Baird's down the road. Get used to showing your face in there.' He smiled at her, impressed by her walking into a room full of MIT detectives and remaining unfazed. 'Now, did you find out anything about Roger that might help us?'

'Well, there was nothing thrown up on his record about any

threats issued to him. But you were right about one thing.' She showed Miller.

'Thanks, Steffi.'

'I'm going over to Matheson's house. I want to talk to him there. Take a statement about last night.'

'I'll come with you,' Purcell said.

Connie Gilmour sat opposite Malcolm Freeman in his office, the smell of furniture polish assaulting her olfactory sense.

'I'd like to see him one more time before he goes away for good,' she said.

'Of course you may. If you give me five minutes, I'll have him brought through.' Freeman got up, and left Connie alone. Then she felt her phone vibrate in her pocket. She took it out, and looked at the screen. Jimmy. His timing couldn't be better.

She debated whether to answer it or not. She'd been grateful he could be with her at the hospital when Monty passed, but she'd heard through the grapevine that he was sleeping with the pathologist.

Truth be told, she was a bit jealous. He seemed to have landed on his feet after he found out Lauren was cheating on him. Not that she wished anything bad for him, but he was the one who'd fooled around on *her*. He deserved to be miserable, the bastard.

She answered it. 'What now, Jimmy?'

She could hear his breathing for a couple of seconds. *Oh God.* 'I'm sorry, I didn't mean that. I'm waiting for the undertaker to bring Uncle Monty through so I can say my goodbyes to him. I didn't mean to take it out on you.'

'It's okay, Con. I understand the stress you're going through.'

'What's up?'

'I'm sorry to tell you this, but Gabriel was arrested a short while ago. Him and his friend, Mitchell Robb.'

'Gabe's been arrested? What for?'

'Robb was arrested on suspicion of murdering his girlfriend. Gabe helped him. We're trying to get to the bottom of it all now.'

'I don't believe it. Gabe wouldn't hurt a fly. Neither would Mitchell. Oh my God. Who arrested them?'

'Percy Purcell.'

'He's a wanker, you do know that?'

'Listen, Con, I know you're upset, but he's a bloody good detective.'

'Oh, don't start defending him, Jimmy. He's arrested two men who wouldn't hurt anybody. You coppers are all alike.'

'Okay then, *you* tell me where Jess Thorn is.'

'How the fuck would I know?' she snapped, and realised Freeman was standing in the doorway.

'I'm sorry, I can come back if this is a bad time.'

Connie hung up. 'No, it's fine. I apologise for the language. Just ex-husband problems.' She got up, and he led her through to a viewing room. Her uncle was lying in the coffin, dressed in one of his best suits. His hair was combed perfectly, and his lips were glued together, making him look as if he was about to smile, sit up, and tell her it was all a joke.

Freeman left her alone with her uncle. She took her phone out and called her boyfriend. She didn't feel like going home alone. Not just now. And she felt that Jimmy was a million miles away. Maybe it was time she drew a line in the sand with her marriage. She made the call and her boyfriend said he'd be there for her.

After ending the call, she approached the coffin, and looked down at the prone figure.

'I'm going to miss you. I'm sorry I made such a mess of things. You wanted to be proud of me, yet I ended up getting a divorce. I feel ashamed.'

She couldn't control herself any longer. She held one of his cold hands, and wept openly.

After a while, she felt her phone vibrate from a text message. She looked at the screen. It was almost as if her dead uncle had answered her.

It was her boyfriend. He was waiting for her outside. Her heart skipped a beat at the thought of seeing him again. He was so handsome. So smart and articulate.

What she didn't know was how dangerous he was.

She was about to find out.

FIFTY-FIVE

Miller was impressed by the white, detached bungalow in Riversdale Road, a stone's throw from Murrayfield rugby stadium.

'This is it,' he said to Purcell, as he pulled up to Tony Matheson's house.

'You been here before?' Purcell asked.

'No. I've never socialised with him.'

'Your dad seems to like him a lot.'

Miller turned to look at him. 'My dad felt sorry for him after his old man died. I remember a bitter young man. Then his mum, sister, and granny died. After that, he was just a pain in the arse. He wanted to go to medical school to be a doctor, but he didn't have high enough grades.'

'You ever thought about becoming a therapist, Frank?'

'I feel bad saying that, but it's true. I didn't have much to do with him.'

'I remember his father alright. My best description of him would be *workshy*. God knows how he ever got into CID.'

'Not that you want to speak ill of the dead.'

'It's true. The one time he really got off his arse was to chase that twat across the roof of the tenement. And he nearly took Roger Robertson with him.'

'Right, let's go and see what Tony remembers about last night.'

They got out of the car, under a bright, but deceptively cold sky, went in through the small, wrought iron gate, and rang Matheson's bell.

There was no answer, so Purcell grabbed the doorknocker, and gave it a good workout. Still no answer.

They walked round to the left side of the house where the driveway was. It was one of the few properties that had a double garage. The structure was painted the same colour as the house, and set well back from the road. Miller and Purcell both looked through the house windows as they went, but couldn't see anything.

Round the back were the bedrooms. The curtains were open, and they were both empty. Miller walked over to the garages, and looked at the garage doors.

'Well, Inspector, I'm concerned about the welfare of one of our officers, so let's get the door opened.'

Miller pulled the handle, and the door slid up easily. And the other one. Both were empty.

'Can I help you?' They both turned round at the same time.

An older man was standing on his side of the fence, looking at them.

'We're police officers. We're looking for a colleague of ours who may be injured. Have you seen him?'

'Tony? Injured? He didn't seem injured when I saw him a little while ago.'

'Did he have his police uniform on?'

'No, he was dressed like he was just going to work.'

'Does he have any other vehicle?'

'No, but there's been a taxi parking outside his house, off and on, for a few days. I thought it was maybe the neighbour across the road, but now it's gone.'

'Thanks. You've been very helpful.' As the old man left, Miller pulled the garage doors down.

'Bloody Herdan,' Purcell said. 'Maybe he's been watching the house. Sounds like he took Robb's taxi last night. He was careless to drop a business card though.'

'Maybe. It could be it's another driver, or it could be he's watching Tony. Maybe he wants to finish what we interrupted. If he's gone in to work, I think we should go to the hospital and talk to him.'

'Herdan's brazen enough to kill Tony in the hospital. I think he's getting desperate.'

They got back into the car, Purcell driving, and headed out to Corstorphine Road, an arterial road that fed the daily commuters from the west right into the city centre. They crossed Ravelston, near where Robb lived. Up one hill, and down the other side, skirting past Sainsbury's on the way to the Western General.

Purcell drove near the car park, looking for a taxi, but seeing none. 'Where would he park if he came looking for Matheson?'

'Try round the back. There has to be a staff car park or something.'

The *or something* turned out to be a loading zone round the back of the building. Herdan's taxi was parked there. There were no doors to get in the back of the building, just the loading doors. Then Miller saw a small staff door. He got out of the car and ran towards it, while Purcell got on the radio, calling for backup.

Then Miller came running back over.

Purcell floored it round to the front of the building, letting Miller out when an ambulance came screaming in behind him. 'Go, Frank, and I'll get out of this guy's way. I'll see you inside.'

Miller ran into the reception area, and approached the woman behind the desk. 'I need to know what level Tony Matheson works on.'

She looked him up in her system and told him.

Miller hesitated, confused. 'Are you sure?'

'Of course I'm sure.'

'Another officer's coming in. Tell him where I've gone.' And he started running again.

FIFTY-SIX

Miller ran for the stairs, his adrenaline level shooting through the roof. He wouldn't be able to wait on the lift coming.

Just as well he was going downstairs and not up.

Down the first flight, his shoes clattering on the concrete steps, his hand sliding down the metal handrail. Not letting go at the bottom, but pulling himself round, and getting his feet to move fast on the next set of steps.

Down one level. Two more to go.

By the time he got down to the bowels of the hospital, his breathing was fast. He went through a set of doors, and came out by the lifts. He didn't know where he was going, so he slid up to the set of rubber doors in front of him looking through the opaque top half. It was dimly lit, with half the fluorescents out, and some of the others flickering. The walls were dirty, and the floor wasn't much better.

He slipped through, past one flap, careful not to let it slap back into place. He saw old posters on the walls; most of them ripped and hanging off. Another set of doors at the far end of this corridor. Yet another set of doors on the right, this time wooden ones with porthole windows in them.

The room beyond was in total darkness.

He ducked, and walked past them. A doorway on the right. A table and chairs under a dull light. A microwave oven on a counter. A kettle. A little corridor off to the left. He walked towards it, and bumped into one of the chairs. He took out a flashlight. The little LED cut through the darkness. There were several doors on the right. He gently pushed on the first one, but the room was empty. Same with the second. The third one had a bed in it.

He got a text on his phone. *Where are you?* Purcell.

He was going to send a reply, but thought it would be better to call, so he hit the speed dial.

He turned, and walked back down the short corridor, and then he heard a noise. He moved forward. When he reached the small eating area, a figure was standing, watching him. He shoved his phone in his pocket as the figure came at him.

A surgeon. What the hell was going on? But he had no time to answer his own question, as the fist came at his face, connecting with his cheekbone. Miller punched back, hitting the man's eye socket, while his right foot shot out and kicked the man in the shin.

The surgeon let out a yell, and pushed Miller backwards, turning to run as Miller fell over. Then Frank was back on his feet, chasing his assailant.

The rubber doors were clacking together. Miller ran full tilt at one, which would have knocked the other man down had he been behind it. He wasn't.

He was nowhere in sight.

He was in what seemed to be like a small warehouse, with a roller door on the left. Cages on wheels lined the corridor, overflowing into this large area. It was darker in here, and filthy. There was another set of rubber doors on the right. Miller looked through the top half, and saw the surgeon farther along.

He went through one half, and let the door swing closed behind him.

The surgeon turned to look at him. 'Hello, Frank.'

FIFTY-SEVEN

Purcell rode the lift to the third floor. When he got out, he walked round the corner to the labs, and was confronted by a door that was marked *Authorised Personnel Only*. So he walked through it. He saw a young man wearing a white lab coat, and asked him who was in charge. He pointed towards an office in the corner.

The door was open, so he knocked on the doorframe. A woman in her fifties looked over her glasses at him.

'Can I help you?'

He brought out his warrant card. 'Superintendent Purcell, Edinburgh MIT. Did my colleague just come in here?'

'No. Have you lost him somewhere in the hospital?'

Everybody's a fucking comedian. 'No. I'm looking for a lab technician who works here. Tony Matheson.'

'Who?'

'Tony Matheson.'

'I'm sorry, none of my staff is called Matheson. Have you got the right lab?'

'This is pathology, correct?'

'Correct.'

'Then I have the right lab.'

'Right lab, wrong person.'

'Well, can you check?'

'I don't need to check, Inspector. I'm the manager of this lab.'

'Superintendent.'

She made a *whatever* face. 'It still doesn't change the fact that I've never heard of the man. And the lab staff regularly get together on social evenings.'

'Is there any way you could check on your computer. I'd be very grateful. This is really important.' He gave her his best boyish smile. *Before I fuck you over for obstructing the course of justice, sourpuss.*

'Why not?' She played around with her keyboard. 'I'm in the intranet now. Tony Mathewson, you said?'

'Matheson.' *For fuck's sake.* Still keeping the smile, which was starting to hurt now.

More clicking, the mouse moving about on the pad with infernal slowness. 'Ah. There he is.' She looked at Purcell. 'What made you think he works in my department?'

'Because he told me.'

'That's where he really works.' She wrote it down on a small, square Post-it sticky note.

Purcell looked puzzled. 'Are you sure?'

'I'm sure. Superintendent.'

'Thank you.' Then his phone rang. 'Hello?' No answer. 'Frank? Hello?' No answer, just muffled noises.

FIFTY-EIGHT

Miller walked slowly towards the surgeon, and saw there was a woman strapped to a gurney. The door to the furnace was open, with the stretcher close to it.

'My, my, two for one. This is my lucky day.' The surgeon was standing at the end of the gurney, looking at him.

'Hello, Tony.' He kept his hands in view, in a non-threatening stance. 'Why don't you just push the stretcher over here, and we can talk?'

Matheson laughed, and pulled the mask down. 'Now what would be the fun in that?' He pulled the gag out of the woman's mouth. 'Do you think I should let Frank take you home?'

'Please let me go,' Connie Gilmour said.

'Let you go? I'm your boyfriend remember? You told me you were falling for me in a big way. We exchanged bodily fluids. You were falling in love with me, I could tell. I was so charming and funny. And a great lover wasn't I?'

She didn't answer him.

'Answer me!' he screamed.

'Yes, yes, you're a great lover!'

'It's over, my friend. Let's go home,' Miller said.

'How did you know it was me, Frank?' Matheson said, ignoring his request.

'It was Roger, to be honest. He was dead, and you had been abducted. Then we were told he'd been placed on the track and run over. Then when I was talking to Roger's widow, she said how you had been going out drinking with him, and requesting shifts with him. If I'd come here and found out I was wrong, then no harm, no foul. Seems I wasn't wrong though.'

'You're so clever, Frank. One of the better detectives. Like my dad. What a waste.'

'It wasn't Roger on the Campbell Estate, so who was it?'

Matheson smiled. 'Arthur King. I killed him earlier and kept him in the taxi. I took the taxi to the estate earlier in the day, and hid it behind some shrubbery. Then when we got there, I just drove it along the track, and then I attacked Roger. I smashed his face with a hammer first, to make him less recognisable.'

Miller could feel the anger rising, but kept it under control. 'That was a bit risky. What if somebody had found it? I mean, a taxi isn't easy to conceal.'

'Well, duh. You're looking for Herdan aren't you? You would have been called out to discover that Herdan had killed King and hidden him in his taxi. It wouldn't be connected to me. I wiped it down to get rid of my prints. However, nobody found it.'

'You thought of everything.'

'I even brought him here and left him hidden while I went to pick up the jakie so I could get him to go into the church. I knew Beam would tell you I was coming. I watched you go in with Purcell.'

'That makes sense; the homeless man said you were wearing a white shirt. It was your uniform shirt. Very clever. But tell me about your game at the estate.'

'Even when Roger was ordering his burgers, I was in the toilets making a treble nine call, reporting a girl screaming. On my burner phone of course. What with all the cutbacks, I knew we were the nearest patrol. So we'd get the shout.'

'Other cars were called out. Again, you took a risk.' *Keep him talking.* He inched closer.

'That was me again. I made another call on my phone, and told them there was even more screaming. After I changed King into Roger's uniform. Roger wasn't happy about that, let me tell you. I had to smack him and tie him up. Then I cuffed him to the inside handrail of the taxi.'

'Then you just sat in the taxi all night hoping to get found. What if we hadn't found you?'

'I only took a little Rohypnol. Best night's sleep I ever had. Not enough so I wouldn't remember the night before mind, but enough so there would be the faintest trace of it in my blood. If you didn't find me, I would have just woken up and made a call after banging on one of Robb's neighbour's doors.'

'So you took Jessica Thorn's keys when you killed her, I take it?'

'Yeah. That made life a lot easier. I dropped off Herdan's taxi at my place, drove over to Robb's street, and parked there. My car's still there. Then I let myself into Robb's garage with his wife's keys, and well, you know the rest.'

Miller could see Matheson was enjoying all of this. 'Where's Roger now?'

'He went where they all went.' He pointed with his thumb to the furnace. 'You should have heard him screaming. It's not a nice thing, burning to death.' He smiled at Connie Gilmour. 'As you're about to find out.'

'You blamed Roger for your dad's death, didn't you? Because he couldn't hold onto your dad as he was hanging over the edge of that tenement.' Miller inched forward.

'Of course I blame him. He could have pulled my dad up, but oh no, weak boy Roger let him fall. Leaving me to live with those two bitches. And that old woman. My mother, sister, and grandmother all lifted their hand to me at one time or another. But I showed them, didn't I? It's easy to tamper with a boiler. Make it look like it hasn't been looked after properly. They knew I was going to Scout camp that weekend, and they planned to stay over. So I went to see granny the day before. And I fiddled with her boiler. It worked a treat. They all died!'

'Please, Tony,' Connie said.

'We could have been a good thing, you and me. Had I not wanted to take care of you all.'

'What did I do to you?'

Miller inched closer, feeling the heat increase the closer he got to Matheson. He could only imagine how Connie was feeling right now.

'Is it because I asked Jimmy to come to the hospital the other night, Tony?' she said.

The smile slipped off Matheson's face. 'Are you stupid? Of course it's not about that. But I think you *do* know what it's about. Do you want to tell him, or shall I?'

'I don't know what you're talking about.'

'Cathy Graham. My sweet Cathy.'

Connie looked away from him.

'That's right. Run away from it.' He gave Miller his attention. 'You didn't know about them, did you?'

'Who?'

'Connie. Ashley. Jess. Michaela. They killed my Cathy.'

Miller thought Matheson had gone off the deep end. 'I thought you said you killed Cathy.'

'I didn't kill Cathy! Aren't you paying attention?'

'Father Beam was attacked by you after he came back and discovered you killing Cathy.'

'Is that what you think? Some fucking detective you are! It wasn't me, it was those four bitches! The man who pretended to be a psycho killer that night in the church was Mitchell Robb.'

'Robb? What about the other night?'

'That was me. I was just copying what Robb had done. I wanted you to think the killer had come back. I copied their own work. They had to pay. Not only did they humiliate her, they took photos after killing her! They killed her, and their pervert boyfriends covered it up! Made it look like some nutter killed her, and then they took photos of her. Then they put one in the priest's office in his church. I mean, how sick can you get?'

Miller looked at Connie. 'Is this true?'

Connie started crying. 'Yes! Yes, it's all true. Gabriel always had a laugh with Cathy if he was round at Monty's house and she was there cleaning. He got it into his head that she would be up for fooling around with us. He knew Father Beam was going to see Monty one night, and that Cathy would be alone in the church, so he convinced us to go round there. After she died, we all left, except Mitchell and Dan. They were busy making the scene look like a killer had done it when the priest came back.'

'Why did you kill her?'

'It was an accident, Frank. We were only having some fun. Swinging isn't illegal.'

'You're the other woman we couldn't identify on the DVD, aren't you?'

'Yes.'

'You were swinging with Gabriel Chase! He's your fucking cousin, for God's sake.'

'I didn't sleep with him. Only the others.'

'Does Jimmy know? About any of it?'

She shook her head. 'No. He doesn't know about Cathy either. It was an accident, I swear. She was there working on her Sunday school stuff, and we tried to get her to join in, but she said no. We teased her. We'd been drinking. Gabe started to get annoyed when Cathy said no. It was Michaela who started it. She was trying so hard to get Cathy to join in, but she said she only loved Tony, and she wouldn't do anything to hurt him. And then she said she was going to tell Father Beam.'

'See, Miller? My Cathy loved me more than anything. She was going to be my wife. Until those scumbags took her away from me.'

'What happened next, Connie?' Miller said, edging closer and closer.

'Michaela grabbed hold of Cathy's wrists, and Cathy started fighting. Next thing we knew, Cathy fell back and hit her head against the sharp edge of the fireplace in the office. She was dead. We didn't know what to do. It was an accident.'

'Why didn't you call an ambulance? Try to save her?' Matheson said.

'We panicked. We didn't know what to do.'

'Liar! You didn't want your dirty little secret to come out!'

'Connie?' Miller said. 'Is that the truth?'

Connie was sobbing. 'Yes! We didn't want anybody to find out we were shagging each other. Satisfied? We didn't know what to do. Gabe called Monty, even though he knew Beam was there. Believe it or not, it was his idea to make it look like she was murdered. He stalled Beam for as long as he could. Beam had said his stomach was acting up and he was coming home. Monty said all we needed was a scapegoat. A fictitious killer to take the blame. It was perfect. You never would have found him because he didn't exist.'

'God, Connie, what were you thinking?'

'We *weren't* thinking that's the whole point!'

'So you took some photos with a Polaroid camera, and shoved one in Will Beam's office. So how come there were still some in Monty's office in his house?'

'We used the Polaroid because, well, if you use your phone, next you know, everything's on Facebook. The camera we had didn't even put a date stamp on the photo. Anyway, Gabe took a few, trying to get the right angle. He put the extras in his pocket. He must have hidden them in Monty's home office.'

'The thing I don't understand is why didn't you just leave her there? Why take her away?'

'When she was fighting with Michaela, she scratched her on the neck when she lashed out. She had Michaela's DNA under her nails. We couldn't leave her there.'

'Tony, how did you find out about what they'd done?' Miller asked.

'I overheard Robb and Connie talking about it through there, when he was giving her one. Simple as that. Robb brings nurses down here for a shag. He thinks I don't know about it. He and Connie were in there, and I heard them. I only went in to have my fucking lunch, and they were at it. Then they started talking about it. Perverts.'

'Through where?'

'There. Where I just found you. In one of those rooms where the doctors used to rest, before they built the extension and abandoned them. Romance isn't dead, eh? He takes women in there with clean sheets, then dumps them for me to burn. Oh, you didn't know I was the furnace man. I lied when I said I was a lab technician. Obviously.'

'And you decided to get them back.'

'If Monty hadn't had a stroke, I would have killed him first.'

'Why did you kill Patricia Wilkinson if she wasn't part of the group who killed Cathy?'

'Well, you've got me there, detective. See, I didn't kill her.'

'You don't have to pretend anymore, Tony. We're going to get you help.'

'I have nothing to lose. I'm telling you, I didn't kill Patricia. You found her, didn't you? In that fucker Herdan's house. He didn't kill her either, because he had already been burnt in the furnace. If I'd killed her, you wouldn't have found her, because she would have been burnt as well.'

'Who did kill her then?'

'Why are you asking me? You're the one with the answers. You find out.'

Another inch closer. 'Connie doesn't deserve this. She *does* deserve to be punished though. I'll see she pays for what she did.'

'Oh, yes, a copper's ex-wife is going to do jail time. No, I don't think so. She'll be better off being punished right now.'

He gripped the plastic body basket, and started to push Connie into the flames.

FIFTY-NINE

Purcell looked over the bottom half of the rubber doors, and saw Miller standing talking to Tony Matheson, who was dressed as a surgeon. And there was a woman strapped to a stretcher near the furnace door. He guessed Miller was trying to negotiate the woman's release, but it would have been easier if he'd been closer. If Miller couldn't reach her, then Purcell certainly wasn't going to get to her.

Miller had kept his phone on, and he could hear muffled talking, but he'd already called for backup. The trouble with that was, if the freight door was opened, then that would alert Matheson, and Connie Gilmour would be toast.

Moving quickly, but quietly, away from the rubber doors, he moved to the door at the side of the freight door. His backup would have to come in this way. They were five minutes out, and he didn't think they had five minutes.

He opened the personnel door, and stepped outside. A box truck was pulling up; ready to drop off whatever it was that needed burning. The driver kept the engine running, and jumped out, walking round the back.

'You can't go in there,' Purcell said.

'Who are you?'

'Police.'

'I've got a delivery to make. And I have to pick up empty cages. My boss will go nuts if I can't drop off.'

'I'll deliver it for you.'

Purcell climbed into the cab of the truck, drove it forward, then put it into reverse. 'Here goes nothing. I hope you're on the ball, Frank,' he said to himself, and floored it.

Miller could see the pure fear in Connie's eyes. The flames were low inside the furnace, but they generated a lot of heat. The gurney was closer now, Connie's head near the opening.

'Was Janet helping you?'

Matheson furrowed his brows. 'Of course not. I pursued her. Used all my charm to get her to go out with me. I discovered she worked for Chase after I sat outside his place and watched who would came and went. Eventually, I charmed Janet, and she went out with me. That gave me access to Monty's house again. Once I'd got a copy of her key, I dumped her. Then I waited a while. As I said, if Monty hadn't had a stroke, I was going to kill him. I needed to be able to get into his house to kill him. In a way I feel cheated that he just died. I started going out with the lovely Mrs Gilmour here after I dumped Janet.'

'Why kill the others then?'

'I had to get rid of Herdan. You had to think it was him. He helped Robb take Cathy away. Robb's going to prison for sure. They all got what was coming to them. Again, to try to throw you off for a little while. Enough so I could put this bitch into the flames. She's the last one, Frank. Why don't you just walk away?'

'You would understand if you were a detective, and not just a lousy special.' *Time to play with his mind, Frank.*

'What did you fucking say?' Matheson took a step towards Miller, but then thought better of it.

'You heard. You couldn't cut the mustard. Yes, they let you be a special, but you wouldn't have made it in the real world. Just like you couldn't make it as a doctor, but you dress like one just to get a hard-on. Like you couldn't be a lab technician, and you ended up as a furnace operator. A job a monkey could do.'

'Of course I could have. I just chose not to. I'm a damn sight smarter than you give me credit for, Frank. Why do you think I'm wearing these scrubs? There'll be no DNA evidence on me. When you're both dead, I'll burn the scrubs anyway. I'll tell them it was Herdan, and he made off. I'm better than them, better than all of you. They'll never figure it out.'

'You keep telling yourself that, Tony. You're just like your dad; you only make it halfway there. My dad said Archie was a lazy bastard,' he said, attributing Purcell's words to his father.

'Jack wouldn't have said that.'

'Of course he would. He was just being polite to you, because he felt sorry for you. In fact, when your dad died, he wanted to ask you over, but I said no. You were a fucking weirdo then as well, and I can see that things never changed! Fucking weirdo bastard!' Miller was getting into his stride now, trying to knock Matheson off balance.

'You shut your fucking mouth about my dad.'

'He was a useless prick! Imagine falling off that roof! Roger couldn't hold him, and it wasn't his fault. Jack said he warned Archie about not chasing that suspect across the roof. There was nowhere else to run, and they knew they had him trapped, but Archie the hero had to chase him. My dad said he was a fucking clown.'

'No! You're lying! Jack wouldn't have said that about my dad.' Matheson's lip trembled.

'He did. You would have been a second-rate copper, just like he was!' Miller took a step forward, as if he was readying himself for a fight.

'Fuck you! I'll fucking kill her right now!' Matheson turned away from Miller. Then the freight door exploded into the warehouse with a crash. The truck kept coming until it smashed into the doorframe holding the rubber doors.

Matheson turned, pushed Connie into the furnace, and hit a button. There was a *whooshing* noise, the gas restricted as a safety precaution until the furnace operator closed the door.

Miller felt as if he was running in slow motion, held back by a giant elastic band as he reached the opening. The increase in heat alerted Miller that somehow, Matheson had fiddled with the override, and even with the door open, the flames were going to come shooting out like flame throwers.

He leaned in, feeling the heat trying to sear the skin from his bones. He would only get one chance at this. He blindly reached out, grasped one of the holes designed to be grabbed by rescuers, and pulled with all his might, stepping back at the same time, pulling, and pulling.

Connie was screaming with only seconds to live, but Miller pulled with all the strength he could muster. After the body basket overcame inertia, the rollers moved it along.

As the flames shot out of the holes in the top of the chamber, the flames from the bottom joined them, but they missed. The body basket went sailing through the air for a few feet before gravity grabbed it, and dragged it down to the floor, where it crashed sideways, and rolled over. Connie still screaming for all her worth.

Matheson ran for the side doors, through the rubber doors, and along the dimly lit corridor, heading for the lift. He pressed the button, reckoning it would be faster as Miller was preoccupied, and whoever was driving the truck would be helping him.

The lift doors dinged, and slid open.

A man was there, and he stepped forward, and punched Matheson in the face. As he fell backwards, the man grabbed him, and rolled him over. He struggled as he felt the cuffs going on.

Andy Watt hauled him to his feet as a group of uniforms rushed out of the stairwell. 'Roger was a drinking buddy of ours.'

'Well, he's burning in hell now!'

Watt turned him round, and pulled his fist back as Purcell came running. 'Andy!'

Watt caught himself. 'Take him away, lads.' He pushed Matheson towards the uniforms.

'It's not worth it.'

'I know, but sometimes this job gets to you.'

'Come on, Frank's with Connie. She's going to the Royal. Then she's going to be arrested.'

SIXTY

Kate had been planning to cook for Jimmy Gilmour, but after the news that his ex-wife had been arrested, he had gone to see her. Truth be told, she felt a vein of jealousy run through her. Maybe they'd get to the point in their relationship when he would feel the same way about her.

She was cleaning up in the PM suite when the door opened. She had her back to it.

'I thought you were already away home, Gus?' she said.

'He is away home.'

She spun round at the sound of the strange voice.

Jared Flucker was standing looking at her. Smiling. He took a step towards her, his hands up. 'You don't have to be scared, Arlene. I mean, Kate. I'm not here to hurt you.'

She picked up a scalpel. 'I swear to God, if you come any closer, I'll kill you.'

'Jesus, calm down. I've only ever wanted to talk to you. I want you to hear it from my own lips... I didn't kill your mother.'

'Yes you did. You were there, for God's sake. A cigarette butt with your DNA on it was at the scene. You were caught there. I saw you!'

313

'As my lawyer said, I was trying to help untie the rope round your mother's neck. I was helping her, Kate. I didn't kill her.'

'Your fingerprints were found upstairs in her living room! You were in the house!'

'Of course I was. I often helped senior citizens into the house with their groceries. Your mum was no exception. So, of course, my fingerprints were there.'

'I saw you kill her.'

'Did you? Think back. Did you actually see me put the rope round your mother's neck?'

There was silence between them for a moment.

'You can't answer that truthfully, because you actually *didn't* see me do it. Because I didn't do it.'

'Stop! You're playing with my head now. You want me to believe that. So when they have another trial, I'll have to say I'm not sure.'

'There's not going to be another trial, Kate.'

'How did you find out about my new identity? Tell me!'

'You had somebody call me and tell me. You wanted me to come here. That's what you said. So we could talk. So now I'm here, and you're going all bananas on me.'

'I didn't get anybody to call you.'

'She's right, me old son.' Another man walked into the suite, and stood looking at them. 'It was me who called you.'

Brian Crane. Kate's ex-boyfriend.

'Brian! Thank God you're here,' Kate said. 'He was going to kill me.'

Flucker stared at his nemesis. 'You? You called me? Why?'

'I let you know where she was staying, because I knew you would go scurrying after her. That's exactly what I needed. You see, there's a possibility I'm going to prison for setting you up, and a lot of other bad stuff I did. But not if she's dead. Lucky for me, we spent one more night together before she was brought up here. She told me her new name, and where she was going to be working.'

Flucker laughed. 'You moron. I'm not going to touch her. I just came here to make her see I'm innocent.'

'Not after I left some stuff in your gaff back in London. More incriminating stuff. Plus, they'll find you both dead.'

'I just said I'm not going to touch her, Crane. You're not much of a detective if you couldn't figure that one out.'

'I'm the best detective the Met ever had, sunshine. That's why I came up with the perfect plan; you're going to fight her, you stab her, but before she bleeds out, she gets you right in the neck. You both die. Game over.'

Kate looked at Crane. 'Why are you doing this?'

'It was me who killed your mother. Nosy old boot thought I was up to no good. I put some stuff in her basement. She came down to see what was going on, and I let her have it. It's her own fault; if she'd just got on the senior citizen bus with that twat, she would have been out, and I would have left her alone.'

Tears were flowing down Kate's cheeks. 'You killed my mum? You were my boyfriend.'

'And you were my girlfriend. One of them. You were surplus to requirements.'

Kate looked at Flucker. 'But you sent me threats from prison.'

Crane smiled, pulling his gloves on tighter. 'Nope, that was me too. In fact, Flucker was never guilty of anything more than being a boring twat. I killed your mother, and I'm going to kill you both. There's no way I'm going to prison.'

The door banged open, and hit Crane.

'Sorry, sir.'

'I thought you were away home, Gus?' Kate said, for the second time.

'I forgot something.' He was carrying a steel tray with some instruments on it.

'It can wait, moron,' Crane said. 'We're having a private talk here.'

'I won't be long, sir.'

'I said, fuck off,' Crane shouted, grabbing hold of the white coat, and pulling it hard.

He had gotten himself close enough to Frank Miller that he was within striking distance. 'You first, Crane,' he said, bringing his arm over Crane's, drawing him in close, and going for a headbutt.

Crane was a street fighter, saw it coming at the last second, and put his head down so his face didn't take the brunt of Miller's force. His right fist came round, and connected with the side of Miller's head. Miller kept hold of Crane, and punched him in the solar plexus.

Flucker grabbed Kate by the shoulders, and pushed her against the wall, shielding her with his body. 'You're safe now,' he said.

Crane doubled over, but knew he was fighting for his life. He charged at Miller, body-slamming him against a countertop. Miller let out a grunt as his spine connected with the top of the counter. Then he brought up his knee into Crane's groin, and the London detective yelled. He punched Miller in the side of the face. Miller lost his balance and fell over. Crane tried to kick him in the face, but Miller dodged at the last minute, and Crane's boot kicked the cabinets.

Then Miller saw a uniform rushing in. A female.

Crane turned round, and laughed. 'Come on then, darlin', let's see how tough a wee Scottish lassie is.'

So Steffi Walker obliged. As Crane's finger came towards her eye, she grabbed it, and twisted hard. Crane squealed like a little girl, as Steffi kept bending it. The detective was forced to follow it, or learn how to finger type with his thumb.

Steffi twisted his hand behind his back, slammed his face down onto the floor, bringing her speed cuffs out, and slapping them on. 'This wee lassie was in the British army.'

More uniforms ran in, followed by Purcell.

'Miller, you lazy sod. Get up off the floor. And you can take that white lab coat off.'

'You took your bloody time.' Miller struggled to his feet, his face feeling as if it had been hit by a bus. He walked over to Crane, and helped him to his feet by pulling him up by the hair.

'Did you get all that from Flucker's wire?' he asked Purcell.

'Better than surround sound.'

Flucker let Kate go, turned, and gave Purcell the thumbs up.

Miller looked Crane in the eyes. 'I'm going to make sure all your pals down in London know you were taken down by that *wee lassie*, as you called her.'

'Shut up.'

'Get him out of here.' Steffi and her colleagues took him out.

'You okay, Kate?' Miller asked.

'I'm shaking like a bloody leaf. But thanks to all of you, it's finally over.' She turned to Flucker. 'I'm sorry I ever doubted you. I did something stupid by telling Crane about me being in witness protection. Neil's going to want to have a word with me about that.'

'I'm just glad you now know I'm innocent,' Flucker said.

Purcell shook his hand. 'I must admit, when McGovern was going over the plan to trap Crane this afternoon, I was a bit sceptical. But you all played your part well. Especially you, Kate. And you're a natural, Jared. Neil says dinner is on him. He and his wife are taking you out to a first class restaurant.'

'That's very kind, but all I ever wanted to know was that Kate was safe.' He looked at her. 'I'll always think of you as Arlene though.'

'I've been called worse.' She gave him a peck on the cheek.

SIXTY-ONE

'You need to buy him a steak for that eye,' Purcell said to Kim as he paid for the round of drinks.

'Don't waste a steak like that,' Watt said.

'Come on, Hazel, you may as well chip in with your opinion,' Miller said. 'It's bash Miller night.'

Hazel laughed. 'No, I think you should have it on your eye.'

'Aw come on, Haze,' Watt said, 'he's already approved your maternity leave.'

'That's not for a couple of months at least.'

'I'm glad everything went alright at the hospital,' Kim said to Hazel. 'You gave us all a scare.'

'It was nothing to worry about. The baby's fine.'

'Well, I'll drink to that,' Watt said.

They were in Logie Baird's, which was just heating up with the Friday night crowd.

'I hear Jared Flucker did well today,' Kim said to Purcell.

'He came up here wanting to convince Kate he wasn't guilty. That's all he wanted to do, but McGovern got wind of Crane coming as well, and he came up with a plan. We all went over it in the station. Flucker agreed to do it. Thank God it went well, and if Frank there didn't fight like a girl, he wouldn't have got a smack.'

'I didn't see you getting your hands dirty,' Miller said. 'And seeing how well Steffi Walker fought, I'll take that as a compliment.'

'They pay me to supervise you lot, not to get my nose broken.'

'So, what's your mother planning to do about the victims who went into the furnace?' Hazel asked.

'Death certificates are being issued to the families. A death certificate was issued for Patricia Wilkinson too, and my mother officially released her body this afternoon. Her funeral has been arranged for Monday.'

'What about Michaela's body in Aberdeen? Did Matheson say what he did with it?' Hazel asked Purcell.

'He brought her down here, and put her in the furnace as well.'

'So Patricia was the only one of the women he didn't put in there.'

'He maintains he didn't kill her,' Miller said.

'He's a psychopath though. And a convincing liar.' Hazel sipped her orange juice.

Miller looked over as the door opened into the bar, and a young woman entered. He walked over to her, and brought her up to the bar.

'For those of you who haven't been introduced, this is Steffi Walker. The newest member of the team.'

'Wow. Already in MIT?' Watt asked. 'What about the others who were waiting to be interviewed next Monday?'

'I'm still doing the interviewing, but there have been no suitable candidates from CID and Steffi has already shown she can more than handle the stress.'

'And I owe you one, Steffi,' Hazel said.

'Now you're all embarrassing me.'

'Just wait 'til we get started,' Kim said.

'Where's Angie?' Watt asked.

'She's with McGovern, down at his office, taking notes for me,' Purcell said. 'She says she'll join us afterwards.'

Miller took Purcell aside. 'You know your timing was perfect this afternoon. A minute later, and Connie Gilmour would have been shut in that furnace, and I wouldn't have been able to get to her in time. It was your distraction that saved her.'

'Shite. Christ, man, you reached into a furnace that had already been rigged, and hauled her out of there.'

'I'm just saying.'

'We work as a team in MIT. Not like the old days when that pair of wankers sat upstairs and barked orders.'

'Steffi Walker's replacing Jimmy Gilmour, isn't she?'

Purcell looked away for a moment then back at Miller. 'I know he's a valued member of your team, but he can't be back with MIT. His wife has been charged with conspiracy to murder. Plus, he can't be trusted.'

'I could always trust Jimmy.'

Purcell reached into an inside pocket, and brought out a photograph. Miller took it and looked at it. There were several people in it, all standing around looking down at a very dead Cathy Graham. One of them was Connie Gilmour. 'How did you know?'

'I didn't. I guessed. I told him if I ever found out he was keeping something from me, I'd have his nuts in a sling. He gave me this. He took it from the pile before we all got to Monty's house after he called. He was protecting his ex, but I think he knew Connie would drop him in it by telling us that he had it. His career would be done after that. As it is, he's lucky to keep the position up at the firing range. Lloyd Masters is a lot more forgiving than I am.'

Paddy Gibb came in, and Purcell bought him a pint.

'Mitchell Robb told us they buried Cathy Graham in Monty Chase's back garden. In the flowerbed. Monty knew all about it. Matheson told us he made Monty have a stroke. By squeezing the carotid. It didn't leave a mark, and the old man already had had two mini strokes as his carotid was ninety per cent blocked. It wouldn't take much to give him a stroke. So after Monty was taken into hospital, he drove up to Aberdeen, and took care of Michaela Savage.'

'That's something we didn't count on.' Purcell said.

'He's singing like a canary now. Harvey Levitt says it's because he wants to show us how much cleverer he is than us. I don't care as long as he tells us all about it.'

Miller took Watt aside.

'Gilmour's gone.'

'I figured as much. Purcell doesn't take any prisoners. Serves Jimmy right. He should have been honest right up front. At least we have a new girl who knows how to handle herself. She'll be better than Gilmour. And Angie Rivers will soon settle down.'

'We'll see what next week brings.'

'I'm glad this case is finished.'

'It's not over yet, Andy. I have a funeral to go to on Monday.'

SIXTY-TWO

'Sir, I feel out of place.' Steffi Walker stood beside Miller in the back row of the Cloister Chapel at Warriston Crematorium.

'Why? You're dressed appropriately, and I'm wearing a black tie. We're both fine.' They were talking quietly as more people came in. Miller looked at his watch, 1:58 pm.

'I mean, this is my first day with MIT. I wasn't even getting my hopes up about getting into CID. I just think that maybe one of the others should be here with you.'

'We're not like that. You'll find that out. Keep your nose clean, and you'll sail through your six months probationary period with us.'

'Thanks. It means a lot what you've done for me.'

'Everything you did, you did for yourself.' He looked round when he saw the coffin being brought in. He scanned the faces in front of him. Patricia Wilkinson's parents were at the front, completely distraught.

The coffin was placed on the conveyor belt, and it slowly moved in before the curtains covered it.

After the doors were closed, the minister, a woman, read the eulogy, celebrating Patricia's life.

322

They sang *Abide with Me* which brought back sad memories for Miller, as it was a hymn that had been sung at Carol's funeral. Afterwards, as they filed out, Miller and Steffi shook hands with Patricia's family, and told them they were sorry for their loss.

They were waiting outside in the cold. The man they were waiting for came outside, and started heading for the car park when Miller and Steffi intercepted him.

'Mr Gates. Good to see you again.'

Stanley Gates stopped, and looked at Miller as if he couldn't place him. Then recognition sparked in his eyes. 'Inspector Miller.'

'I thought that was a very nice service the minister gave Patricia.'

'It was indeed. She was a nice girl. She and Ashley were very good friends.' He looked wistfully up at the grey sky for a moment. 'At least the Wilkinsons got to say goodbye to their daughter.'

'Wasn't Mrs Gates coming today?'

'No. She wasn't much of a friend to Patricia.'

'But you were.'

Gates' eyebrows furrowed. 'What are you insinuating?'

Miller took his hand out of his pocket. 'I think this is yours.' He opened the palm of his hand and Gates looked down at the black, jacket button that lay there.

'What are you talking about? Mine?'

'Forensics found it under Patricia's bed.'

'And you think it's mine? Don't be ridiculous. I'll be onto the chief constable about this.'

'He was already briefed this morning.'

Gates was about to walk away when he stopped. 'Just what the hell are you saying here?'

'I'm saying that, as we speak, the forensics team – armed with a warrant – are going through your wardrobe. Will they find a jacket with a button missing?'

Stanley Gates laughed. 'That's pathetic. You forget what I do for a living. The procurator fiscal won't bring charges on such a flimsy piece of evidence.'

'And yet I don't hear you denying it, Mr Gates,' Steffi said.

'Listen to me, young lady, this is nonsense, and I won't listen to any more of it.'

'We also have her diary,' Miller said. 'Of course, it's not just the button, but that will place you in her bedroom. And you were there, weren't you? Being her lover.'

All the air went out of him then, and there were tears in his eyes. 'Yes, yes I was.' His voice wasn't so combative now. 'You don't understand, Miller. My wife is a drunk. I met Patricia through Ashley. We fell for each other. I was in love with her.'

'Yet you killed her.'

'It was an accident. We were larking about on her bed. She was pretending to rip my clothes off. The button must have come off then. Later on, we were being very, *energetic*, shall we say? She fell backwards off the bed, and I heard something snap. Then she didn't move. I panicked. I sat there for hours, wondering what to do. Then I saw her Polaroid photo printer. I took a photo of her, and stuck it on her gas fire. Then I rolled her up in a rug. I went and got my Range Rover, and drove her to Herdan's house. I'd heard on the TV that you were looking for him. So I went into his house, and left Patricia there, hoping you would think he had killed her.'

'Not knowing that Herdan was dead all this time.'

'I was selfish. Just thinking of myself.'

'Mr Stanley Gates, I'm arresting you for the murder of Patricia Wilkinson.' He read him his rights, and Steffi brought the cuffs out.

'Please, no. It's undignified. People will see.'

'And the way you left Patricia was dignified?' He nodded to Steffi. 'Cuff him.'

They made sure that Stanley Gates was in full view of the other mourners as they took him round to the car park where Andy Watt was waiting with a car.

'So, how do you feel now?' Miller asked Steffi, as she closed the door on Gates.

'Just another day at the office,' she said, smiling.
'You'll go far,' he said, and they both got in the car.

AFTERWORD

I'm sure taxi driving in Edinburgh has changed greatly over the years, but I knew somebody a long time ago who drove a taxi, and I drew on this for my research. My taxi company is made up, but as far as I'm aware, the taxi computer was real, and so was the zoning. Things have no doubt moved on, but for the purposes of my story, this is how it is.

For those of you who are interested in such things, I got the title for this book from a song in the Tears For Fears album, The Hurting.

I would like to thank my friends on Facebook, some old, some new, but who I care about. It's always a laugh reading some of the posts with my breakfast. A big thank you goes to Julie Ann Stott, Wendy Haines and Jeni Bridge for their support and enthusiasm. Good job, ladies!

Also thanks to David at the Police Scotland Service Centre in Bilston for his help on Special Constables.

And to my daughters, Stephanie and Samantha, who never fail to let me know when I'm slacking. (Hulu is research, I'll have you know!)

Thanks go to my wife, Debbie, the rock in my life, who isn't afraid to tell it like it is. I love you.

And last but not least, to all the readers who buy my books. Your support really does mean a lot. Without you all, there would be nothing. So from the bottom of my heart, a very big thank you!

Thank you all for the reviews. They really do make a difference and I'd appreciate it if you left an honest review for this book.

All the best my friends.

John Carson

New York

October 2016

ABOUT THE AUTHOR

John Carson is originally from Edinburgh, Scotland, but now lives in New York State with his wife and family. And two dogs. And four cats.

website - johncarsonauthor.com
    Facebook - JohnCarsonAuthor
    Twitter - JohnCarsonBooks
    Instagram - JohnCarsonAuthor

Made in the USA
Las Vegas, NV
26 July 2021